The Blue Man

First published in 2022 by Leilanie Stewart

The Blue Man Copyright © 2022 Leilanie Stewart

ISBN: 9781739952327

The characters, events, names and places used in this book are fictitious or used fictitiously. Any resemblance to real persons, living or dead is coincidental.

No part of this book may be reproduced in any form or by any means without the express written permission of the publisher.

All rights reserved

Thank you for supporting independent publishing.

Website: www.leilaniestewart.com
F: facebook.com/leilaniestewartauthor
Twitter: @leilaniestewart
Instagram: @leilaniestewartauthor

The Blue Man

Leilanie Stewart

Also by Leilanie Stewart

The Buddha's Bone

Gods of Avalon Road

Prologue

They say he comes across the mud flats when the mist rolls in. They say he comes under the cloak of dark and a bright full moon; that was how it was on the night it happened, that fateful night.

The Blue Man, bathed in eerie blue light. The light from the moon, shimmering over unearthly mists.

He wears a blue Balmoral and is dressed in dark blue plaid with a travelling cloak over his left shoulder. If you see the mists come in, and you're caught out near the mudflats on a moonlit night, you should carry salt. Salt will ward him off. Salt over your left shoulder. Salt will blind the Devil.

He wasn't always a devil. Devils often start as men. Once, long ago, on a cold moonlit night, a man died and a devil was born. The devil known as The Blue Man.

Chapter one

Sabrina – September 2020

What would she look like? How long had it been; my brain paused to work out the number of years. We had last met when we were eighteen, back in the year two thousand. A new millennium. Or the end of the world, according to the Mayan calendar. I forced my brain back to the present, and away from dark shadows. Now we were both thirty-eight. Twenty years. Our lives had diverged, taking us down different paths and we had lost touch.

Twenty zero zero. Back then she had been slim, blonde and bubbly. I had both envied her for all the attention she had got so easily from boys and loved her, for we were as close as sisters. We had worn each other's clothes and shoes, written each other letters that we would secretly slip into the other's school bag, to be found and read in private after the school day was over. We had been the best of friends for three years, from fifteen until eighteen. Until that day. The day it had all unravelled.

Twenty twenty, pandemic year. My thoughts couldn't help themselves from redirecting to the negative; Northern Ireland in August had only recently opened out of lockdown. But this was a fresh start for Megan, and I, and indeed the whole country. There she was; time for me to safely compartmentalise any old dusty thoughts and let the ghosts of the past have them again. There she was. Still slim, though now looking a tad on the too-thin side; her legs drowning in her regular-cut jeans, her hair more dirty-fair and streaked with grey than vibrant bottle-blonde. She wore a duffel-coat that was more middle-aged comfort-seeker than young, club-ready teen. Her blonde hair was still the same length – just below her shoulders and her face, though recognisable, was more careworn with fine lines around her eyes and mouth. What would she think of me? Heavily pregnant and two stone heavier than she had last seen me.

"Megan," I said, resisting the urge to give her a warm embrace. "Lovely to see you."

"Awk, look at you. I love the burgundy hair dye, it suits you." Megan gestured widely with her arms, admiring my pregnant girth. "You look amazing."

"Aye, not long to go now," I said, rubbing my stomach tenderly.

We walked into the coffee shop and ordered our drinks at the counter; a decaf coffee for me and a mint tea for her.

"When was the last time we saw each other – during the A-levels, I think?" she said.

"A wee bit after that I think. We got bleutered down at Holywood Seafront. Or was it Vicky Park?"

"Must've been a good night then if we can't even remember." Megan laughed, but her smile faded soon after. "Do you remember what Louisa-Mae did to me?"

My shoulders tensed; I hadn't expected her to bring it up so soon. "Sorta. School got pretty bad towards the end."

"I would've got a flippin' A in my A-level Technology if it wasn't for that nasty piece of work."

"They turned on me too – Louisa-Mae and Lauren. They thought I was the one who touted to you," I said.

Megan's eyes glimmered with happiness in camaraderie at my revelation. "Is that right? I didn't know they were total bitches to you too."

I sniffed. "Aye, but I shot them down in one go – I'd been at the dentist on the morning it happened."

Megan peered at me over her cup, held just below her bottom lip. "The thing is, I don't even remember who actually told me what they'd done. My memory of that time is hazy. Maybe because it was all so horrible."

I sighed at the memory of Louisa-Mae. Maybe a bit too loud, for Megan slid a sideways glance as if to ask for an elaboration, though I kept my thoughts to myself. Back then, to say that Louisa-Mae had been the most dominant personality in our whole year group was an understatement. Brass-neck bully was more apt. And Megan. Poor Megan. She had been easy pickings.

"Do you remember the Blue Man?"

Megan's closed question came out of nowhere, jolting me from my melancholy reminiscences. The hairs on the back of my neck stood up as another painful memory was forced to scuttle out of its dark corner.

"Vaguely." I paused to drink my decaf coffee, hoping she would bring the topic back into light, not darkness.

"I saw him for the first time on that night after Louisa-Mae sabotaged my project."

A chill ran through my body, as though my blood had turned to ice. "I remember. How could I forget?"

Megan's brow furrowed. "You're saying, you saw him too?"

Why did I have to dig myself into a hole? I could easily have made a non-committal grunt and let my feigned boredom pave the way onto another topic. Especially after what we had been through. All that we had been through.

"I'll never forget his ice blue face. And those moon-white teeth pulled back in a grimace." Megan's eyes became unfocused at a point somewhere behind my left shoulder. With a shiver, I drew my shoulder close to my neck, protecting it from an unseen foe before my rational mind set in: we were in a café, in broad daylight. Our lives had changed, moved on from the horrors of the past.

Yet if that was the case, why did I feel frozen? I wanted to change the topic, but my tongue was rigid in my mouth. Megan needed to speak, had waited twenty years to say her piece.

"I saw him a couple of times over that summer, but the last time was the worst. After that, I couldn't take it any more. Do you know I left Belfast after that? I moved to Derry and went to Ulster to study Marketing."

The University of Ulster. Not bad for Megan, considering all she had been through. Warmth flooded me at the change in conversation. "That's great, I'm so glad you did something creative. What was Derry like?"

"Amazing. That's how I met Paddy. He's from Derry, he was studying Law at the University of Ulster and we met in the queue getting our student cards." Megan's face lit up at the mention of her husband. "We're living at Holywood Arches now near my mum, we just bought a house. We lived in Derry for a while as I got a great job for an advertising company and he was working for a local law firm. I would've stayed there if I'd had my way – it was Paddy's idea to move back to Belfast. The only downside about living back home is seeing Louisa-Mae around. She's still living in Belmont. She never left. She got really fat, you should see the size of her waddling around. Hobbles around with a limp too – you remember how she fell down Sydenham Bridge? I'll never forget it. Fat bitch got her comeuppance that night. Can you believe she's still smug though after all that? The way she smirks when she sees me. It reminds me of everything I'd rather forget."

I wanted to forget it too; or at least move on in the conversation. I sipped my tea and said nothing.

Megan's happy face changed to a smirk. "But you know who I saw at the Housing Association the other day? Lauren. She was applying for a council house – she has five kids now, with three different fathers and none of them are sticking around. She's not even working, such a layabout. Can you imagine that with all those kids? What a nightmare."

Hmph. I'd never taken Megan to be so snobbish before; looking down on others because they were poor, or fat, and she was settled with a mortgage and a husband. Not that Louisa-Mae and Lauren didn't deserve Megan's wrath. But her judgemental comments dug up my own insecurities. What would she think if I told her that I was bankrupt, that my flat and car back in Liverpool had been repossessed? What if I told her that Jake and I lived in a privately rented one bed flat with shabby furnishings and cracks in the walls just off the Cregagh Road? What did she think of me looking like a ten-tonne-Tessie?

Maybe time to change the subject. "So how's your mum and your brother?"

"Mum is good thanks. But I'm not very close to Stuart, to be honest." Megan shrugged and gave an indifferent sniff. "He lives in the house I grew up in over in Mersey Street, so that my mum can take care of him – she moved to a new house just off the Beersbridge Road when she remarried. Stuart was diagnosed with schizophrenia in his early twenties."

"Oh, I didn't know that." I trailed off, about to say that I was sorry to hear it, though glad I held my tongue. Maybe she didn't see it as a debilitating disability. In any event, it didn't seem she cared too much.

"Stuart drives me mad. He's too much of a burden on my mum, and she's in her sixties now, she could do without it."

"Doesn't he have a social worker, or a psychiatric nurse? You know, someone professional who helps him?"

Megan nodded. "Both. But he's so off the wall, it seriously would take an entire mental hospital to look after him. He's obsessed with radioactivity – he thinks everything is contaminated. He makes all these metal dishes that he thinks intercepts it. His house is full of them. I don't visit him much anyway as I don't want to be reminded of the Blue Man. You remember the yew tree thing, in the back garden?"

My heart sped up as Megan's eyes bored into mine, waiting for a response. My lips stayed shut, unable, or unwilling to comment on a part of my life that I would have wiped from memory if I could. That was besides the fact that it was awkward; we were two old friends who were only getting to know each other all over again. Too much information, too soon; and too painful. Time for another change of topic, however forced.

"So, are you working in Marketing now?"

Megan shook her head. "I'm still looking. I'm doing some temping work for a recruitment agency in the meantime, mostly just admin work."

She shrugged, my indication that the topic should be dropped.

"What about you? You were always very bookish, always reading something in the school library. Did you become a librarian?"

I chortled. "Not exactly, but close. I'm an English and Drama teacher, but it's harder to find work here than in England, so I'm doing substitute work right back at the place where we started."

Megan's mouth dropped, theatrically. "You're having me on? Back at our old school?"

I nodded. "It's changed though from when we were there. There's a wider choice of subjects now compared to when we were at school and more support for both the staff and pupils. I think it's better overall."

"It couldn't have been worse. I really felt so alone back then, like nobody would help me." Megan tossed her hand dismissively. "Is your husband an English teacher too?"

"No, he's a cashier at a bank. We met in Liverpool when I was over there doing my teacher training at Edgehill. He's from there," I said. "His mum will be coming over next month when the baby is born. It'll be her first grandchild."

A slow smile spread across Megan's face. "Speaking of babies, I have some other news to share. Did you know that I'm expecting too?"

"A way on, you're not are you?" I grabbed her arm. "That's lovely news. When's the due date?"

"February. Awk I'm chuffed, you know, something nice to brighten up the New Year. It's always so depressing after Christmas. That's why Paddy and I moved back from Derry. We wanted to be near my mum so she can help, since it's her first grandchild and everything."

I grinned. "Our babies can be play dates. We should meet up after they're both born."

Megan grinned too. "That would be grand."

Chapter two

Megan – September 2020

I'm not really sure how I felt about seeing Sabrina today. I suppose it was good. I guess it helped that she had put on a lot of weight. That sounds really bitchy, but it was for more sanitised reasons than purely schadenfreude: her changed appearance helped me to separate back then, in 2000, from now, like I was meeting a different person. On a selfish note, I'm glad I didn't get fat though. Sabrina had always been so beautiful, in a dark, exotic way, what with her Spanish ancestry and all. Even if she didn't know how lovely she had been, it had been hard to compete with that, back in those days. But now? Well. Shallow of me, maybe, but it was good to be the yummy-mummy while she was more of a big mama.

Where the flippin' hell was Paddy anyway? He said he was going to stick around, be there on standby, be ready to pick me up. It put me in mind of that part of *Aliens* where Ripley was thinking Bishop had left her stranded. Sure, if I couldn't even rely on him to make the flippin' bed in the mornings when I told him to, why did I ever think he'd remember to pick me up?

Two short toots jerked me out of my musings. I jumped, clapped a hand to my chest and stood up from the cold metal of the bench.

"What are you doing waiting around there for? Catching a bus somewhere?" Paddy's eyes crinkled as he smiled.

"Took you long enough! Imagine leaving your poor wee wife stuck on some bench in front of City Hall when she's expecting and all, that's good of you!" I grinned back and jumped in the car.

His smile melted into his normal, neutral expression. "How did it go? Everything alright?"

I shut the door and hugged my arms around myself. "It was okay."

"Okay?" Paddy pulled out of the bus stop lane into the traffic. "Okay enough to see her again, or okay I'm legging it out of here?"

I clamped my seatbelt and stared ahead at the cars in front. "Awk, it wasn't that bad you know. It was okay enough that I would see her again."

We slowed at the traffic lights. There she was, Sabrina, waddling across the intersection.

"That's her." I jerked my head forward. Sabrina passed by without seeing us.

Paddy nodded in approval. "Not bad."

I spun to face him, and dug an elbow into his side for good measure. "What's that supposed to mean?"

Paddy was stoic. "I just meant, she fits the image I'd pictured from the way you described her."

I huffed, watching Sabrina's retreating back. "Well that's funny. Cause I don't remember telling you that she was a fat pregnant woman. When we were eighteen, we used to be able to wear each other's clothes and shoes and all, you know, we were the same size."

"Just the Spanish part, I meant," said Paddy. As the lights changed and we drove on, Paddy's eyes flitted to the mirror. Only a split second – he didn't know I'd seen him look – but he had taken a second glance at Sabrina.

Maybe it was a bad idea to see her after all. Suddenly I wasn't a confident, mature thirty-eight year old woman with a husband and a career. Suddenly I had been whisked back in time to that awkward eighteen year old, along with the petty rivalries that came with it. Like boys.

I caught hold of myself. This was my husband of four years I was talking about, not some dyed-blonde teenage boy in a bomber jacket. Paddy loved me. He would never choose Sabrina over me. Friends before men, we had said at the time. But not so; not when it really came down to it. Sabrina and I had patched things up, after Johnny. But maybe patching things up was like sticking a plaster over a cut. It helped it to heal on the surface. But maybe under the skin, that old wound had still been festering, all these years later.

The car inched along through traffic on Chichester Street. Paddy must have read my mind that I wanted some head-space after seeing Sabrina, for he cranked the radio up and we drifted into silence. I watched the shoppers pass by: old grannies lugging their trolleys, young mums shouting at kids to hurry up, a couple of workmen in high-vis vests and hats laughing on a corner beside their scaffolding. And then-

My heart jolted in my chest. A bagpipe player busking on Arthur Street. He wore a green and red kilt and had an orange-haired 'Angus' hat on. The frightened child inside me wanted to escape; shove Paddy aside and hit accelerate, ram through the cars and vans ahead, but we were stuck in the congestion. Instead, I took a deep breath through my nose and exhaled slowly through my open mouth.

"What's wrong, babe?"

Paddy must have heard my audible gasp then, for he turned the radio down. Was I really that bad? Such a lack of self-control, letting my animal brain override my sensibilities. I tutted and shuffled in my seat. "Ah, nothing. I just saw something that reminded me about this – thing – in the past."

My caring hubby put his hand briefly on mine and squeezed. "That hasn't come up for a while now," he said, his voice an octave lower.

"I know." I sighed. "I'm on top of it though, it's okay."

"You've been saying it's okay a lot today too," he said, shooting a quick glance my way.

I shrugged my shoulders and wrapped my arms around my middle once more, hugging myself. "I mean, I'll be okay in a wee bit." I cranked the radio up again, but not before I heard him say, *I don't know if you should see Sabrina again.*

My eyes flitted to the wing mirror, but we were making speed now, and so the bagpipe player was long behind us. That poor man in the orange 'Angus' cap and kilt. He was just an innocent busker. I forced myself to think it: not the Blue Man. The bagpipe player reminded me of the Blue Man, but he wasn't him. The Blue Man was a part of my past, not present.

I shook my head; a physical act to initiate a much-needed mental shake-up, bringing myself into the present. Maybe Paddy was right, maybe seeing Sabrina had been bad, after all. Maybe it was too soon. Too raw.

I closed my eyes and listened to the pop song playing on the radio, solidifying me in the present. Reminding myself that I was in the here and now calmed me. Louisa-Mae was in the past. Lauren was in the past. I shivered. The Blue Man was also in the past.

Sabrina was part of the past too, but now had ventured into the present. Did that mean other things from the past would follow? Sabrina had been through it all with me; she had been there from the start.

That night. That horrifying night. The night the Blue Man came.

As we crossed the bridge leaving Belfast City Centre behind us, my eyes stayed on the road ahead, passing in a grey blur and my mind drifted into the grey blur of the past. I was only lying to myself if I thought that Sabrina hadn't stirred up parts of my memories that I would rather have kept suppressed. But maybe good would come from bad, if I could find a way to deal with those fears from two decades ago, once and for all. It would be like having a proper burial for the Blue Man, funeral and all, and finally laying the horrors to rest.

Chapter three

Megan – April 2000

"Where did you hear that story?" I asked.

An uneasy silence followed. Glancing at Louisa-Mae and Lauren, I could tell that I wasn't the only one spooked. Lauren's wide blue eyes were glassy and full of fear. Louisa-Mae kept a blank face, but in the silence I heard her swallow a dry lump in her throat.

Sabrina sat back on her haunches, looking pleased at how her story about The Blue Man had affected us. "Everyone round here knows it. I mean, if you grow up round my way anyway. Youse are all snobs from Belmont, and all. "

"Don't call me a snob, I'm from Avoniel, my Da told me the story. I already knew it, so there," said Lauren, tossing her dark, permed hair.

"Aye, I forgot you were a *millbag* like me," Sabrina laughed, digging Lauren in her ribs.

"You're from Sydenham, she's from the Newton, she's more *millie* than you so lap it up!" Lauren jabbed her thumb at me and made a *lapper* face, bunching her tongue under her bottom lip.

"I'm not from the Newton, I'm from Mersey Street," I protested.

"Same difference," Lauren shrugged.

"You're just trying to cover up cause you got scared. You didn't know the story did you? You're just lying to be hard," said Sabrina.

The pair of them were starting to do my head in. I glanced at Louisa-Mae. Still no reaction. She sat there with her legs folded under her, saying nothing, then took a swig of White Knight from the bottle and wiped it on the back of her hand.

"Aye, dead on." Louisa-Mae rolled her eyes. "You're full of shit Sabrina. If you're going to tell a story about the bogeyman you should do it to a bunch of wee kids, you'd get a better reaction."

Sabrina's face fell. "I'm dead serious, it's a real story. It happened over there on the banks of the Connsy, near this here park, so it did. In fact, weird coincidence but he was born almost exactly a hundred years ago. He was born at the turn of last century, and now it's the new millennium."

I glanced across towards the mudflats on the banks of the Connswater River. The water was deep enough to drown a person, and the pools of oil from the shipyard beyond that were now floating on the surface of the black water gave it a sinister quality that I recalled from my early years. *Don't play there*, my granny had warned. Was it because a man had died, for real, right there?

But Louisa-Mae was unconvinced.

"Yeah right, I suppose the Aztec calendar predicted that he would be born again in the year 2000, just cause it's the millennium this year. He'll probably be born on Halloween night too, on a full moon, with a bunch of witches dancing around a bonfire. Piss off." Louisa-Mae took another swig of White Knight and spilled it all down her front. Lauren and I fell about cackling.

"Sure, we must be the witches then. Who's up for starting a boney?" said Lauren.

Louisa-Mae shot her a dirty look, probably for siding with Sabrina. Sabrina said nothing, but sat smirking at winning a victory over Louisa-Mae, no doubt.

"It's like all those other ghost stories you hear, like the banshee at Scrabo Tower and the floating nun haunting Inch Abbey or something." Louisa-Mae flapped her hand dismissively. "Go on Sabrina, why don't you tell us about the Leprechauns playing tricks on us in the trees. Oh look, I think I see one over there."

We all turned to the clump of trees near the river. A wet splat hit my cheek; I wiped a sticky trail of White Knight down my face and rubbed the stream of bubbles off my denim jacket.

"Screw you!" I wiped my cheek. "What did I do?"

"Nothing, you were just an easy target." Louisa-Mae laughed then shook cider over Lauren and Sabrina too. She tossed her long strawberry-blonde hair, looking like a proud lion. "That's what you get you pack of sluts."

"Oi. What're youse lot doing here?"

Johnny's voice. Before I even turned, heat flooded my face. Lucky for me the sun had already set, or I would have been *pure* scundered. I swivelled my head and watched him stride across the grass with his mate Daz. His blonde hair hung in curtains around his eyes and he was wearing the denim jacket and blue jeans combo that I liked on him the best. Such a *screw*.

"Hiya Johnny," I said, then cleared my throat to get rid of the annoying too-high-pitched croak that had come out of my mouth.

Johnny didn't answer me; he was looking at Louisa-Mae. "Alright there skivvy." He prodded her back with his toe. Louisa-Mae sucked in her lip and rolled her eyes before rounding on him.

"See if you call me that one more time, I'll seriously knock your block off, dirtbag."

Johnny and Daz sniggered before Louisa-Mae jumped to her feet, suddenly sober even after downing all that White Knight, and swiped at Johnny's head. I watched her chasing him away into the bushes.

"What did he mean, skivvy?" I asked.

Lauren smirked. "Louisa-Mae doesn't want it getting round, but since it's just youse. Mr Crawford made her carry his Technology folder and bag the other day cause he said he had a sore arm."

"And did he?" I said, my eyes searching the bushes; no sight of any of them.

Lauren pulled a face. "What do you think, does he look like he's hurt? He's loving it that he made a mug out of her to the teacher."

"He fancies her, it's obvious," said Sabrina.

An alarm went off inside me. "Do you think she fancies him too?"

"Nah, not Louisa-Mae. She likes someone else." Lauren stuck her chin out, loving the fact that she knew something that me and Sabrina didn't.

I turned my attention back to the clump of trees and bushes. Daz limped out, his breath coming in heavy rasps. Clearly winded he said, "that mate of yours is a right geg."

I looked past Daz, my eyes scanning the bushes. No sign of either Johnny or Louisa-Mae. "You don't think she's *seeing* him in there, is she?"

Lauren's forehead wrinkled. "Ugh, as if she'd see Johnny dirt."

I tutted. "What do you call him that for?"

Lauren's face switched from furrowed brow to ecstatic in a split-second. She pointed her finger at me. "Ah, you fancy him, don't you? You dirtbird! You kept that one a secret, alright."

My face was burning, scorching hot. "No I don't, he's boggin'."

"Megan dirtbird!" Lauren rolled over with laughter on the grass. She sat back up cross-legged and waggled a finger at me. "Megan and Johnny up a tree, k-i-s-s-i-n-g, Megan said would you finger me and Johnny said yes cer-tain-ly!"

Her singsong voice grated in my ear. I looked to Sabrina for help, but she shrugged her shoulders at me and flicked a look of pity my way.

"That's disgusting, you're a dirt-y wee git," I said. My eyes flitted once more to the bushes. Still no sign of Louisa-Mae or Johnny. My imagination was beginning to fight the restraint I'd put on it – and it wasn't good. What if Louisa-Mae got there first? I wasn't sure I wanted to make a move on sloppy seconds, even if it was a screw like Johnny.

The Blue Man

Louisa-Mae stumbled out of the bushes first, almost completely doubled over and squealing with laughter. Johnny followed, his face and neck beetroot.

"What're youse two up to?" said Lauren, her voice tainted with impatience. Louisa-Mae's sidekick didn't like to be kept in the dark anymore than the rest of us did.

"Go on Sabrina, tell him. He doesn't believe me – about your Blue Man," said Louisa-Mae.

Sabrina's eyes widened. "He's not *my* Blue Man. I only told you what I'd heard."

Inwardly, I breathed a huge sigh of relief. Hopefully telling Johnny about Sabrina's ghost story was all they had been up to in the bushes alone for so long.

"I even got that *header* there to look around, cause I told him I heard a choking sound coming from the mudflats – and then I snuck up on him and scared him. It was a cracker – you should've seen his face!" Louisa-Mae rolled over on the grass holding her stomach.

Sabrina's face was fearful. "How did you know the way he died? You said you'd never heard the story before."

Silence fell. As the last of the twilight gave way to darkness, the only sound was the wind whistling among the trees.

"You're joking? He didn't die in the mudflats, did he?"

Sabrina nodded. "So the story goes. He was murdered out on the mudflats, but not before he had sold his soul to the Devil."

I jumped to my feet. "Right, can we stop with this flippin' ghost story now, the joke's gone far enough.

I'm hungry. Who wants to walk up to the chippy with me?"

Louisa-Mae's laughter cut through the silence, this time accompanied by Lauren's. "Ah, you wee feardy-cat, you actually believe all that bollocks about the Blue Man, don't you?"

I didn't answer. I wrapped my arms around myself to shield from the evening chill and marched away across the grass towards the gate.

"Here you, don't walk away from me. Are you seriously that scared?" Louisa-Mae's voice behind me was high-pitched and insistent. I didn't answer. The grass rustled as the sound of running feet approached. I felt a hand slip into the left pocket of my denim jacket. Louisa-Mae held my makeup bag high, her face pulled into a taunting smirk.

"Give it back," I said, stretching my hand out.

"Nah uh-uh," she said, in a tone of delighted sadism. "You can't leave now, we all know you wouldn't go anywhere without your bag of slap."

As I walked forward, Louisa-Mae stepped backwards, until she turned and dashed for the bushes. With no choice in the matter, I tore after her. Leaves slapped my face and I swiped with both arms, ducking under branches.

On the other side of the overgrowth, Louisa-Mae teetered on the riverbank. She extended her arm out holding my make-up bag over the mudflats. My eyes dropped to the oily effluence from the nearby Shorts Brother's factories. She wouldn't really do it, would she?

"Give it back, right now," I said, choosing a low, threatening tone.

The Blue Man

Bad idea. It seemed to have spurred her on. For a horrible split second I watched my make-up bag arc through the darkening sky, the blue glitter twinkling in the last remnants of twilight. It hit the mud with a wet squelch and sat forlornly, half-lodged in it.

"Go and get it now, I dare you." Louisa-Mae turned to look over her shoulder and shouted, "Megan's gonna see if the Blue Man really is out there, in the mudflats."

A flurry of feet and rustling leaves announced the others arriving: Lauren, Daz and Sabrina stood on the riverbank looking at where Louisa-Mae pointed, proudly showing off her handiwork.

"It's an offering to the ghost of the Blue Man," said Louisa-Mae, and then in a theatrical voice added, "Woo!"

I turned on my heel and headed for the gate.

"Wait, Megan, I'll come too," Sabrina called, though I didn't wait for her; I didn't want to give Louisa-Mae the satisfaction of seeing me annoyed. Sabrina would catch up, she was my friend. I wasn't so sure about Louisa-Mae. Sure, she was a good laugh and all; nights out with her were always good craic. Sometimes she could be a really great friend, like when she gave me iron tablets the time my period was so heavy. But other times, like tonight, she proved she could be a real bitch.

As I passed through the gate, tidal smells on the breeze struck me full in the face; mudflats and the smell of decay. Probably dead sticklebacks, or crabs, coming from the riverbank at low-tide. Nothing more. Anything more was a story about the bogeyman to scare kids. That's what I told myself.

Chapter four

Sabrina – April 2000

Saturday night had gone well. Too well; better than I could ever have planned. I hadn't counted on the story of the Blue Man causing a bust-up between Louisa-Mae and Megan, but so it had. Megan had been sucking up to Louisa-Mae now for how long? I counted on my fingers. Since January: four months. Megan was supposed to be *my* best friend, and over the past twelve weeks, I'd had to watch her buddying up to little miss popular. Why? What was so special about Louisa-Mae?

Louisa-Mae had it all: she had nice orangey-yellow hair that was like the colour of a sunset and she had a pretty face. She was posh, or at least lived in a good area in Belmont. Her parents had decent jobs and she lived in a gorgeous house. On top of all that, the boys always seemed to fancy her first. Why did she have it so easy, yet she was still kind of a bitch?

If it wasn't for the bitch angle, I would've *pure* hated Louisa-Mae. But the bitch angle made me feel a bit sorry for her, like, what had to be wrong for her to act so horrible at times? Megan was the only one I'd told that to; but now I was wondering if I could trust her to keep secrets. She was sucking up to Louisa-Mae so much and all Louisa-Mae did was treat her like shit.

Speak of the Devil. Louisa-Mae breezed into our form room, her long, orange hair flying behind her in perfect waves. She had the usual 'I'm better than you' look on her face with her nose stuck up, but today she looked even more arrogant. What on earth could she be extra smug about? Everyone was talking about how she'd chucked Megan's make-up bag into the mudflats, and the majority agreed with what I'd thought for ages: that Louisa-Mae was sort of a bitch.

Louisa-Mae strode straight to Megan's desk and stood, looking down her nose at her. For a moment, I thought she was going to tip the desk over on Megan, or kick her under it, or something else horrible that I couldn't think of, cause I wasn't so nasty myself. But she didn't. Instead, she reached inside her Pierre Cardin handbag and brought out a glossy salmon-pink make-up bag.

"Megan. I didn't mean to be a total dick there on Saturday. Thought you might need a new make-up bag."

Megan's mouth hung open as she took the bag off Louisa-Mae and opened it. "But – these must've cost a fortune. My stuff was old, and all."

Louisa-Mae's self-satisfied grin widened. "Don't worry about it. But we're all made up now, aren't we?"

Megan's wide eyes said it all as her fingers scuttled over the array of eye pencils, lip glosses and brushes inside. "You even got my favourite foundation."

I clenched my teeth. Louisa-Mae had been forgiven without even so much as an apology. She really had a right cheek.

"Here, you'll love this one," said Louisa-Mae. She grabbed a silver pencil and popped off the lid. Without asking if it was okay or not, she grabbed Megan's chin in her left hand and tilted it upwards, so that Megan faced her, then carefully drew a silver line under both eyes. "It matches the blue-grey of your eyes."

Megan snatched her pocket mirror and surveyed the damage, wrinkling her nose; an affect that gave me a jolt of guilty satisfaction. "Nah, I don't like it, it makes me look like a tart."

Megan started rubbing it off with a cotton wool bud that she wet with her own saliva. Louisa-Mae looked down at her, her mouth puckered. She watched Megan apply neutral brown eyeliner, and I watched Louisa-Mae's displeasure with a dash of ecstasy that was electricity in my veins.

"Brown is too boring," Louisa-Mae said, spitting each word out. "You need something to brighten it up."

She snatched a tub of cream blusher and started dabbing it on Megan's cheeks. Megan tried to bat her hand away, but Louisa-Mae was on a mission.

"Here, leave off her, she looks far too done up like that," I said. My protests on Megan's behalf went unheeded.

"Overdone, like a cooked chicken," Louisa-Mae laughed. Quick as a whippet, she grabbed a bottle of glitter lip gloss and brought the applicator to Megan's lips. Louisa-Mae's hand on her chin held Megan's face with such force, it gave her fish lips.

"I said enough!" said Megan. She backhanded the applicator in Louisa-Mae's fingers. It shot across the classroom and hit the whiteboard, leaving a foot-long, glossy pink streak as the glass bottle shattered.

Louisa-Mae pointed at the smeared whiteboard and threw her head back cackling.

"Alright, wind your neck in, it isn't that funny," said Megan. She huffed as she crossed the room and rubbed at the whiteboard with her sleeve.

But Louisa-Mae was having none of it. She strode over to Megan, opened a tube of bronze liquid foundation and squeezed it all over her face. Megan jumped backwards, the liquid spilling all over Mrs Miller's desk, books and papers.

"Oh my God, you nut-job," Megan gasped. "You've really done it now. I'm not taking the blame for that."

At that moment, as Megan began to back away from the soiled desk, the classroom door clicked open. Mrs Miller walked in. The other girls in our form, who had been giggling during the lip-gloss-whiteboard charade, scattered back to their desks like cockroaches scuttling under rocks. The teacher's eyes travelled from Megan, to Louisa-Mae and then to the whiteboard and her smeared desk; her lips pulled into a taut line.

"Who did this?" said Mrs Miller.

Louisa-Mae looked straight at Megan. Mrs Miller's eyes followed, resting on Megan for an explanation.

Megan shook her head. "It wasn't me. It was the Blue Man."

***

Lauren sniggered as she passed me the R.E. textbook. I looked at the picture of Jesus hanging on the cross with two Roman centurions standing to one side. Lauren had drawn a speech bubble from the first Roman's mouth with the slogan, 'How's it hanging?'

I laughed behind my hand as I drew a speech bubble from the second centurion's mouth, reading, 'It wasn't me. It was the Blue Man.' When I passed it back to Lauren, she spluttered and passed the book forward to Natasha in front, tears streaming down her face. Natasha heaved with suppressed laughter and passed the book onwards. After the book made its fifth turn from desk to desk, Mrs Miller noticed.

"Alright. Who did this?"

Holding the book up on display to the class was the wrong move; all thirty of us erupted with laughter. But no responses.

"Lauren, this is your handwriting. Go outside and wait in the corridor."

Lauren walked out, her face beetroot.

Mrs Miller frowned as she studied the second speech bubble: mine. I smiled to myself. Quite crafty to have made the handwriting loopy, and sloping backwards to the left. Not like my angular, forward-facing writing.

"Who else defaced the book? If there is a co-conspirator, you'll also be in trouble."

With Lauren, Louisa-Mae and Megan sent out of class, no-one knew for sure that I had done the other graffiti. Mrs Miller gave a disgusted look at the class then walked out into the corridor. Hushed whispers and giggles broke out the moment she had gone.

"Who else did it?"

"Was it you, Sabrina?"

"Did Louisa-Mae do it?"

"Ssh, listen! Lauren's getting a bollocking!"

Even though we all fell silent, it was hard to hear Mrs Miller as she was keeping her voice intentionally quiet. A moment later, the door whooshed open, blowing papers off the teacher's desk. Mrs Miller appeared in the doorway looking livid.

"Get outside here now, Sabrina."

I grabbed my bag and plodded toward the door. Lauren avoided looking at me as I went into the corridor. My so-called mate was a tout. What a wick one.

"You two follow me."

We fell in line behind Mrs Miller as she led us on a death-march to Mr Simpson's office. The vice principal would go through us, for sure.

From the corner of my eye, I could see Lauren's face angled directly at mine. My own face burned with anger at her betrayal. As if reading my thoughts, she whispered under her breath.

"I didn't tout on you, I swear. She just knew."

I put my finger to my lips.

"I think she saw you laughing."

I flapped my hand at her to shut her up.

As soon as Mrs Miller opened the door to Mr Simpson's office, I saw Louisa-Mae and Megan standing in front of his desk, their faces sombre. Lauren and I filed next to them, all of us facing the vice principal as he sat in his chair. Mr Simpson rose in one swift motion like he was a man half his age. He leaned forward on his knuckles and as he loomed across the desk towards us, his face turned puce, a vein protruding in his forehead.

"You four hallions had better explain yourselves."

A snigger escaped Louisa-Mae with her poor self-control; saliva arced across Mr Simpson's desk and left a wet splat. The vice principal looked at the droplet, then at Louisa-Mae and each of us in turn, his eyes practically bulging with rage.

"Do you find it funny? Well I don't. I don't think you'll be too amused when I call up each and every one of your parents and tell them that their daughters have been defacing school property."

Louisa-Mae pressed her lips together. Her eyes were glassy as she struggled to contain her laughter. "It wasn't us, Sir," she said, her voice choked.

"Then who was it? Who smeared lotion on the whiteboard and all over Mrs Miller's desk?"

"Lip-gloss," she corrected. "And foundation." The audacity of Louisa-Mae, talking back to the vice.

"I don't care what it was. I want to know who put it there!"

Her face sobered, her voice becoming composed. "It wasn't us. It was The Blue Man."

I couldn't believe my ears. Louisa-Mae was pushing it too far. We'd all be thrown into General Detention, at this rate.

"Stop lying to me!" Mr Simpson shouted. "I don't think you realise the trouble you're in!"

Or the isolation room.

Mr Simpson spun to target Lauren and I with his anger. "And now I see this."

The open R.E. textbook lay on his desk. He jabbed a finger at the speech bubbles surrounding Jesus. This time I didn't laugh. Neither did Lauren.

"Which one of you defaced this book?"

"It wasn't us. It was The Blue Man."

Lauren spoke in a low monotone, as though she were drugged. Or hypnotised.

"Oh it was, was it? Well, since the Blue Man can't foot the bill, I'll be dividing it between all four of your parents. Starting tomorrow, the four of you are suspended for three days. Now, get out of my sight!"

Chapter five

Sabrina – September 2020

As I walked away from the café, in the opposite direction to Megan, a sort-of antsy feeling overcame me, like being keyed-up for no reason. Well, not for no reason. After all, hadn't I just met with my high school best friend, who I had been wanting to track down since forever ago, but hadn't seen in twenty years? Wasn't that enough reason to be full of nervous energy, right there?

I glanced over my shoulder with a wave of embarrassment before I got into my second-hand, well-loved Skoda Octavia, even though I knew Megan was far away in the opposite direction and wouldn't see my beat-up transport. I chided myself aloud with a sigh. Yes, it was true that my car needed duct-tape on the door handle of the driver's side to keep it shut and yes, it tended to stall at traffic lights and occasionally need pushed to get started again, but it was *my* car. Besides, cars were simply transport; it didn't matter if someone drove a gorgeous new Porsche, or a second-hand Skoda Octavia that they had bought off Gumtree for £400. I shrugged to myself. Maybe I was trying to convince myself, but that was okay.

I parked in a free spot near the flat that Jake and I rented just off the Cregagh Road and walked around the corner to Woodstock Road to browse in a charity shop for bargain books. The rack out in front usually had decent reads; maybe a bit of retail therapy would do me some good after my wave of insecurity about Megan seeing the state of my car. There was always room for more books for a self-confessed bibliophile. My hand thought otherwise though, my fingers fumbling around the wallet in my coat pocket. I had a £20 note, enough money for the next couple of night's dinner for Jake and I. Besides, in less than a fortnight, I would be finished work and off on nine month's of statutory maternity pay. Not a happy thought. Three months of close to full pay, then my payments would drop off a cliff – a huge cliff – into an abyss that would see me through the winter. Even Jake's salary as a bank cashier would be squeezed tight on our maternity budget. Beggars couldn't be choosers, so we would have to stretch what we had. I pursed my lips as I turned away from the bargain book rack. Books were a luxury that would have to wait.

I crossed at the traffic lights, my mind on the twenty pound note and what that would get me for dinner. I probably shouldn't have had a decaf coffee; should've had a herbal tea like Megan had and saved myself a couple of quid. Pregnancy had changed my taste buds too; the decaf had left a bitter aftertaste in my mouth that I would have been happy to do without.

My feet led a robotic march through the grocery shop, picking up essentials for the next few days. I slung the shopping bag over my shoulder, feeling lopsided. As if I wasn't enough of a *pure* heifer to start with. Should I call Jake to meet me? It was his half day at work so he would be available, if I asked him. Nah, too lazy; our flat was mere streets away. The exercise would do me good.

Our flat was number four of six in a dilapidated townhouse, with weeds growing through cracks in the brickwork and chipped paint on the window sills of the front facade; and that was for starters on the outside. What would Megan think if she saw it? Guess I'd never invite her, now that I knew of her snobbery about wealth – or lack of it. It had raised an ugly little part of me too though; I had always considered myself somewhat of a spiritual person, the kind who didn't care about material wealth, the sort who would have easily given up all of her possessions and gone away on a Buddhist retreat in Tibet. Yet, here I was worrying about what an old friend that I hadn't seen in decades thought of me. Why did I care? It was a question I pondered as I stepped over the uneven, broken tiles of the garden path leading up to the entrance to the flats.

"Oh, hello Sabrina love, how are you getting along?"

Betty, the midwife who lived in Flat one with her partner, a painter. Betty was a vibrant Jamaican woman who had moved over from London. I had warmed to her immediately for that reason, as Jake and I had lived in London for a year when I worked on my first teaching job after my PGCE and it brought back good memories of our time living in Tottenham. I warmed to her even more when I found out her name was Betty. It was such an antiquated name that harked to an old world now rapidly fading. Would any babies of my own child's generation be called Betty? Bettys were fading into obscurity, a soon-to-be extinct breed. But such a lovely name! Maybe if I had a girl, I'd give her Betty as her middle name.

"Hiya Betty. Nearly there now, just over a month to go."

"Are you drinking enough water? It'll help with the swelling in your ankles." She eyed the bag of messages slung over my shoulder. "And you shouldn't be doing the grocery shopping either, get that husband of yours to help out!"

I smiled as I fumbled with the front door key. "You're too good to me Betty."

She grabbed my arm, stopping me before I went into the communal hallway. "Oh and another thing. The washing machine is broken. Kevin has reported it to the Estate agents, so they should be sending someone round today to get it fixed. Just thought I'd save you two a trip down with your basket."

"That's awfully good of you letting me know." I stepped into the entranceway and reached for the pile of mail on the desk.

"I think there's a new tenant in Flat five above you, moved in yesterday."

I sifted through the envelopes, keeping my eyes peeled for anything addressed to Flat four. How long was Betty going to keep me talking? Much as I loved her company, my bladder was going to give at any minute, seven and a half months of baby weight bearing down on it.

"There's something odd about him though. He came down, about a half hour ago, to collect his post. He was wearing a blue hoody over a blue skirt."

Betty had got my attention; I looked up from the pile of envelopes to search her face. "What do you mean, skirt? You mean, like a kilt?"

"No, it could have been a towel tied around his waist." Betty's usual jovial demeanour was gone, serious for the first time since I'd known her. "That wasn't what struck me as odd though – he didn't bother to take down his hood, even when he saw me coming out of the laundry room. Surely if you were meeting your new neighbours, you'd say hello and show your face, wouldn't you? But no greeting, nothing."

I stared at Betty, not sure what to say. The fact that such a sociable woman as Betty was unsettled had me rattled. I needed to stay level-headed though; assuming it was a kilt was simply my paranoid mind making unseen connections that were more leap than step. Kilt. Probably it had been seeing Megan that had left me rattled, not what Betty was telling me about the new neighbour. Megan reminding me of the Blue Man.

Still, it made for a nervous trek up the stairs to our flat on the first floor. I kept my fingers crossed in my pocket that I wouldn't bump into the man in Flat five on the way up and was happy in the knowledge that Jake was home to alleviate my fears – however irrational.

"Jake? I'm home," I called, the moment I pushed the door open.

"Hey honey. How did it go with – Melanie?"

"Megan," I said. "Actually, I think it went well. The weird thing is, it was like nothing had changed, it was as if we'd seen each other yesterday not two decades ago. We just slipped back into this comfortable groove with each other."

Jake got up from the sofa and came into the hallway, kissing me on top of my head as I kicked off my shoes.

"That's great. I'm glad it went so well. I know you'd been wanting to get in touch with her since before we even met."

"You wouldn't believe it." I laughed. "She's even worse than me about not doing the whole social media thing. I searched for her from time to time and then randomly a couple of months ago her profile popped up, so I added her and then we got messaging. If not for that, we might never have linked up again."

I followed Jake into the room to the left of the hallway, that served as both kitchenette and living room, and flopped down on the sagging green velvet settee.

"It was nice of her to come and meet you in town. Didn't you say she lives in Sydenham?" said Jake.

"No, Holywood Arches. Town is best for us both as it's the neutral ground we need to give our friendship a fresh start – we have no history there. She's pregnant too, isn't that the funniest thing? The baby won't be due until February though."

"Something more you two'll have in common then, that's good," said Jake. "You could invite them both round when our little spud is born."

I rubbed my belly, grinning widely. "Er – I don't think so. Megan wouldn't be much impressed with this place. I mean, we live in a run-down wee shithole, and all."

One corner of Jake's mouth rose in a smirk. "You're kidding right? It's not like you to care about such things. Is she really so stuck up?"

I dropped my hands in my lap and shrugged. "Maybe it's not about her, it's about me. I mean, what would she think if she knew our flat in Liverpool got repossessed? It was a poky place, you couldn't have swung a cat in that wee hovel, but it was ours. Now we're paying someone else's mortgage to live in a dive, because nobody in their right mind would give me a mortgage since I'm in the red."

"Ah, but if she knew the circumstances," Jake went on.

I flapped my hands, ignoring him. "Nobody over there gave a rat's arse if you were renting or a homeowner, or what sort of car you drove. Not that there's anything wrong with my wee Skoda, sure it gets me to where I need to be, but I guess I miss Liverpool – I didn't feel self-conscious like I do here. There's this unspoken rule over here that whenever you meet up with old school chums that you somehow have to be the most successful. People here judge you on what sort of car you have and whether you own your house or not. It's such a materialistic place and I hate feeling like a loser."

Jake pulled me into a cuddle and I happily took the chance to melt into his warm, snug armpit. "Maybe if she knew about how we lost our money, she might be more sympathetic."

I pulled his heavy, warm arm tighter around me. "Somehow Megan as she came across to me today doesn't seem the type to feel sorry for anyone."

He squeezed my shoulder, massaging the nape of my neck. "But it was a brutal court case, and an even worse accident."

A memory filled my mind: of a quiet road with no cars; of the school where I worked as an English teacher on the other side; my wrist-watch showing that I had ten minutes to get to class and the puffin crossing just a few feet too far ahead. I had cut between the parked cars. One had pulled out, oh so quiet, oh so fast, and I had turned at the last minute, distracted by thoughts of being late to lessons.

"Yeah, well the judge knows best, I suppose." I let my voice trail off as I forced the image out of my head; me flying up over the bonnet, smacking against the windscreen, crashing onto concrete. "He found in that driver's favour because I was in the wrong. I should have gone to the crossing."

Jake scowled. "He was a misogynist if you ask me. He didn't even take into consideration how that wanker was over the speed limit for a school zone, nor the fact that you were hospitalised for three months."

As if in response, my knee twinged. The metal plate helped, but I would have a limp for the rest of my life. "All he cared about was that the driver had right of way and I shouldn't have been jaywalking."

"Well," Jake sighed. "Paying that bastard's costs as well as our own solicitor's fees is the first and last experience I want to ever have in court."

"Same here. Belfast is a fresh start all over again. I mean, it's my home and all. That court case has given me a fresh perspective on living back here. I just wish people weren't so judgemental."

Jake stroked my hair. "Not your mum though, she's been great."

"I know, I'm lucky. She told me she wanted us to stay until I was over the depression, but I felt like we were imposing. Her house over there in Ashmount is so small."

Jake kissed the top of my head. "I know honey. As much as she loved having us stay, we were getting in her way. Plus, it was hard having to tiptoe around and whisper during the daytime, so as to let her sleep off her night shifts in that care home. She's a trooper, doing that work during a pandemic."

I sniffed. "I know. I wish she didn't have to do care work in case she catches covid, but she loves the chats she gets with those auld grannies and grandas, you know? She's done it now for twenty years, I think she'd be depressed if she did anything else."

Jake looked around our kitchenette and threw his arms wide. "We don't own this place, but at least it's our space until we get back on our feet and can buy again. Besides, you shouldn't care what people think, honey. You barely know your old school mates anymore and if they don't accept you as you are, then screw them."

His words interrupted my dour thoughts. Jake was right. I smiled. My lovely husband always talked sense. "Thanks sweetie, you're right. Maybe if I didn't feel so insecure about life generally, then Megan wouldn't have made me feel so self-conscious."

Jake's eyes crinkled as he pulled a silly grin. "What's there to feel self-conscious about this place? It's a palace. We have a sofa, don't we? A *proper* sofa. We only had a sofa bed in that hovel in Toxteth where we lived after the flat got repossessed. This is *luxury* in comparison."

I threw my head back with laughter. "You're absolutely right – appreciate the little things."

At that moment the kitchen light swung as a thud upstairs resounded through the ceiling. An opportune moment to tell Jake about our new neighbour. "Here, Betty in number one was saying that there's a new fella upstairs. Apparently he's an oddball."

I swallowed, thinking of the description of him dressed in a blue skirt and hoodie, but couldn't bring myself to mention it. Honestly, it made me feel sick.

"Yeah, I heard him talking to David in number three across from us, out on the stairs while you were away. Really thick accent. Couldn't tell if it was a broad Belfast accent, or Scottish."

Scottish. The sickness in my stomach was welling. Not since my early days of pregnancy did I feel like I needed to purge my body; of the decaf coffee, the memories Megan had stirred and my paranoia at the new tenant living above us.

Surely it had to all be a coincidence? An unfortunate one, a horrible one, but a coincidence nonetheless.

"I think he got into an argument with David as he dropped his cheesy chips all over his doormat on the way downstairs and didn't make much effort to clean it."

I sighed. This was no time to be irrational. My pregnancy hormones were running high, that was all.

"Is something wrong honey? You look pale."

I looked Jake straight in the face; time to be honest. "I need to tell you about some things that happened over one summer, back in 2000."

Chapter six

Megan – April 2000

I took a swig of *Buckfast*, winced and swallowed.

"See? Told you it was good." Louisa-Mae smirked, looking like she was struggling to hold in laughter.

"So what wee lads are coming tonight? You said there would be boys."

Louisa-Mae and Lauren exchanged sly grins. "You're such a tart, Megan. You're just gagging for it, aren't you?"

I felt my ears burn but was thankful that they were well hidden under my hair. It had taken me an hour to straighten it all, given how thick it was. And for what? If Johnny didn't show up, I would have wasted my time.

"Johnny's been invited, don't worry," said Louisa-Mae, reading my mind. The heat from my ears flooded forwards into my cheeks; there was no hiding it now. I turned my face away.

I shrugged. "I'm not fussed if he shows up or not. I was just wondering how you got round to inviting any boys when we haven't even been in school for three days."

She tapped her nose and gave me a sly look. "I have my ways."

Suspension hadn't been half bad. My mum had given me a dirty look and had cold-shouldered me for, like, an hour after she got the call from Mr Simpson. Not that I cared; it had given me some peace to watch *Jerry Springer* by myself while she huffed in the kitchen. She eased up when I told her that it was Louisa-Mae's fault and that all I had done was get caught up in the madness. The only bad part was missing out on all the gossip – and not seeing Johnny. I glanced at Louisa-Mae and unease tugged at me. How did she manage to invite him if, like me, she'd been suspended for three days. Did she have his number?

Say My Name by *Destiny's Child* blasted out of the stereo in Louisa-Mae's living room and I couldn't help but feel it was a reflection of how I wanted Johnny to think of me. We'd been so confident getting dressed and doing our make-up in Louisa-Mae's bedroom upstairs, but now that we'd nothing to do other than wait for the fellas to come, doubts snuck into my head. Like, were we too dolled up? We were all wearing dresses instead of jeans: me in a grey pinafore over a white polo jumper looking very sixties with my cream foundation and beige lips, then Louisa-Mae looking all fake-tanned and busty in her blue chequered baby doll dress that suited her strawberry blonde hair. Lauren had on a black mini skirt and her 'ninety-percent angel' belly-top with her dark, permed hair in a high ponytail in a scrunchie and Sabrina looked all *Lisa Loeb* with a classic little black dress to match her black framed glasses and newly layered long, dark hair.

"Here, do you think we should get changed into jeans? You don't think we look like we're trying too hard?" I said.

Louisa-Mae smirked. "Are you worried Johnny'll think you look like a slutbag?"

Lauren cackled, but thankfully Sabrina didn't laugh.

"Who said anything about Johnny? It's not like I fancy him, or nothing."

She smirked. "Aye, right."

The doorbell rang, saving me from any further awkwardness. A new song started: *Smooth* by *Santana* blared out of the stereo as Louisa-Mae strode to answer the door, followed by Sabrina and the song put me in the right kind of sexy mood, ready for the fellas arriving. I trailed out after Louisa-Mae into the hallway, wondering if Johnny would notice my new dress.

Johnny, Daz and their mate Rab stood on the doorstep. Johnny's eyes dropped to Louisa-Mae's chest bulging over her baby-doll dress; I averted my eyes, secretly seething.

"Alright, Blondie?" said Johnny. Heat rushed into my face as he smiled at me; me, not Louisa-Mae or Sabrina. Did that mean Johnny fancied me, not them lot?

But no; my hopes were knocked back as he went on, "I heard about you and The Blue Man. The Blue Man did it. Brilliant! That's so class."

Ack well, so he didn't fancy me. Still, he liked my comeback to Mrs Miller about the lipgloss and foundation. I glanced at Louisa-Mae. Had she been in touch with Johnny over the three day suspension; had she told him?

"Is Chris gonna be here too?" said Johnny to Louisa-Mae.

Louisa-Mae shook her head. "My duffus brother's staying at his mate Willy's house. We've got the place to ourselves all weekend."

Wish my mum would've trusted me to mind the house for the weekend. Mind you, Chris was older than Louisa-Mae and my dirtbird brother was three years younger. I would've had to mind Stuart along with my house if it was my party.

We went back into the living room. Louisa-Mae had planned the party well; dozens of bottles of *White Knight* covered the table, along with two twelve-packs of *Carly Special*, at Lauren's request. Absolute boke if you asked me, though they did get you bleutered faster.

Who Let the Dogs Out? by the *Baha Men* blasted out of the radio. Johnny sang along, pointing his fingers at Louisa-Mae and Lauren. I suppressed a mean-spirited smile; this was a good sign that Johnny didn't fancy Louisa-Mae after all. The opposite actually – he thought she was a minger. My path to sticking the lips on him, maybe even later getting to buck him, was clear.

I sat down on the two-seater sofa, watching Johnny though his eyes were now on the booze. He glanced at me as if sensing that I was looking at him and I held his gaze, then let my eyes drop to the space on the sofa beside me. I gave two short nods to reinforce that I wanted him to sit. Johnny cottoned on to what I wanted, but with a flirtatious smile, he winked and walked to the window where he planted his arse on the ledge. His eyes lingered on me for a split second over the top of his Carly Special can before darting to his mate Rab as they fell into conversation. The warm feeling from our connection, however small, stayed with me even as Daz plonked himself next to me instead.

Daz passed me a plastic cup. I looked at the brown liquid as I took it from him. *Buckfast*. "Louisa-Mae said it's your favourite."

Louisa-Mae; the friggin' joker. "Aye, alright then."

He clanked his can of Carly Special against my cup in a sloppy *cheers*. We both slurped simultaneously.

"You seeing anyone then?"

Hmph, forward. So that was the score then, Daz fancied me? Sure, he wasn't boggin' or nothing; at least he wasn't a ginger bap. But he wasn't my type either. I looked across to Johnny, who held the blinds back as he peered out across Louisa-Mae's driveway and said something to his mate Rab that I couldn't hear over the loud music. Why couldn't Johnny have sat beside me?

Lauren, hovering over near the stereo with her drink, caught my eye and I knew she'd overheard what Daz had asked me.

"Well, are you? Who're you seeing?" Daz went on.

Lauren cocked her head towards Daz, goading me to answer. I smirked at her over the rim of my cup, a cheeky answer forming in my head.

"The Blue Man."

Daz guffawed. "Aye, dead on. That joke again. Chris told us you'd said that to your Form teacher."

I made the connections in my head: Louisa-Mae had told her brother, who'd told Johnny, who'd said to Daz.

The door knocked again and Louisa-Mae let another two fellas come into the hallway. Johnny, Sabrina and I poured into the hallway for a nosy.

"This here is Stevie and Craig," Johnny introduced. He pointed to us in turn, showing his mates. "Ginger-snap here is Louisa-Mae. Barbie doll is Megan and Specky is Sabrina."

Louisa-Mae hit Johnny a kick to his shin, while Sabrina pulled a face and I grinned to myself. *Barbie doll. Blondie.* Compared to Ginger-snap and specky. Maybe he did fancy me after all?

"Look what I got," said Stevie. "poppers."

Johnny looked at Louisa-Mae. "You game for it?"

Louisa-Mae twisted the cap off and inhaled, throwing her head back dramatically. High as a kite, she galloped back into the living room.

"What about you, trouble?" Johnny looked at me.

I shrugged, trying to be casual. Didn't want him to think I'd never done it before. "You go first. How do I know it's the good stuff?"

Johnny puckered his mouth as though to say he didn't believe me. He sucked in the vapours. "Your turn."

I looked at the small, brown bottle that he thrust under my nose, and took a deep breath. Everything around me became clearer, the lights on Louisa-Mae's front doorstep becoming brighter. After less than a minute, the feeling passed and a sickness welled. It was a horrible sensation, though I did my best to keep a neutral face.

"Good, isn't it?" said Stevie.

I wrinkled my nose. "Nah, it's not strong enough for me. It had no effect."

The boys laughed, clearly impressed. Stevie jerked his thumb my way. "She's hard!"

Aye, hard as a friggin' marshmallow. I turned away from them to go back into the living room. I was light-headed and needed to sit to settle my stomach. Getting bleutered was enough for me.

Inside the living room, Louisa-Mae, Lauren, Daz and Rab stood near the drinks table, their heads together, but when I approached they all fell apart. Louisa-Mae and Rab were red-faced and awkward. My eyes flitted between them; did Louisa-Mae like Rab? Maybe she had mistaken me *raking* around with him just before, on the sofa. Did she like him, but think I was making a move?

I shot her an exaggerated smile then nodded towards Rab, as though to say 'what's going on'? Louisa-Mae rushed to me and grabbed my elbow.

"Come on. Girl chat, now." I let her lead me lead me by the arm into the kitchen. "Somebody likes you."

"Who? Johnny? Did Rab tell you that?"

One of Louisa-Mae's eyebrows shot up. "So you *do* like Johnny?"

I shrugged. "A bit. Did he say something to Rab?"

She rolled her eyes. "Forget Johnny. I'm talking about Daz."

I sighed. "Oh right. Aye, well... he's alright I suppose."

Louisa-Mae gave an appeasing smile. "He's a nice enough fella. And he's funny too. Well? Do you want to *see* him or not?"

I shook my head. "Who does Johnny fancy, then?"

I looked past Louisa-Mae out through the open kitchen doorway towards the hall. I could make out Johnny's back and the edge of someone's black dress off to his right. I craned to look further. A horrible sinking feeling grew in my stomach. Sabrina.

Without giving any further thought, I marched across to the open kitchen doorway. "Sabrina, come over here a minute."

Sabrina shot me a puzzled look as she came into the kitchen.

"Sabrina, don't *see* Johnny." The words tumbled out of my mouth, a wee bit too fast, a wee bit too desperate.

"What? Why not?"

"Cause I like him. Please Sabrina, don't stick the lips on him. I was hoping to see him tonight."

Sabrina blushed, a deer-in-headlights look on her face. Louisa-Mae's eyes sparkled at the obvious drama. I seethed; at both of them.

"Why didn't you tell me you fancied him? How was I meant to know? You never said nothing," said Sabrina.

I swallowed, too embarrassed to apologised and too desperate not to plead. "Here – I know. I'll do your Technology homework for you if you don't see him. How about that? You know your book nightstand project? I'll design your preliminary sketches, and all."

Sabrina lowered her eyes, her long eyelashes sweeping her cheek as she looked at her feet. "It's a bit late for that. We already *saw* each other. He stuck the lips on me just now."

My ears melted at those words. The bottom of my stomach fell out. I wanted to be sick over Sabrina's guilty face, over Louisa-Mae's wide open gloating mouth. Instead, I clapped my hands over my face and pressed my fingertips into my burning tear-ducts.

Enough of all that. I pushed between my so-called friends and stomped out through the door into Louisa-Mae's back garden. I heard Louisa-Mae stopping Sabrina from coming after me, but I wouldn't have cared even if she did. Sabrina was supposed to be my best friend, but there she was, taking the boy I fancied from right under my nose. Some friend.

Why was my head so dizzy? I'd only had one cupful of *Bucky* and one whiff of poppers, but my brain might as well have been swimming. I clenched my hands into fists, squeezing until the knuckles went white. How good would it feel to punch Sabrina. She was my so-called best friend; if she really knew me so well, she would've picked up on the fact that I fancied Johnny. She must've known, but chosen to stick the lips on him anyway. Sabrina was no friend of mine.

With no outlet for my anger, I dragged my fists down the side of the wall, shredding the skin on each knuckle. The pain felt good. Dark lines streaked the bricks, just visible in the growing nightfall. I let the tears pour freely, letting all the pent up frustration pour out into the darkening garden.

"Megan, you alright there? Where were you, I was looking for you?"

Daz's voice floated across from the back door, the distant sound of dance music pumping across the house. He closed the door and the music muffled. We were alone.

I sniffed. "I'm okay."

Daz came closer. In the growing twilight, I had to strain to see what he was holding. A cup of Bucky in one hand, open can in the other. He stank of beer. I snatched the Bucky off him, twisted the lid and downed the whole quarter bottle in one go.

"Go easy there, you header," said Daz, though he sounded more impressed than worried.

Header was right; I felt so pissed my head was spinning.

A twig snapped at the bottom of the garden. I looked beyond the shed, but could only see shadows among the bushes. In the dim evening light, everything looked blue. My eyes stopped on a large, navy-blue mass that drew my attention.

"Here, Daz. What's that big blue thing over there?" I said, pointing.

Daz craned his head. I could make out his eyes, squinting to see through the darkness.

"It's just the wheely-bin," he said.

I shook my head. "Nah, it's not the right shape. It's more rounded, you know."

"It's probably some bin bags, or something." Daz took along swig of beer and turned to me. He took a step closer, coming up right beside me.

The last thing I wanted was Daz sticking the lips on me; especially beer lips. I walked away across the grass towards the shed to get a closer look at the dark blue shape. A chill shot through me fast as a lightning bolt; my feet froze to the spot. The large, blue shape was a man-sized mass, like a person crouching in the bushes. There was a head and rounded shoulders; on top of the head I could discern the outline of what looked like a Scottish Balmoral, like the type a bagpipe player in traditional Scottish clothing would wear.

He comes under the cloak of dark and a bright full moon.

I swayed on the spot, the inhalations from the poppers, and the thick, tarry Buckfast getting the better of me; was it a whisper on the air, or a voice in my head?

He comes under the cloak of dark and a bright full moon.
I looked up at the full moon above. *He comes.*
"Oh my God, it's the Blue Man!"

I shrieked and turned to run, crashing into Daz; he had followed me across the lawn. Daz grabbed my arms, steadying me. I buried my head in his denim jacket and closed my eyes, nausea washing over me.

My heart pounded, almost as much as my head. Cackling laughter broke out from the direction of the open kitchen doorway: Louisa-Mae.

"You fell for it, you dopey bitch." Louisa-Mae snorted. "I should be a voice actress."

Shame washed away my fear. Sabrina's stupid ghost story had got me *pure* creeped-out, that was all. Not the Blue Man, only a stunt pulled by Louisa-Mae.

Still, the Blue Man had got my head *turned*. Fear and paranoia; why couldn't it be love instead? I'd rather have my head full of Johnny, a real person, not a ghost. Instead, Johnny had hooked up with Sabrina, and all I was left with was the fear caused by a story that she had started. If it weren't for Sabrina, I wouldn't have even heard about the Blue Man. The stuck-up bitch had Johnny, and all I was left with was her ghost story. I seethed. Fear and paranoia; I didn't feel like myself. It wasn't a pleasant thought.

Chapter seven

Sabrina – September 2020

Orange lights from passing cars danced across the ceiling. I rolled my head to the side and grabbed my phone on the nightstand: three A.M. Wasn't three in the morning the Devil's hour, the time of day when demonic activity was at its highest? Why did I know that information; watching too many horror movies, no doubt.

In the still of the early hours, all I could hear was the rhythmic pulse of music from flat five above. I felt the beat in my chest: *dah-dum, tish, dum-dum-dum, dah-dum, tish, dum-dum-dum.* The melody wasn't discernible, only the drum beat of whatever music our new neighbour was listening to. How irritating, not only that he had cranked the song on just after midnight, but the fact that he played just the one song on a constant loop. Dah-dum, tish, dum-dum-dum. It was all I could hear in my head, all I could feel in my temples, all I could sense as the deep base tones rebounded off my very bones. The insipid rhythm vibrated throughout my body keeping me awake.

I rolled my head to my left and looked at Jake. He was still out for the count. How could he sleep through such a racket?

Not that I'd been sleeping well anyway. Seeing Megan yesterday had unsettled me more than I had at first thought. Not to mention finding out from Betty about the new creepy fella in the flat above, and the added details from Jake about him having a thick accent, possibly Scottish. Too many coincidences in such a short space of time. After all that I had laid bare the truth of that horrible, fateful summer to Jake: how four gullible teenage girls had chanced upon the enigma of the Blue Man, and how it had torn us – individually and as a group – apart. Rehashing all those old memories had been a strange and disturbing experience; my own voice in my ears had sounded detached, a monotone that wasn't mine. I might as well have been hypnotised, talking as though having an out-of-body experience. It had been an eerie feeling to relay something to Jake in that manner, and one that I was glad I would never have to repeat now that he knew the truth.

Dah-dum, tish, dum-dum-dum.

Ugh. What the hell was that song anyway? None of the melody made it through the ceiling, the notes filtered by plaster, wood and carpet. Only the pulse, the Devil's heartbeat, resounding straight from the maw of hell. Yes, too many horror movies and too much time to brood on what the fella upstairs was doing in his flat.

"Jake." I nudged my sleeping hubby with my elbow. "Honey, I can't sleep. The music upstairs is keeping me awake."

Jake grunted, smacked his lips twice then proceeded to snore. Glad it wasn't waking him up at least. Still, it meant I had to deal with the problem in Flat five myself. I swung my legs out of bed and used them as a lever to flip my pregnant-bulk upright. Not an easy feat; for a few seconds I flailed like a turtle on its back before my uncooperative body acquiesced and I found myself sitting on the edge of the bed.

I padded across the carpet without a sound and grabbed my dressing gown off the hook on the bedroom door. My body wanted bed, but my mind would never – could never – be able to rest until I found out what was the deal with the new tenant above.

Dah-dum, tish, dum-dum-dum. The pounding music from above goaded me on. I had a mission, yes, and I wouldn't fail.

I was already in the hallway outside our flat when I realised I hadn't brought my key. My motivation began to wane at the thought of retrieving it from the nightstand next to my bed; I had to go on. I pulled the door of our flat closed just enough to look like it was locked should any neighbour pass by on the communal landing, though not shut tight enough that I risked locking myself out. If Jake couldn't be stirred by my talking in his ear, then he certainly wouldn't wake up if I had to bang on the door.

Dah-dum, tish, dum-dum-dum. My jaw was set, my mind determined. Yes, I would press on.

My slippers made a soft rustle on the underlay as I walked across the landing towards the stairs leading upwards. A subconscious decision no doubt, but I didn't lift my hand to flick on the light as I passed the switch. I didn't want to telegraph my arrival; I had to catch the man off guard. As much as I wanted the music to stop, a nagging part of my mind had to know what the song was. It was water torture on my brain to hear the rhythm, but not know the song.

The emergency exit sign above the fire escape on the left case an eerie green glow over the stair well that highlighted the decrepitude of the building, throwing shadows across the uneven walls and showing stains on the brown carpeting. As I ascended, my heavy bump weighed me down, my own heartbeat racing from over-exertion and something else; fear? What should I be afraid of? The tenant above wasn't likely to be a psycho, was he? Doubt slithered into my thoughts. Jake had said the new neighbour in Flat five had argued with the other neighbour across from us in Flat three. What kind of person got himself into an argument with a fellow tenant when he was new to the building?

Come on, Sabrina, toughen up. Whether he was an argumentative arsehole or not, surely he would draw the line at fighting with a vulnerable, heavily-pregnant woman who simply wanted the music to be turned down? I would find out soon enough, at any rate. Besides, Jake was only one floor below, should I need him.

I stepped off onto the landing for Flat five and six above, trying to ignore the huge house spider in the corner that hung in its ominous web, ready to taunt me. Beware of The Blue Man, it seemed to say. Turn back. Stay away.

I brushed the metaphorical spider web out of my mind instead. Be rational, Sabrina, I willed myself. The tenant in Flat five was a new neighbour, certainly not The Blue Man. No, definitely not The Blue Man. The new neighbour was a real, living, flesh and blood person and the Blue Man was a–

My thoughts froze; I was not about to scare myself off this mission by giving myself the heebie-jeebies over a menace from the past. No, there was a time and place for the Blue Man – and this wasn't it.

Dah-dum, tish, dum-dum-dum. The beat went on. Strange that even as I approached Flat five, the song wasn't any clearer. I thought that this close, I would at least have been able to make out a tune, or even a few words. But no; just the drum beat, pounding annoyingly in my temples.

A line of light showed below the doorway of Flat five. I couldn't say how, but seeing it relaxed me. Phantoms resided in darkness, people lived in light. I sighed, allowing myself a long exhale that reset the fear-gauge in my body. I felt my racing heart slow down and approached the door.

The sliver of light snuffed out.

The incessant beat of the song on a loop stopped.

My feet stopped too, as my mind took a moment to think through my next plan of action. This was unanticipated. Did that mean the man in Flat five knew I approached? Such a notion was absurd; I walked silently in my slippers and in any event, there was no peep-hole window on the door.

No heebie-jeebies! I gave myself a mental shake-up and padded forward to the door of Flat five. Rat-a-tat-tat. My knuckles struck a sharp beat on the wood, loud enough to announce my presence and show that I meant business, but not too noisy as to be hostile.

No response. I counted to twenty in my head and knocked again: rat-a-tat-tat.

The light remained off. Not a sound could be heard behind the door, even as I inclined my ear close to the wood.

Surely the man hadn't gone to bed, right as I happened to arrive at his door? It could have been the case, of course, though would have been a strange coincidence. Not to worry anyway. The music had stopped, and that was my prime objective in going to Flat five in the first place – aside from wanting to see the mysterious, and sinister-sounding, new neighbour for myself.

I turned away from Flat five, feeling a massive psychic weight slide off my shoulders. Relief coursed through my veins warming my body. I didn't realise how tense I had felt at the prospect of meeting the unsavoury new neighbour until the need to meet him had been eliminated. Thank goodness he had shut off the music of his own accord. I padded downstairs with a spring in my step, despite the weight of my baby, and the skulking spider nearby. As I descended the last couple of steps towards the landing leading to mine and Jake's flat, my eye flicked upwards. A dark gap showed in the doorway of Flat five, visible between the wooden bannisters. I stumbled in my slippers, almost falling on my face, and grabbed hold of the hand rail. An audible click reached my ears. No, I hadn't imagined it; the person in Flat five had opened the door and was probably – likely – watching me go downstairs.

My stomach had bottomed out with a jolt. Adrenaline propelled me across the landing to my flat. I slipped inside, shut the door and clicked the lock. In the dark hallway of my flat with Jake, I still didn't feel safe; the heebie-jeebies were too close to home. I hurried into the bedroom, closed the door tight, flung my dressing gown back on the hook and slid into bed. Only then, snuggled against Jake's large, safe warmth, did I relax.

But not for long. Dah-dum, tish, dum-dum,dum.

Dah-dum, tish, dum-dum-dum.

I stared at the dark ceiling and blinked a few times. What could this mean?

My rational brain kicked into gear. One of several explanations. Firstly, that Mr. Flat five was a paranoid nut who hadn't actually turned the music off in the first place, but had lowered the volume when he had heard me approach his door, and had turned it back up now that I had gone. Secondly, that Mr. Flat five was a psycho who was playing games with me; he had turned it off to trick me into a false sense of security then, just as I thought all was well, had cranked the music up again. Thirdly, that Mr. Flat five was a sociopath who had no empathy at all and hence had never turned the music off in the first place; it had appeared that way only because I could hear it more clearly in my flat that the stairwell or landing.

Unease wormed its way back into my gut; none of those explanations were positive. Explanation one was the best of a bad bunch, though living below a paranoid nut was still unsettling.

Dah-dum, tish, dum-dum-dum.

I grabbed the pillow and clamped it against my ear. The rhythm didn't diminish; if anything the pillow amplified the chords in a different way, making the deeper notes reverberate off my ear-bones in an even more torturous manner. I wanted to scream. Instead, I pulled the whole pillow on top of my face and pressed down on it with both hands. Self-smothering was preferable to musical-torture.

This was ridiculous. If I were to salvage any amount of decent sleep, however miniscule, then I would have to find my ear defenders. The silicon plugs were in a drawer, somewhere. It was either that, or face going back upstairs to confront Mr. Paranoid nut. I swung my legs out of bed and levered myself upright once more. Silicon plugs it was.

I crossed the bedroom to the large chest of drawers by the window. The small plastic box with the silicone plugs was behind my make-up bag in the top drawer, I was pretty sure of it. Without needing to turn on the bedroom light, my hands found their way to the right spot and closed around the palm-sized box. Goal-in-one. A vestige of decent sleep would be mine, in not too long.

I turned to make the short trek back to bed when it occurred to me that the music upstairs had stopped. There had been no dah-dum, tish-dum-dum-dum for at least fifteen seconds or so; the whole time I had rummaged for my ear defenders. Was the fella in Flat five a mind reader? Had he sensed that I had found a solution to beat him at his game, and pulled the plug, lest he be a sore loser? Now who was the paranoid nut?

A creak on the landing outside our flat door punctuated the dead silence. I held my breath, not sure whether to scurry into bed or stomp to the front door and confront the threat – whether real or imaginary.

Instead I stood still, like a frightened rabbit.

Bom-bom-bom.

Three knocks on the door of our flat, Flat Four. Three knocks at three thirty A.M., half way through the demonic witching hour. Three knocks a taunt to the trinity – a response that insulted the Father, the Son and the Holy Spirit. Or so the litany of horror movies I'd watched told me.

I wiped my brow with the back of my hand; I was being irrational. Too many horror movies had tormented my brain, filling it with absurd ideas, spooking me. With a renewed fervour, the logical, adult part of my brain revved into gear and I strode to the front door full of confidence. Quick turn of the bolt and–

Nothing. Nobody on the landing, or stairwell going up. I walked to the bannister and looked over. Nobody downstairs either. Unless this guy was Usain Bolt, there was no way he could have sprinted back up to Flat five – definitely not without any sound.

I turned back into my flat swallowing a dry lump in my throat. Whatever had taken place tonight, whether rational or supernatural, was connected to my meeting with Megan earlier in the day. Of that, I had no doubt. Life was telling me that now was the time to deal with the Blue Man, and lay the past to rest, for once and for all.

Chapter eight

Megan – September 2020

Victoria Park was teeming with people; not surprising since it was a sunny autumn day. Dog walkers passed us and families with young children on scooters. The warmth – and the crowds – should have lifted my spirits. Instead, I felt a chill that seared through my body, right to the bone.

"Babe, I think we should go home," said Paddy. His voice sounded distant in my ear, like he was speaking through a wind tunnel.

I shook my head, the coastal breeze blowing in off Belfast Lough tossing blonde strands across my face. "No, seriously. It makes me feel better. I need time to think after seeing-" I gulped sea air. "Sabrina."

We had parked the car across from Sydenham train station, then crossed the bridge over the bypass into

Vicky Park. To the left were the Harland and Wolff cranes and factories from the glory days of Belfast and the grey triangular tops of the Short's Brothers industrial buildings. Straight ahead, effluence from where the Connswater River met the Lough. To the right, before the land owned by George Best Belfast city Airport, was mudflats were once lay...

Lay...

"Megan, what's on your mind? You look white as a ghost."

I chortled. "That sounds about right. I was just thinking that over there, you have the old Harland and Wolff shipyard." I swallowed, allowing myself the courage to go on. "And somewhere out there, in the mudflats out on the Lough, was where he came. Came and died."

"Who?" said Paddy.

"Don't make me say his name," I said, shaking my head.

"Whose name?" Paddy's eyes burrowed into my temple.

I looked away from him, out across the oil-slick water. "I was sure I'd told you this before. Have I really not said anything about – the Blue Man?"

"The Blue Man? No, never. Is this anything to do with your A-level Technology work and Louisa-Mae?"

I sucked air into my lungs. "Yes. They're all tied in together. The Blue Man is the other part of the story that you have to know for it to all make sense."

There, I had said it. The cat was out of the bag. Paddy and I had been married for four years, together for eight, and all this time I'd never – not once told him the whole truth about that summer.

If I had, I wonder if he would have even married me?

No time to worry about that now. Paddy watched me, like a faithful labrador waiting to be tossed a bone. What a bone I had to tell. I sighed, bracing myself.

"When we were eighteen, in the summer of our A-levels, the four of us were close – Louisa-Mae, Lauren, Sabrina and I. We were typical teenage girls, into make-up and seeing fellas from school, but not trouble in any way. That all seemed to change after a story Sabrina told us, right here in this park one night."

"Let me guess – about the Blue Man?" said Paddy.

I nodded. "It sounded like folklore at first. Just this story that the Blue Man appeared on moonlit nights when the mist came in over the mudflats. That sort of creepy rubbish designed to scare naughty kids to bed. But the more I found out about the man behind the urban legend, the more it seemed real, like he had actually been a real person. Someone who was connected to the local history, someone with a real vendetta against the people who wronged him, you know, who stole his power. And that by digging into his story, we were – the four of us – tying our fates together with his."

Paddy said nothing. He blinked a few times, seeming like he was processing what I had told him.

"Babe, not to sound cynical or anything, but isn't that all a bit – over-dramatic? Like, did you ever think that maybe the whole thing was made up?"

I was quick to answer; maybe a tad defensive. "By who? Sabrina?"

"Exactly. You told me ages ago that she was good at English, right? You were the designer among the four and she was the storyteller."

Now it was my turn to pause. I stepped off the concrete path onto the grass. "Sabrina was good at English, but she wouldn't have made up a story like that."

Paddy hopped onto the grass beside me. "Why not? Maybe she did it for kicks, to scare you all. Get a reaction, you know? I'm guessing you were all drinking that night she told you the story?"

"Diamond lightning, Diamond White... White Lightning." I waved my hands dismissively. "White Knight, I can't remember the flippin' name. Something that we drank that got the job done."

He shrugged. "Well, that explains it. Sabrina was a talented storyteller, end of matter."

I climbed a grassy bank and looked out across the mudflats, letting my eyes travel beyond to Belfast Lough. "No, Sabrina knew the story cause everyone from Sydenham all the way to the Newton did – her nanny and some of the auld men who worked in the shipyard. I even heard stuff about him – the Blue Man – that Sabrina didn't know. She was as surprised as the rest of us were when she found out more of the background about his life – and his death."

"Alright, fair enough." Paddy skimmed a stone across the waves. "But how did a ghost story cause four girls to, you know, turn bad. Get into trouble. Did you really all fall out over an urban legend?"

Hmph. It hadn't escaped my attention that Paddy's voice dripped with disdain as he said *urban legend*.

"It wasn't a superficial matter, what happened between the four of us. I'm convinced that the chain of events changed everything. My life for one has never been the same. I'm still haunted by it. I'd be surprised if Sabrina isn't still traumatised too." I cast a sideways glance at Paddy. "You should be thankful, in a way, for the Blue Man. If it wasn't for what happened, I never would have left Belfast. If I hadn't gone to Derry, we wouldn't have met."

Paddy guffawed, his eyes crinkling. "He's quite the match-maker, this Blue Man of yours. A regular cupid, if you ask me."

"Don't mock him, love, you're tempting fate with talk like that." I shivered and rubbed my arms, hoping to get some warm blood flowing into my body, to chase away the chill of the past.

Paddy wrapped his arms around me and pulled me into a tight, warm hug that erased the ghost of yesteryear, if even for a brief moment. "Alright, I believe you, I'll be serious. But let me say this one thing, just this once. If the Blue Man is real, why didn't he keep following you around all these years? Are you saying he just, well, evaporated or something?"

I wasn't sure if Paddy was teasing me or not, though his expression was flat, enquiring. I had to trust him. "He didn't disappear. We found out a way to beat him at his game."

"So you exorcised him?" Paddy added, his face still sober.

"Not quite. I suppose you could say we tricked him into leaving us alone."

Paddy looked out across the Connswater River; I could tell he was deep in thought, as I was. "And now you're worried that seeing Sabrina again might attract him back out of the spirit world?"

I nodded; I couldn't bring myself to answer, as though a confirmation would make the inevitable happen sooner. "Ghosts feed on energy. I hadn't thought about him much in the past twenty years. I'm talking, two or three times in a couple of decades. But since I saw her today, it was like picking a big scab off an old cut, and like, finding out there's still pus underneath, and that it's been festering. I've been thinking about him non-stop. Even seeing that busker in town, that Scottish fella playing the bagpipes. It's like the Blue Man is sending me a sign that he's back."

Paddy skimmed a stone into the water. "Maybe he'll go away again then, if you don't see Sabrina any more. Leave it at that – one catch-up coffee. If you really don't want to cut her off entirely, you can stay friends on Facebook."

I turned away from the muddy riverbank. "It's not enough. We've opened an old wound. It has to be – treated. Disinfected. I mean, if I stopped contact with her now, it wouldn't be enough. The memories are all stirred up now, I wouldn't just be able to forget about him."

"Never say never." Paddy took my hand in his. "If you want to forget her – and him – it's not a bad idea. Just remember you're a different person now, not that troubled teenage girl. We all do things in the past that we regret – God knows I sure did – but it's the here and now that matters. You're my wife, the woman I love, and we're going to have our first child. Let's focus on the present."

Paddy's strong, warm hand enveloping mine made me feel safe. Maybe he was right. After all, hadn't I successfully buried the memories for twenty years, to the point where I hadn't even told my beloved soulmate about that horror, from the summer when Sabrina and I were eighteen? Paddy was the voice of reason – and sense.

I dropped down onto the grassy bank and rolled onto my back. The blue sky above whisked my troubles away, as though the Blue Man – and all the pain of the past twenty years – had never existed.

Speaking of pain; a prickle on my left shoulder forced me to push myself up onto my elbows.

"Ouch!" I pulled the offending object off my skin and looked at what was in my hand. It was a thistle, the stem withered and drooping, the purple flower flattened.

All the blood ran from my veins. "See? I told you. It's a sign. He's giving me a sign. Throw it away, we have to go."

Paddy looked from me to the thistle and tossed it, nonchalantly over his left shoulder. "It's just a thistle. Why don't we go and get some lunch and forget about all this stuff about the Blue Man."

Easy for him to be so casual. Just a thistle. I wished it was nothing, an insignificant weed. But I couldn't.

"Don't you see, Paddy? Do you know what the thistle is? It's a symbol – the national flower of Scotland. The Blue Man, when he was alive, was Scottish."

Paddy shook his head. "Babe, it's just a weed. They grow everywhere. It doesn't mean anything."

"Maybe not to you, but I know what it means. It jabbed me on my left shoulder. The left shoulder is where the Devil sits. I know what it means, only too well. It means it's too late for me, love. I'm already in trouble. He knows I'm here."

Chapter nine

Sabrina – April 2000

"Oh my God, Megan absolutely fell for that, she's such a dopey bitch!" Louisa-Mae shrieked, her shrill laughter filling the kitchen. The commotion brought everyone else scurrying in around us. Everyone except Megan and Daz, who were still in Louisa-Mae's garden.

"She really thought she saw the Blue Man." Louisa-Mae bent double over her kitchen sink, choking. "I knew it would scare her, but I didn't think it would work that well."

Outside, Megan was huddled in Daz's arms. Daz shot a devious grin through the window when he saw us watching, locking eyes with his best mate, Johnny. Megan cried on his shoulder, oblivious, as he consoled her.

"What did you do?" I asked.

Louisa-Mae caught her breath with one hand on the kitchen sink. Her chin jutted proudly. "I got Chris to help me make a scarecrow earlier out of bin bags stuffed with newspapers. We dressed it in one of my dad's work shirts and trousers, blue ones, and Chris even found an old Granda hat from somewhere. Well, it's not a Scottish Balmoral, but in the dark it looks dead creepy. I was planning to wait until we were all drunk and bring it in the house to scare all you lot, cause you'd all think it was the Blue Man, but Megan found it behind the shed!"

A punch in my ribs knocked the wind out of my chest; Louisa-Mae had jabbed me in the stomach to get my attention. "Oi, look at this."

I followed the line of Louisa-Mae's finger pointing out the kitchen window. Daz had stopped consoling Megan and the pair had their lips locked, their arms like tentacles all over each other.

"Megan strikes again," laughed Lauren, sidling up on the other side of Louisa-Mae. "Who doesn't that girl stick the lips on?"

"Erm, nobody. Face it, she doesn't walk like a cowboy for no reason. The girl looks like she was bucked over a horse backwards," said Louisa-Mae. Both her and Lauren cackled. Johnny, Rab and Stevie looked amused, but said nothing.

I turned to Johnny. "Is that why Daz wanted to see her, Megan I mean? Cause there's a rumour that she's easy?"

Johnny gave me a knowing smile. "Everyone knows she spreads her legs easier than butter."

I was about to walk away to get myself another drink from the living room when Louisa-Mae grabbed my arm. "Don't go yet, show's just beginning."

Daz's left hand had crept below Megan's short, grey pinafore dress, fumbling under the folds.

"Dir-ty wee hallion," said Lauren, "She knows full well we can see them."

"She doesn't care, she's stocious," Louisa-Mae remarked.

I broke free of Louisa-Mae's grip. "I need more Bucky."

Watching my best friend get fingered by a chancer, to her own humiliation, was not my idea of entertainment. Who the hell knew why Louisa-Mae and Lauren found it so funny? They were meant to be Megan's friends, but honestly, they carried on like two complete bitches sometimes. Who needed enemies when you had mates like that?

A sniff behind me alerted me to Johnny's presence; he had followed me through to the living room. He cracked open another beer. "Were you in on the scarecrow gag?"

I shook my head. "That was all Louisa-Mae. She's quite the mastermind."

Johnny gave a quick glance behind each shoulder, then shot me a lopsided smile when he saw that we were alone. His sexy smile made my stomach jolt. I'd always found him cute, but when he smiled like that, he looked a total screw. He shook his blonde curtains out of his face and leaned closer, about to kiss me, when Daz came bursting into the room.

"Did you see us out there? Did you?" Daz danced around Johnny then stuck two fingers under Johnny's nose. "Whiff that. Fishy fingers."

"You're disgusting," I said.

Daz gawped at me through heavy lids. "Oh right, didn't see you there. Don't tell her."

How could he not have seen me, unless he was stoned? Nothing but a *pure steek*. Megan could do better; Daz was *pure* scum. Scummier than scum.

Megan sidled into the room behind Daz, looking proud as punch. I had to warn her. Leaving Daz to gloat to Johnny, I tugged Megan by her sleeve out into the hallway. We'd barely got out of earshot of the boys when she whisked her arm out of my grasp, her lip curled.

"Megan, don't bother with Daz."

Her voice was sour. "Don't tell me you like him? Johnny not enough for you now, you need to have Daz as well?"

"What? No – Daz is no good. I wouldn't keep seeing him if I were you."

Daz swaggered out into the hallway and wrapped his arms around Megan's waist from behind, planting his chin on her shoulder. "What am I missing, girls?"

Megan grabbed Daz's arms and pulled them tight around herself. "I'm not you, Sabrina."

I watched Megan lead Daz upstairs. Daz glanced back over his shoulder, his tongue hanging out like a hungry dog, and exchanged smirks with Johnny.

Louisa-Mae, Lauren, Rab and Stevie flooded out of the kitchen and joined Johnny and I in the living room. My cheeks grew hotter the more I drank. At some point, Rab lit a huge spliff and passed it around. I recall Lauren giving me a blow-back and my head became muddled. A big house spider crawled across my knee as I sat one the sofa; normally a monster on my bare leg would have sent me screaming, but I casually flicked it off and necked more Bucky.

"I need a piss."

Louisa-Mae's downstairs toilet was closer, and therefore a more achievable feat than the bathroom. I managed the trip there, and was on my way back, when I heard Louisa-Mae and Lauren's voices.

"But Sabrina's still a virgin." Lauren's voice.

"Yeah, exactly. We need to get her bucked." Louisa-Mae. Callous. Calculating.

"Johnny'll do it. He's not Johnny dirt for no reason." Lauren again.

"Why do you think I set them up? He was going to try it on with Megan tonight until I told him Sabrina was up for it." Louisa-Mae's voice sounded flirty. Dangerous.

"Aww, you are a right sneaky wee article." Lauren drew each word out, impressed. "You knew Megan liked Johnny and you set him up with Sabrina to shit stir."

"Ssh! It's more fun this way. Anyway, Sabrina's such a tag along. She's little miss *pure*, but she just needs to lose it already."

"Who's this you're talking about then getting bucked?" Johnny's voice. I peered around the corner of the doorframe, enough to see Johnny with his arms around Lauren and Louisa-Mae's shoulders.

"Nothing. We were just talking about how Sabrina's gonna buck the life out of you tonight. She's a wild one, that one. It's the Spanish blood in her." Louisa-Mae pulling all her skills of persuasion, Lauren sniggering alongside.

"Shut up now, she'll be out any minute," hissed Lauren.

"No she won't, she must be dropping a huge turd in there, taking this long." Charming, Louisa-Mae. That was my cue to enter. I acted like I had heard nothing, grabbed my cup of Bucky in one hand and Rab's spliff in the other and started dancing.

"Yeooo!" shouted Johnny, joining me in the middle of the living room floor.

Louisa-Mae and Lauren flashed looks of surprise, with a side dish of jealous, as I drew the attention of all three boys to myself. That would serve the two conniving bitches just right. Virgin, indeed. How did those two *millbags* find out that I was a virgin? I hadn't even told Megan that, as I was too ashamed to be a virgin at eighteen. But the way they talked about trying to get me bucked – like my fanny was another object of entertainment for Louisa-Mae. I gritted my teeth and closed my eyes as I danced with Johnny, blocking out the sight of the two manipulative cows. The next thing I knew, we were kissing again; long, and slow, and wet. He tasted vaguely of Tayto Cheese and Onion crisps. Hmm. Great to eat, but not so good on someone else's tongue as an aftertaste; though he was hard to resist. He was such a screw.

When Johnny and I pulled apart, they were gone: Louisa-Mae, Lauren, Rab and Stevie.

Had they paired off and gone to separate rooms to buck each other? No; too fast for that. Louisa-Mae and Lauren hadn't seem particularly interested in either Rab or Stevie. My curious mind was only beginning to think of other ideas for what they might be up to when Megan's shrill, terrified scream rang through the house.

Johnny and I looked at one another before hurtling upstairs. Johnny took the stairs two at a time, darting ahead of me. We both burst into the master bedroom, Louisa-Mae's mum and dad's room, where laughter rang out, mingled with shouts of protest. My eyes struggled to take in the scene: Megan breathing heavily on the floor in a huddle where she had clearly fallen off the bed, clutching her pinafore dress to her chest in a feeble attempt to cover her bra; Daz lying spread-eagle under a thin sheet and laughing nervously; Louisa-Mae's bin-bag 'Blue Man' face down on the floor at the far side by the wardrobe. At the foot of the bed, the four perpetrators were bent doubled in hysterics.

"That was fucking magic!" gasped Lauren.

Louisa-Mae cast me a *sleekit* glance. "You should've seen it, Sabrina. They were bucking away with Megan on top, and Rab just lobs the Blue Man scarecrow on top of them. Fucking epic!"

Johnny guffawed with his mates. I laughed along with the joke too, but stopped when I saw Megan's tears. Black mascara ran down her face.

"Megan, are you okay?" I asked.

Megan rocked forward onto her knees, one limp hand still shielding her stripy bra. Her back arched as she heaved and the contents of her stomach spilled onto the floor.

The room fell silent; all except for Louisa-Mae, who struggled to supress her laughter.

"Awk, wee chicken, are you okay?" Louisa-Mae's sarcastic croon did nothing to hide her unsympathetic smile that thrived on the entertainment. I gritted my teeth; how could she be so heartless as to revel in someone's misery to that extent? Just as I was feeling the urge to punch her, Louisa-Mae dropped to her knees and started mopping the vomit with a box of tissues from her mother's bedside table. It was more than I would have been able to do, my squeamish side turning my guts at the mere sight of vomit, phlegm or blood.

Johnny looked at me. "She'll be okay. See? Louisa-Mae'll take care of it. C'mon."

He tugged one of the pinafore straps of my dress, his fingertips a light touch, enough to guide me out of the room, but not coerce. I was in control. I was still in charge.

We walked along the landing to an open, dark doorway next to the bathroom. The decor inside – black and grey bedspread and a weights bench – suggested that it was Louisa-Mae's older brother Chris's room. I didn't switch on the light as I shut the door behind us. But I made sure to slide the bolt shut to give us privacy. No point allowing Louisa-Mae any opportunity to throw the scarecrow Blue Man in on top of us.

Chapter ten

Megan – April 2000

My head was still banging with a stinking hangover, but my arm was steady as I added the last few letters of the alphabet onto the board: X, Y, Z. I was about to put the lid back on the marker, when I remembered that I needed to add 'yes' and 'no' in each corner. How else would we be able to make contact with the spirit world if not for that?

I sat back and admired my handmade Ouija board. Not bad for a Sunday afternoon. My art skills never let me down, even if my brain was mush.

"Are you sure we should really be doing this, though?" Sabrina's lip curled downwards, her eyes round and fearful. "I mean, on a Sunday and all?"

Louisa-Mae's face crumpled into a pitying smirk. "Aww, wee chicken, don't tell me you're scared? It's the Lord's day, what better day to do it on? The connection should be stronger."

I looked down at my craftsmanship. Part of me hoped I'd done it wrong and that it wouldn't work. Sabrina had a point; I wasn't a church-goer, but maybe it was bad luck to do it on a Sunday.

"I'm with Sabrina, though. What if it's – what's the word? Blasphemous? What if we all get cursed?"

Louisa-Mae's eyebrows shot upwards. "Woo-hoo-hoo! Listen to Little-Miss-Big-Boots here, using fancy words. I'm surprised you knew such a word when you got twenty-nine percent on the last R.E. test, you did the worst in the class."

"Maybe she swallowed a dictionary last night instead of dick!" Lauren grabbed my Ouija board with both hands and banged it down on top of my head. "Get it? Dictionary, dick?"

"You're lucky I've forgiven youse pair after throwing that flippin' Blue Man scarecrow at me and Daz last night," I said. I snatched it off her and shot her a foul glare; not that it mattered as both Louisa-Mae and Lauren threw their heads back laughing.

"We already told you, it was Rab, not us. It was his idea to chuck it at you – and he was the one who actually did the chucking. If you want to blame someone, take it out on him," Louisa-Mae spluttered.

"Fine then, whenever you two have wised up, let's give this a go." I twisted my face into what I hoped was a menacing smirk. "Anyway, it's your house. If this goes wrong and we summon a demon, it'll all come down on you."

Louisa-Mae fell silent right away with a pucker-mouth that made her chin wrinkle. I allowed myself a chuckle at her reaction, then inhaled to reset myself; if we were going to contact the Blue Man, we needed to get serious.

She snatched my hand and slammed it onto the cardboard pointer I had made, which sat on top of the Ouija board. It was the only indication Louisa-Mae gave that she was mad at me. I noticed that she took Lauren's hand much more gently and set it on the cardboard. She even placed Sabrina's hand on the pointer without force, and I'd always got the impression that Louisa-Mae didn't like Sabrina that much, even if she had never said so. Then again, did Louisa-Mae really like *anyone*? Well, maybe except for Lauren.

"Have you ever done this before?" Lauren had a deer-in-headlights expression, not one that I'd ever seen on her usually confident face. She stared at Louisa-Mae waiting for her answer.

"Un-huh." Louisa-Mae tossed her head in an authoritative manner. "Once at my cousin's house when we were stocious. Now, can we be quiet? It won't work if there's interruptions. And don't break the circle, no matter what. Right?"

I noticed that when she said 'right', Louisa-Mae rounded on me. What made her think I'd be the one to wreck the séance? Flippin' cheek! Sometimes she could be bold as brass.

Yet, part of me felt a shiver of thrill. If it weren't for Louisa-Mae, who else would have been game for playing a Ouija board? She could always be counted on for excitement. Maybe that was why I overlooked some of the other things about her. Like, that sometimes, *sometimes* she could be sort of nasty.

A deep breath. I needed to focus my thoughts. I was game for a laugh.

"Is there anyone there?" Louisa-Mae's voice had a slight, wavering edge giving it a mystique, like a Medium in a horror movie. Lauren sniggered, her face pink from suppressing laughter.

"Don't laugh, you flippin header! It won't work if we muck about." Louisa-Mae's voice barked in Lauren's ear.

Lauren looked huffy. "Alright gurny-gub, if it means that much to you."

Louisa-Mae sighed. "Let's all do it properly this time, alright? No laughing and no cheating."

Silence fell; proper silence, not anticipating-laughter silence. I breathed out through my nose, feeling my heartrate slow down. Had my heart been racing? I hadn't noticed. What was there to be afraid of? The Blue Man?Nah; this was all just a laugh, wasn't it?

Louisa-Mae started making large circles on the Ouija board with the pointer and everyone's hands followed her lead, pushing too. Soon all four of us were in a groove so that it became unclear if any of us, or none at all, were actually making the pointer move.

"Is there anybody there? Have we made contact with anyone?" Louisa-Mae swallowed, her throat making an audible squelching sound. Her face was flat, giving away nothing but the quaver in her voice gave it away; she was nervous.

The pointer landed on 'yes'.

An ear-splitting din made me reflexively clamp both hands against my head to save my hearing: Lauren and Louisa-Mae had both screamed at once. Lauren threw her hands up and Sabrina clapped both of hers against her cheeks, but nobody pushed their chairs back. The circle remained unbroken.

My heart hammered as we regrouped with our hands on the pointer.

Louisa-Mae's voice audibly shook. "Are you a spirit?"

The pointer stayed on 'yes'.

"Do you want to make contact with one of us in particular?"

The pointer didn't move, still on 'yes'.

"Is it...me?"

The pointer slid to 'no'.

"Is it Lauren?"

The pointer stayed on 'no'.

"Is it Sabrina?"

Still 'no'.

A two second pause. Lauren, Louisa-Mae and Sabrina all looked at me, their eyes wide.

"Is it Megan?"

The pointer slid to 'yes'.

Instinctively I stood up, but Louisa-Mae grabbed my wrist with her other hand that wasn't on the pointer. "Don't break the circle."

There was a desperate, wild urgency in her face that I'd never seen before. That expression alone was almost enough to stop me leaving the table. Almost. I pushed my chair back with my leg.

"Don't Megan. Come on, you aren't a feardy-cat, are you?" Louisa-Mae's voice was soft; not a taunt so much as a prompt for me to continue.

"We're all in this together," Lauren added. "We won't let anything harm you."

I looked at Sabrina, but she said nothing. Hard to tell if her glasses made her eyes look watery, or if it was just light from outside reflecting. I kept my hand on the pointer and used the other to slide my chair back in, then sat down. Louisa-Mae gave me a reassuring smile. Her chest heaved as she took a deep breath and continued.

"Are you one of Megan's relatives?" said Louisa-Mae.

The pointer moved to 'no'.

"Are you someone that she knows?"

The pointer moved to 'yes'.

Louisa-Mae paused, her eyes roving the board. "Can you tell us your name?"

The pointer began moving in a figure eight shape across the board. It completed two loops before resting on the letter 'N'. Next it landed on 'O'. Then 'R', followed by 'M', 'A' and 'N' again.

"Norman," said Louisa-Mae. "Is that your name? Norman?"

But the pointer hadn't stopped moving, tracing more figure eights on the board. Letter by letter, it spelled out the word 'James' and 'McMurray'.

"Norman James McMurray? Is that the name you were known by when you were alive?"

The pointer landed on 'no'.

Louisa-Mae blinked at the board. Her blank face looked as confused as I felt. "What name were you known by here on earth?"

The pointer began making figure eights again. It landed on the letter 'B'. Then 'l'. I watched the rest of the letters follow until they spelled out a word: Bluman.

"Bluman?" said Louisa-Mae, one eyebrow raised.

A creeping chill trickled in through every pore in my body. "He missed a letter, the letter 'e'. Not Bluman. He meant to spell Blue Man."

Another pause. This time we all looked at one another, the fear in all our faces visible. "Are you the Blue Man?"

The pointer showed 'yes'.

"Do you have a message for Megan?" Louisa-Mae went on.

The pointer began making figure eights, first slowly, then gaining speed. First it stopped on 'J', followed by 'O', then 'H', and finally two 'N's and a 'Y'.

"Johnny?" Louisa-Mae's voice rose to a squeak.

"What about Johnny?" I said, cutting in. I knew that Louisa-Mae was supposed to lead the session, but I couldn't help myself. My mind raced; I had so much I wanted to ask. Did Johnny fancy me? Had he planned to make a move on me at the party last night, before Sabrina stole him away? But it wasn't what spilled out of my mouth. "Did Sabrina buck Johnny last night?"

Sabrina's mouth fell wide open. Before she could answer, the pointer shot across the board.

'Yes'.

I pushed my chair back and marched out of the room before anyone could see my tears. How could my best friend have betrayed me like that?

"Megan, I didn't," Sabrina called after me. "The board is wrong, we only kissed."

"Aye right," I shouted over my shoulder. I walked into the kitchen and stood looking out across the garden. Footsteps behind me let me know Sabrina had followed me in.

"I swear to you I didn't."

"You knew I liked him – I told you not to see him, right here, yesterday, or have you conveniently forgotten that conversation?"

"I know, you did," Sabrina sighed. "But I told you it was too late – he'd already stuck the lips on me by then."

I spun round and faced her, heat surging through my cheeks. "And after that, you went on upstairs and bucked him, right in Louisa-Mae's brother's bed."

"I didn't." Sabrina put her hands up in protest, but it didn't matter. I didn't believe her.

"How could you do that to me? I thought you were my best friend." I clenched my teeth to fight back tears.

Sabrina's eyes narrowed. "No, I thought you were supposed to be *my* best friend, but here you are accusing me of something I didn't do because you believe a piece of cardboard, rather than me. That's some friend."

I hesitated, formulating my thoughts. "So you're saying, you didn't buck Johnny?"

"Yes. I didn't want to go on about Johnny and me, cause, I'm scundered about it and all." Sabrina blushed and hung her head. "But since you don't believe me, I might as well say it. I'm a virgin."

I had forgotten that Louisa-Mae and Lauren were there until they announced their presence, hovering behind Sabrina in the doorway, by sniggering.

"I knew it," said Louisa-Mae, "Told you she was frigid."

Sabrina shot a scowl over her shoulder at Louisa-Mae. "I'm not frigid, piss off."

"Oh, I can't wait to rip the *pish* out of Johnny for this – imagine Johnny dirt not being able to get the knickers off a wee girl!" Louisa-Mae fell on Lauren's shoulder in a theatrical, and irritating manner. I ignored her and turned to Sabrina.

"You swear on your mum's life you didn't buck Johnny last night?"

Sabrina nodded. "I swear on my mum's life. I'm telling you the truth. We kissed and he started getting all touchy-feely, you know, but I pushed him off and he was so bleutered he rolled back on the bed and fell asleep. The wee shite snores too, so I didn't even get a good night's sleep. And he did this."

Sabrina turned around. In the back of her little black dress was a small, but perfect circle.

"The numpty had a feg in his hand while we were seeing each other and when he fell asleep it burned a hole in my new dress." Sabrina rolled her eyes.

An image of Johnny, passed out drunk and spread-eagled flitted into my mind. I imagined his arms lolling out at either side of his intoxicated body and the cigarette singeing Sabrina's dress. It was enough to make me laugh.

"Sorry Sabrina." I covered my mouth with my hand, supressing my laughter. Once I had composed myself I went on. "But you mean it – that's you all done with Johnny. You swear?"

She wrinkled her nose. "You better believe it. Between that and his cheese and onion breath kiss, we're over."

My laughter faded as another thought popped into my head: the Ouija board. "If it wasn't about Johnny, then I wonder why the Blue Man got in touch with me? And why did he lie about you bucking Johnny too?"

Chapter eleven

Sabrina – October 2020

I scooped the teabag out of my mug and dumped it in the sink. My mind was elsewhere as I poured the milk in, making it too white. Shit. Another teabag in the mug; what a waste.

As I set the spoon down on the counter, a small brown bug crawled out from behind the dishrack and sped across towards the kettle. What sort of bug was that anyway? It wasn't a woodlouse; the body was rugby-ball shaped and it had less legs. Was it some kind of wood beetle? An earwig, maybe? All I knew was that it was the third bug I'd seen in the past week.

The new neighbour in flat five had moved in a week ago. I hadn't yet bumped into him, though his incessant music played every single night without fail. Dah-dum-tish-dum-dum-dum. Over and over again, it had long since ingrained its torturous rhythm into my head.

Jake was annoyed by it too, though he was happy to keep the peace and wear ear-defenders at night. Ear-defenders worked for me too, though I chose not to wear them. There was something off, something threatening about the man upstairs, and when I felt scared, I couldn't relax. What if I missed another confrontation between Mr. Flat Five and another neighbour, for example? Eavesdropping on him gave me a meagre sense of security, a fragment of control over the less-than-ideal living situation.

I took a sip of tea and looked at the time on my phone. Jake wouldn't be home for another couple of hours. My eyes cast across to the basket of laundry. If the machine in the laundry room under the stairs was free, I could get it all done and hung up by the time he was home.

I braced the basket against my left hip and stretched my arm over it to hold the rim. There was no way I could carry it in front of my huge bump, and in any case, I needed my right hand free to open the door. Once I'd locked the flat, I tucked the key in my trouser pocket beside my phone and set off downstairs.

As I approached the laundry room under the stairs beside Flat two where Betty lived, no whirring sound emanated from within. Three month's experience living in the building had taught me that the busiest time for laundry was first thing in the morning, before the other tenants went to work, and the quietest time was mid-afternoon, like now. I relaxed in the knowledge that I wouldn't have to lug my full, heavy basket back upstairs to wait for another time. This was my slot for the washer and drier.

I yanked open the stiff door, preparing to pull the light cord only to find it switched on already. The laundry room was occupied by a man I hadn't met before. He was about five foot ten and his blonde hair was tied in a man-bun on top of his head, the bottom half shaved close to the skin. The smell of cheap cologne masked the heavy odour of cigarettes and he wore a blue hoody over black and white checked pyjamas. My laundry basket slipped on my hip and I jerked it back into place. It was the neighbour from Flat five. He was sorting his laundry into smaller piles of boxers and t-shirts and didn't look up, even though he must've seen me from the corner of his eye.

"I'll be done in a minute," he said without lifting his eyes from his laundry. His accent was thick and Jake had been right; his brogue was half Northern-Irish, half Scottish.

"Er, no rush, take your time," I said, taking another half-step back.

"What flat are you in then?" He turned his head a fraction, though still didn't make eye contact.

"Flat four."

He cast his eyes upwards to the ceiling as though picturing the layout of the building. "That's the one below me. I'm in Five."

I tucked a loose strand of hair behind my ear. "Oh, right. So you're my new neighbour, then?"

He finally turned to look at me. One of his eyes was hazel and the other pale, ice blue. What did they call that anyway? Heterochromia? My brain was full of random crap that I'd picked up from watching too many horror movies; in this case, a film where a girl became possessed by a demonic spirit and a sign that let the exorcising priest know she was possessed, was that one of her eyes had changed colour. Funny that I could recall the details, but not the name of the movie. Aware that I was staring too long as I thought of the film, I dropped my gaze to the washing machine.

"You don't own that bicycle that's chained to the railing outside, do you?" His brow furrowed, making it seem that he was accusing rather than asking the question.

"Me? I don't cycle. I could hardly fit on a bike anyway in my state." I gave a casual guffaw to break the tension and patted my oversized bump.

The neighbour didn't return my laughter. "You wouldn't know owns that bike, by any chance, would you?"

I found myself shaking my head. "I don't know all of the neighbours in this building."

This was turning out to be an interrogation, not an off-the-cuff encounter. The man still frowned as he returned his eyes to his laundry, dumping the boxers on top of the t-shirts and bundling them into one armful.

"Well, if you do find out who owns it, you wouldn't tell them to move it somewhere else, would you? It blocks my motorbike. I work nights doing deliveries and I get back in quite late, so it's hard to see coming back in the dark. I'd be liable to crush it one of these days and we wouldn't want that to happen now, would we?"

My forehead tensed. What was it about the way he said *we wouldn't want that to happen now, would we?* that implied he didn't believe me when I said it wasn't my bicycle? Unease clawed at my chest, raked at my throat, stripping it of saliva. I stepped back, almost touching my back against the hallway wall to let him come out of the laundry room. He breezed past me and I could see the sinews of his forearms as his hoody sleeves were rolled up. He had a wiry, muscular build. Together with the edge to his personality, that hinted at instability under the surface, I felt vulnerable and cornered. If he had chosen to turn around and lash out at me, I would've been powerless to defend myself.

Ack, nonsense. There I was indulging myself in histrionics. Pregnancy hormones allowing my mind to wander. Not every new neighbour in life had to turn out to be a sociopath, like in films. But the idle thought gave me a brainwave: he wouldn't be a stranger to me if I knew his name.

"My name's – Sandra, by the way."

I had been about to say Sabrina, but the lie slipped out of my mouth of its own accord. Maybe it was my instinctive mistrust of the rather dodgy stranger, who was now my new neighbour, but I felt the need to get more information from him before giving him any of my own.

Not that it mattered; my fake name bounced off his retreating back as he marched towards the staircase. He stopped on the bottom step and turned his head, enough to look back over his left shoulder. "You can call me En-Jay. Everybody does."

"En-Jay? Like the letters N and J?"

"Aye that's it," he said, continuing on up the stairs.

Hmph. Taciturn and cryptic. I expected nothing less of the new 'oddball' neighbour, as Betty had described him. I cast my eyes across to the door of Flat two, hoping that Betty was home and would come out to relieve my tension, allow me to vent about Mr. Oddball N.J. of Flat Five. But there was no sound within. Betty was probably working her shift over at the Midwifery Unit in the Mater Hospital.

Instead I relieved my arm of its burden: the laundry basket. I dumped it on the floor and started stuffing clothes into the washing machine, though it was a robotic task; my mind was elsewhere. What a strange fella. Wasn't it weird to introduce yourself by way of a nickname rather than your full name? Was it a sign of disrespect that he didn't want me to know his proper name? Was N.J. even his real name? He could've concocted a random nickname to fob me off with; how would I know any differently? Oh well; who was I to talk anyway? Case of the pot calling the kettle black when I'd told him my name was Sandra.

I loaded the washing powder into the machine drawer and pressed the button to start a cotton cycle. So N.J. rode a motorbike and delivered takeaway food late at night. His music, the insipid *dah-dum-tish-dum-dum-dum* always pounded through our ceiling late at night; no earlier than the witching hour. If he worked a late night job, then that would make sense; he was putting the music on to relax as soon as he got through his door.

The tension in my shoulders released; at last I seemed to have deduced a piece of his character that made sense – or at least, was a *normal* thing to do. Everything about N.J. so far, or that I had built up in my head about him from anecdotes by Betty and Jake, as well as my own observations, had made him appear to be abnormal. Hermit-like or worse; antisocial. Yet, to come home after a day of work and listen to music to relax was as guy-next-door as you could get. There wasn't anything sinister about N.J. in Flat five. My imagination was simply too good sometimes; and my love of horror movies too strong.

I slipped out of the laundry room into the empty hallway and made my way to the stairs. As I climbed towards the first floor, my unease of before began to grow again. If there really wasn't anything sinister about Mr. Flat five then why did I still feel uncomfortable? Was it because of his abrupt, accusatory attitude when we spoke? No; I had come across my fair share of arseholes in my time, so I wasn't particularly fazed by that.

Then what?

The nickname. It wasn't not knowing his real name that upset me, it was the nickname itself. N.J. triggered a feeling, a memory buried deep inside the litter of my mind. What did 'N' stand for anyway? Nick? Maybe Neil?

Or Norman.

I stumbled on the stairs, my toe catching the edge of one step, and fell forward. Luckily my hands caught the step before my bump did; lucky I hadn't fallen the other way and tumbled back down. I had to be more careful; I continued my ascent holding the hand rail.

Norman James: N.J. It had been twenty years since I had heard that name, not since the day the four of us – Louisa-Mae, Lauren, Megan and I had played the Ouija board. Norman James McMurray.

My heart hammered and the breath left my chest as though a boa constrictor spiralled my body, squeezing ever tighter. Pins and needles in my hands gave way to a cold sensation. I hurried towards my flat.

My fingers wrestled with the keys until the lock clicked. I had to calm myself; a panic attack was no good for my baby. I bolted the door from the inside and raced to the bedroom. Why couldn't Jake come home early?

Alone, afraid, there was nothing I could do. I ran to the bed, got under the cover and wept. Norman James, the Blue Man – it was all the same to me. The entity that had tormented us in 2000 had returned, in one form or another, even if nothing more than painful coincidence and a stirring of hateful memories. For now.

Chapter twelve

Megan – October 2020

Thank goodness I was allowed to wee.

I pulled up my maternity leggings and smoothed my summer dress over them before flushing and washing my hands. The midwife must have thought I had a goldfish-memory when I had to double check that I definitely didn't need a full bladder for the scan. No, wee away, she had said. It wasn't like the twelve week scan where the baby was so small you basically needed a full bladder to help the ultrasound imaging show up clearer. Now that it was my twenty week scan, the halfway point in my pregnancy, my baby was big enough to show up regardless of whether I needed to wee or not. Lucky for me, I could relieve my bursting bladder before the ultrasound.

Paddy smiled at me as I came out of the disabled toilet and joined him in the waiting room. We would probably be called at any minute. I was so thankful that he had been able to get the time off work to come with me. It meant a lot that he could be there. Some of my friends had moaned about their partners, saying how they couldn't be arsed going to pre-natal appointments with them, or any of the 'Getting ready for baby' sessions where you learned about foetal brain development and the types of drugs you could access on the big day. Paddy was a man in a million. He was every bit as excited as I was about our first baby.

"Babe, did you remember to switch off your phone? I think it interferes with the ultrasound equipment."

See? Such a diligent husband, just as committed to our soon-to-be family life as I was. I smiled at him as I sat down on the hard plastic of the waiting room chair and rooted around in my bag for my phone. When I pulled it out, I noticed the blue light flashing to show a private message notification. Sabrina's name popped up. Curious, I clicked through.

"Not long til your big scan then... exciting! I'll be thirty-six weeks on Wednesday, eek!"

I stared at the text until my eyes hurt from the backlight. How on earth did she know? I hadn't told her how far along I was.

"What's wrong?" Paddy's eyes bored into the side of my face.

I showed him the message from Sabrina.

"I didn't realise you'd decided to keep texting her." His brow creased as he peeled his eyes off the text and met my gaze.

"I didn't. She just texted me out of the blue."

"You must've told her about the scan." His voice rose an octave at the end, making it a question.

I shook my head. "I definitely didn't. I might've told her the due date, but that was all."

How creepy. I reread the message. What a coincidence in timing that her message arrived just as I was in the waiting room at the Midwifery Unit. Nobody but my mum and a few other relatives knew about the exact date of my scan. Sometimes Sabrina freaked me out. It wasn't the first time she'd appeared to have *extrasensory perception*, if that was a thing. I'd once heard, back in our schooldays, that her great-grandmother had been a gypsy fortune-teller, a psychic, over in Madrid. I don't know why I'd remembered that random piece of useless knowledge all these years later. Maybe it was because Sabrina sometimes scared me with her uncanny knack for intuition. Maybe the bad things tended to stick because they were frightening.

I held my thumb on the button and powered my phone down.

"Are you going to reply?" Paddy asked.

"No." I slipped my phone back in my bag. "It weirded me out. I'm going to ignore it."

Paddy massaged my neck and shoulders. "I'm sure there's nothing to it, she probably just guessed that this is the halfway point since you told her you're due in the spring. It's not like she hacked your phone and read the messages to family."

He chortled, but I didn't. What if Sabrina had done something like that; snooped on my phone. She had my phone number after all. That was apparently all it took. "You don't think she would've though, do you?"

Paddy grimaced. "I was joking, babe. But seriously, if you distrust her that much, I don't know why you met up with her in the first place?"

I forced a laugh. "You know what? It isn't even about Sabrina. Of course I don't think she'd do that. It's just me being hormonal I suppose. I get too paranoid."

Just then the midwife called my name. I hugged my arms around my bump and stood up, feeling like an elephant wearing a tent, and let Paddy lead me to the radiography room.

Paranoid. It was hard *not* to be paranoid. All of my recent contact with Sabrina, and other events since, had been peppered with coincidence. Firstly, the fact that we were both pregnant with our first children at thirty-eight. Secondly, that after I had seen her there happened to be a busker as we drove through Belfast city centre who was wearing a kilt and a Scottish Balmoral hat, similar to that eerie phantom, the Blue Man. Thirdly, that right after the busker I had found a thistle in Vicky Park, a symbol of Scotland, directly after I had talked about the Blue Man with Paddy. Now, Sabrina had texted me in the spookiest coincidence of all, on the exact day of my scan. Could it be fate, however sinister, intervening? Why were the three of us: Sabrina, myself and the Blue Man interlinked?

The midwife directed me to lie down on the gurney. I stretched myself out on the paper towel sheet and pulled my dress up to expose my stomach, tucking the fabric under my boobs. I rolled my maternity leggings down to the top of my knickers and took the sheet of paper towel that the midwife handed me. She instructed me to tuck it into the elastic of my leggings to protect them from the gel needed for the ultrasound. The midwife then began rubbing the gel all over my bump. The cold, wet sensation was enough to pry me from my thoughts of fate and coincidence. Probably a good thing, for if left to my own devices, such notions of Sabrina and the Blue Man could become all-consuming.

The sonographer pressed the ultrasound wand onto bump above the belly button and looked at the screen. He pressed hard, the feeling uncomfortable.

"Now, don't be worrying about little Jack or Jill in there, they're very padded. They won't feel this at all." The sonographer smiled at me, making me realise I must have looked as anxious as I felt.

The screen showed a series of blurry grey blobs that swam in and out of focus, much like a kaleidoscope I had as a kid, only in black and white not colour.

"That's the baby's heart right there. We're going to check that the blood is flowing correctly in and out and that all the parts are well developed. You just try to lie back and relax."

He started using medical terminology as he spoke to the midwife, who typed into a computer. Left ventricle this and inferior vena cave that. Too technical for me. I watched the soothing pulse of my baby's blood flow and spoke soothing words to him or her in my head: don't worry, sweetie, mummy is watching you from out here.

"There's a minor VSD." The sonographer frowned as he dictated to the midwife.

I raised my head. "What's a VSD? Is something wrong with my baby?"

He turned to me, pursed his lips, then gave a tight-lipped smile that seemed forced. "Right there, you have the left and right ventricles. In between those is the septum. Now normally, the septum would be closed. But here you can see a tiny, miniscule gap. A VSD means a ventricular septal defect, a slight hole in the wall between the ventricles."

"What does that mean? Is the baby going to be okay?" said Paddy.

"In your case, yes. A hole this minor might still close on its own. If not, there's a chance that it may cause a heart murmur, or maybe no symptoms at all, though the child may have to see a doctor regularly. Just for checks, you see."

I stared at the screen, watching the rhythmic pulse of my baby's blood flow. His or her heart seemed so strong. Maybe it was wrong of me, but I was angry at the sonographer. He could've told me the good news – that my baby would be fine – before telling me about a heart defect.

After checking the baby's heart, the sonographer talked me through all of the other checks: brain, face, limbs including length, all the internal organs and asked me if I wanted to know the sex of my child, before his tiny penis showed up on the screen. A boy, a sweet son. My concentration zoomed in and out as he spoke, the minor defect still playing on my mind.

"Aww, would you look at that." Paddy's voice jolted me back to the present, in time to see our baby scratch an itch on his face; four perfect fingers across the bridge of his nose. The level of detail you could see was incredible.

"What's that behind him?" I added.

Behind our baby's left shoulder, amidst the swirling dark void on the screen, showed a brief, grainy image. Two narrow, black slits looked like smiling eyes. Below them, what resembled a long, straight nose and underneath that a dark, grimacing mouth. The features were most definitely full-grown rather than childlike, and had more of an angular, male aura, though didn't distinctly resemble a man. But as the sonographer moved the ultrasound wand elsewhere, the image was lost.

"Go back, what was that?" I pleaded.

The sonographer moved the wand back to the baby's head, but he had turned now as though camera-shy and was facing towards my spine, his little body curled like a letter C and his head tucked into his shoulders. It was almost as though something had frightened him and he was retreating to safety. My blood must have dropped ten degrees.

"Megan? What's wrong love?" Paddy's face as he turned to the sonographer and midwife was white, his wide eyes reflecting the light from the ultrasound screen.

"Please don't worry. Your child will be fine," said the midwife.

"It's not that. There was something in there with him," I said.

"What are you talking about, babe?" Paddy squeezed my hand, something he always did when he was worried about me.

"It looked like a face."

The sonographer smiled. "The ultrasound waves bounce off all your internal organs and create echoes that are picked up by the probe. Your baby moving around may have created a discrepancy in the image that was displayed on the monitor."

I shook my head. "It was more solid than that. It was like another person was in there with him."

"I know that you'll have some things to process after today. But we will be in touch. The support is here. We'll be giving you more information about what you can expect," said the midwife.

They weren't listening to me. Was I the only one who had seen the entity on the monitor?

"In the meantime, I've got a few lovely photos of your baby from today's scan. You can keep those until you meet him in a few months." She handed me a series of black and white printed photos of the ultrasound. It should have been a sweet and precious memento of our soon-to-arrive child. But I couldn't bring myself to look at them. What if the images had picked up that menacing face swimming behind my innocent baby? Without looking at them, I took the scan photos and tucked them in my bag.

Chapter thirteen

Sabrina – May 2000

I glanced at Megan's Technology project. The large egg shape, about the size of a human head that she had carved out of balsa wood, was beginning to take the form of a male face.

"What are you making for your project?" I nodded towards her design.

She shrugged. "Not sure. I've got an idea, but it might be rubbish."

I glanced at the A3 design brief she had drawn over the weekend. There was an oval face in the middle, coloured blue in watercolour, with pencils and pens in various colours sticking out the top of the head. Instead of eyes, the design had rugby-ball shaped eye slots; the left eye read 'Saturday' and the right eye showed '2 February'. Instead of a mouth, the circular shape showed a clock face.

"It's going to be a desk companion for an office worker. It'll tell you the day, date and time at a glance. The person can put all their pens and pencils in the holes that I'll be making on top.

I found myself nodding in approval. "Megan, that's fantastic. I wish I was so creative like you. You'll definitely get an A-star."

Her idea wasn't shit, mine was in comparison. I glanced at the cut pieces of MDF wood for my own project. There was nothing imaginative about my redesign of a reading stand with a light, built-in bookmark and snack tray attached.

I looked again at the face Megan had sculpted from balsa wood and down at the blue-faced drawing. She wouldn't have, couldn't have?

Could she?

"Erm, Megan." I jabbed a finger at her sculpture. "That's not the Blue Man you're making, is it?"

Megan smirked, her eyes reducing to slits. "That would be weird, wouldn't it? If I *was* designing the Blue Man, I mean."

I processed her words. "So, is it or isn't it the Blue Man?"

Megan's smile faded until I was left looking at her intense blue eyes, boring into my face, daring me to challenge her. "He's a funny looking fella, so he is. Imagine the amusement he'll give to a bored office worker, or an accountant tired of working out taxes."

I scoffed. "You could call him 'Norman the Nanotechnologist'."

Megan's mouth curled into a scowl. "Why do you say that?"

"Well, he's got all those pens and pencils sticking out the top, sort of defying the laws of physics. So he's a physicist, a nanotechnologist," I said.

"Not that. What makes you think he's called Norman?"

I paused, formulating my answer. Why was Megan getting so prickly?

"Alright, wind your neck in. I just said Norman cause the name popped to mind, that's all. You could call him Johnny the Judicial Assistant instead – he could hold all the pens for the judges in court," I joked.

My joke fell flat; Megan looked livid. "I'm not obsessed with him, if that's what you think."

"Obsessed with who?"

Her face was tinged pink. "You know who I mean, so don't let on like you're clueless. Norman James McMurray, for your information."

It was true; Megan had read my mind. Her blue drawing was obvious. Whether intentional or subconscious she had drawn Norman James McMurray, a.k.a. the Blue Man. Now was not the time to press my point, not when she was building up into one of her *moods*. It was time to defuse the situation, with a bit of crafty deflection.

"There's only one fella I think you're obsessed with – and that's Johnny Montgomery."

The pink tinges in Megan's cheeks spread until her whole face was beetroot. "Awk, well you caught me out. Here, did I tell you about the other night?"

Phew. Megan had taken the bait. "No. When?"

"Monday. Guess who turned up at my house?"

She meant Johnny, but it was my only opportunity to rake her about, now that she was back in a good mood. "Not Daz? No way!"

Megan mocked me with a *lapper* face. "Screw Daz. I'm talking about Johnny."

I peeled a splinter off one of my MDF pieces, absent-mindedly. "What did he want?"

She tossed her head, sending a curtain of blonde hair flying off her shoulder. "He said he was in the area, so he thought he'd come and call on me. Like, does that not sound like the biggest excuse you've ever heard? Johnny lives in Cairnburn, nowhere near Mersey Street, so what was he doing in my area, right? And how did he know where I live?"

I shrugged. "Yeah, I suppose that does sound sort of funny when you put it like that."

She let her mouth fall open theatrically. "You're having me on, right? He must fancy the knickers off me to come to my house. That's what Louisa-Mae said anyway, and I think she's right."

My stomach had already sunk a notch at hearing how Johnny had turned up at Megan's house, and it definitely bottomed out at that; Megan had confided in Louisa-Mae before me. She didn't consider me her best friend anymore.

"Awk, Sabrina, you're not still after him yourself, are you?" Megan's voice had a ring of fake sympathy to it.

My face must've looked like it was tripping me then. I forced a smile. "Johnny? No offence, but he's boggin'. Cheese and onion breath, remember?"

She puffed out her chest, ignoring me. "Anyway, we went down the entry behind my block of houses." Megan lowered her eyes, looking coy. "We shared a joint and took a couple of Diazepam that he'd nicked from his Ma's medicine cupboard. It was such a cracker night. And that's not all we did."

I stared at Megan, like I was seeing her for the first time. Only a short few months ago, Megan had said that she didn't mind having the odd bottle of White Knight, or Buckfast or whatever, but that she'd never try drugs of any sort. A spliff was one thing, but popping tabs was another.

"What is Diazepam anyway?"

She shrugged. "Who the flippin' hell knows? But it made me so spaced out, it was brilliant."

I paused, digesting the last words she had said: *And that's not all we did.* "Did you and Johnny *see* each other?"

One corner of Megan's mouth curled upwards. "Un-hun. More too. I went down on him in the bushes."

I couldn't help gawping and had to compose my face again before speaking. "You dir-ty wee hallion! So are you going to see him again?"

She tilted her head, giving me side-eye. "Maybe. He said he's going to call round again on Friday."

Friday. Megan always went out with Louisa-Mae, Lauren and me on Fridays, so I suppose that ruled out our usual plans. I thought it best not to say anything though; no point letting her know how hurt I felt. I was third best now, behind Johnny and Louisa-Mae.

I tucked my hair behind my ear, trying to be casual. "Oh right, so what are youse going to do then?"

"Don't know. I'll see what he fancies." She turned back to her balsa wood man and started carving features onto it with a file: nose, cheeks, lips.

Maybe I would try another tack to let her know I felt miffed. "Louisa-Mae won't be too happy when she finds out you've ditched our plans for Friday. Remember we said we were going to go to the Strand?"

Megan wrinkled her nose. "We can go to the cinema anytime, she'll understand. This *is* Johnny we're talking about here, not just any wee lad."

I turned back to my random assortment of cut MDF pieces, but my mind was elsewhere. What was the big deal about Johnny? Fair enough, he was a total screw with his blonde curtains and sexy smile. But Louisa-Mae called him Johnny dirt and I kind of believed her on that; he seemed to chase any wee girl to see who would spread the legs for him. That was mainly why I didn't let him buck me when he tried at Louisa-Mae's party. Megan though; that was another matter. I glanced sideways at my distancing friend. You wouldn't think she bucked every fella who stuck the lips on her; she looked like butter wouldn't melt with her hair tied half-up, half-down in a low ponytail and her school skirt at the proper length, just above her knees. She wore tights too so you couldn't see her bare legs. All of that was on purpose, of course. Megan said it made her look like 'a right wee Christian girl', giving us all a laugh. My own school skirt was rolled to halfway up my bare thighs, my white school socks pooled around my shins. I looked like a tart in comparison and the funny thing was, I was still a virgin, while Megan had bucked half the boys at the school next door, but looked pure like an angel. The boys hollered at me and called me all the slutbags of the day, while Megan singlehandedly squashed any rumours about her easy reputation simply by looking angelic. That left her free to buck another wee fella weekend after weekend – and get away with it.

"Here, Sabrina. What do you think?"

My thoughts diverted away from Megan's love life to her sculpture. Her balsa wood model had started to take shape with a distinct forehead, nose, cheekbones and neck.

I shrugged. Better steer clear or Norman this time.; for my own peace of mind. "It looks like a man."

She shot me a sneaky grin. "Look closer."

"Johnny? Wee girl, you're obsessed." I shook my head, more to myself than her. "I mean, he's a bit of alright, but he's not flipping Michaelangelo's David or nothing."

She wrinkled her nose. "Johnny? He's my boyfriend, but I'm not that smitten. Alright, credit where it's due. You were right. It's the Blue Man."

"The Blue Man? Away on." I shook my head, one eye on her creepy sculpture. Wouldn't have surprised me if it had suddenly sprung to life, possessed by the dreaded ghost himself. "Well all I can say is, I hope he gives you the A-star you deserve. No phantom figure in the world would help me get a decent grade. I'll be lucky if I scrape a C."

Megan grinned and kept filing her balsa wood design, bringing life to the sinister presence of the Blue Man, if only in sculpture. Wonder if she was smiling about the fact that I complimented her art skills, or the fact that she now knew I thought Johnny was a screw? Johnny hadn't bothered to turn up at *my* house – maybe he *did* really fancy Megan. Still, I wasn't going to give Megan the satisfaction of letting her think I fancied her boyfriend.

I flicked a piece of balsa wood shaving off the table, finding it therapeutic to cleanse myself of all-things-Megan, even if only emotionally. Johnny had stuck the lips on me at Louisa-Mae's party and after that, he stopped chasing me. Johnny had stuck the lips on Megan after calling to her house and now he was making plans to see her again on Friday. I clenched my teeth. Megan always got the boys. Maybe they saw her as blonde and bubbly, and me as her boring dark-haired, brooding friend. Was it because I didn't let Johnny buck me that he stopped chasing me? I started slotting my MDF pieces together to assemble my reading stand, but my thoughts were on Johnny. My Ma always said that girls needed to play hard to get; if you gave boys what they wanted then they would stop chasing you and go after another girl. But the opposite had happened with Johnny. I hadn't spread the legs for him, so he'd gone after my so-called best mate and left me in the lurch.

Boys were complicated. Maybe I should've bucked Johnny. He would've moved on to Megan anyway, but at least I'd have lost my virginity to a total screw.

"What are you thinking about?" whispered Megan. "You're thinking about knob, aren't you?"

I scrunched my face up on purpose. "Ugh, we're not all sex on the brain like you are, wee girl. I was thinking about my Tech project, for your information."

"Aye right. You should've seen the way you were smoothing your hands over those bits of wood. Come on, admit it. You're gagging to get bucked, aren't you?"

My face burned. "I'm not having this conversation. Can we change the topic?"

I grabbed a hammer and started joining the corners of my reading stand with nails. A throbbing pain erupted in the tip of my thumb as the hammer missed it's target.

"See what I mean? That's sexual frustration, so it is. I'm going to ask the Ouija board what boys fancy you and then we can get you set up at the next party," said Megan with amusement in her voice.

I set the hammer down and sucked the tip of my thumb, soothing the pain. "You're not going to try that thing again, are you?"

"What do you mean 'again'? I've been playing it practically everyday in my bedroom since that day at Louisa-Mae's house. It's great craic, it's been telling me all sorts of stuff."

I gawped at her. "Don't you know you should never play Ouija boards by yourself? Seriously, you know me, who reads more horror books than me? It makes you vulnerable to possession."

Megan rolled her eyes. "Aye, as if Christopher Pike and Dean Koontz and R.L. Stine are experts on occult stuff. You read too much horror, you numpty. Fiction is make-believe."

I gritted my teeth. "What do you think they base their books on? They research true-life horror to get their ideas."

"Yes, mummy, I'll be a good girl and stop playing with the nasty Ouija board."

Megan was impossible. "Aye, catch yourself on. But see if anything bad happens to you? Don't come crying to me. And don't say I didn't warn you."

She tutted. "You've a right cheek anyway. It's your fault I got interested in all this scary stuff in the first place. You were the one who told us all the story about the Blue Man."

I bit my lower lip. Not this again.

"But you know what?" Megan leaned closer. "I've found out so much more about him that any of youse lot knew about. I've been talking to him. He's been telling me all sorts of stuff."

I had a feeling that as much as I didn't want to know, Megan was going to tell me anyway.

"He predicted that Johnny and me would start seeing each other. He said his name was Norman James McMurray and that he used to be a welder at Harland and Wolff. He lived down in Mersey Street. Don't you see? That's where I'm from."

I sighed. "Megan, to be honest, I don't really care. I don't want to—"

"Ack, away and shite, yes you do want to know, so you can stop your lying." She pulled a face, taunting me. "He came over from Scotland when he was a boy as his dad got work at the shipyard. He started seeing this woman called Maureen Ann Boyd. But he got her pregnant before they could get married and that's where it all started to go wrong."

I tutted. "Yeah right, and I'm sure their families didn't approve, and they were poor and struggling and he probably lost his job."

Megan's lip fell into a flat, taut line. "How did you know?"

"Cause I'm psychic." I spat each word with added theatrics. "No, I'm having you on. Seriously, listen to what you've just told me. You haven't said any real detail there, it's all so vague. Everybody in the nineteen hundreds or whenever worked in the shipyard. Everybody was poor. And loads of people came from Scotland, half of Ulster is of Scottish origin!"

Megan folded her arms. "Alright then, little miss sceptic. For your information, I went and looked them up. They were real people."

I chortled. "Sure they were, them and a million other Norman James McMurrays and Maureen Ann Boyds. Everybody and their Da was called Norman back in them days!"

"So you're saying you no longer believe in the Blue Man, the story *you* told us about in the first place?" Megan huffed. She glared at me with a steely gaze and I looked away.

"No, I'm not saying that. It's just – I'm your friend – I want you to be careful. Playing with Ouija boards can lead to bad things happening."

Megan snorted. "You're my friend, aye right. Some friend. You can't just be happy for me and Johnny. Well, he picked me, so maybe you should get over it."

Johnny? Megan had got me completely wrong. The bell rang at the worst possible moment. Megan whisked her balsa wood carving away and shot an accusing glance back over her shoulder at me, like her Blue Man design was the most precious thing in the world and I might harm it. I stood there watching her, with my mouth hanging open and no words to fill the void.

Chapter fourteen

Megan – May 2000

My hands trembled as I touched the pointer. I took them off it, shook them and flexed my fingers, then set them back on the Ouija board. Flippin' Sabrina was getting inside my head with all her nonsense about how it was dangerous to play the Ouija board by yourself. What did she know? Reading too many stupid horror books, her head was always buried in some scary rubbish or other from the school library.

I cleared my throat, took a deep breath and breathed out through my nose, then began. "Hello. Is anybody there?"

A few figure eights around the board and then the pointer landed on 'yes'.

"Is it you again, Norman?"

Yes.

Relief swept over me. In the past few weeks, Norman James McMurray, my very own Blue Man, had become a better friend to me than my own so-called best mates. I knew so much about him, and he about me. Turned out we had quite similar backgrounds. His dad had been a wife beater, as was mine. My dad had left home when I was four years old, after throwing my mum out onto the garden path in front of the neighbours and breaking her leg. Norman's dad had been a violent alcoholic who had eventually left Norman's mum, Norman and his three younger siblings.

I glanced at the note Sabrina had tucked into the front pocket of my school bag. Secret notes was our fun way of talking about the things we couldn't say in words, but that needed to be told. The note was crumpled, as I had read it so much. Now I needed to ask Norman what he thought about it.

"Sabrina said she isn't jealous of me seeing Johnny. Is that true?"

No.

I seethed. Sabrina was a lying little so and so. Wait till I saw her tomorrow. She was lucky it was Friday night and I had plans later with Johnny; I was in such a horrible mood at her lies, I might not be able to bite my tongue. Thinking of Johnny mellowed my mood, a wee bit. I didn't want to get myself worked up before seeing him. Best to turn the topic over to more questions about Johnny.

"Where is Johnny going to take me tonight?"

S-e-a-p-a-r-k.

I blushed as the next question popped to mind; though I knew I could ask it. Norman and I had no secrets.

"Is Johnny going to buck me at the Seapark?"
Yes.

All my blood flooded my face at once and it swam, in a headspin. "Does Johnny fancy me more than Sabrina, or Louisa-Mae?"
Yes.

I wanted to fan myself with my hand as I was so hot, but didn't dare break the connection with the pointer; my fingers gripped it tight, ready for more questions. "Louisa-Mae tried to set me and Johnny up at that party at her house. Is that cause she knows we make a good couple?"
Yes.

After a couple of loops around the board, the pointer spelled out: r-e-a-l-f-r-i-e-n-d.

"Real friend? So Louisa Mae is really my friend?"
Yes.

"What about Sabrina?"
No.

A couple more figure eights on the board, then the pointer spelled out: s-t-e-a-l-j-o-h-n-n-y.

"Steal Johnny? Like hell she will! That wee tart can keep her mitts off him."

I sat back in my chair, fuming. How dare Sabrina have it in mind to steal Johnny off me? I looked at her note. She said she wasn't jealous of me and Johnny and that she didn't want him to come between our friendship; friends before men, she wrote. Yeah right. Norman was telling me Sabrina's real feelings, her true mind. He was a ghost, he could see into people's thoughts. Well, my own mind was made up. Johnny and me were going to buck tonight, at the Seapark, before slutbag Sabrina could get the leg over him first.

There was still another question about Sabrina that I needed to get off my mind, before I could move on with my evening. I focused my thoughts.

"Does Sabrina have psychic powers?"

Yes.

A-ha! I was onto something now. Time to dig further. "Does she have ESP?"

Yes. Followed by letters. My eyes read the words Norman spelled.

"Great-grandmother-Madrid," I read aloud. "So, Sabrina inherited her powers of extrasensory perception through her maternal ancestry?"

Yes.

Wow, what a revelation! I quickly formulated more questions. "Is that why Sabrina reads all those horror books – because she doesn't really know she has a gift, but she's subconsciously learning about it?"

Yes.

My mind was well and truly blown. I thanked Norman and ended the session there. My head was spinning with all the information. It was incredible how little I really knew my friends, for a start. All this time, I'd thought that Louisa-Mae could be kind of nasty at times, but it turned out she was my real friend, while Sabrina had been my best mate for the past three years and there she was, plotting to make a move on my boyfriend.

Speak of the Devil; the doorbell rang. I glanced at my bedside alarm clock. Johnny was on time; that had to mean he was keen. I'd heard the saying that you should keep a boy waiting for a wee bit and if he really liked you, he'd stick around. But this was Johnny, not any other boy. I quickly added a dusting of bronzer onto my face and neck before practically dancing down the stairs to answer the door.

"Alright, Blondie," he said, giving me a crooked smile. My stomach clenched; he was such a flippin' screw.

"Where are we going?" I pulled the front door shut behind me and stepped out into the cool evening air beside him.

Johnny shrugged. "You wanna get the train? I thought we could go for a walk down by the seafront in Holywood?"

I grinned to myself; Norman was right. The Blue Man was as true as his word. He said that Johnny was planning to take me to the Seapark in Holywood, and now Johnny had made the suggestion without any coaxing from me. It made me think back to the first time the four of us – Louisa-Mae, Lauren, Sabrina and I – had done the Ouija board on the morning after the party. Norman had said Sabrina had bucked Johnny, but Sabrina had insisted that she never bucked him. Sabrina had even gone as far as to swear on her mum's life that she didn't have sex with Johnny. But Norman was a truer friend to me than Sabrina; I believed him, not Sabrina the slutbag.

Well, one thing was certain; fate was going to take its course. Johnny and me, this was our night. I felt confident that my new best friend, Norman James, was watching over us, giving us his blessing. As we walked to Bridge End station to get the train to Holywood, I slipped my hand inside Johnny's. He turned to give me a smile, gave my hand a squeeze and onwards we went towards the train station. Norman was right. With his blessing, I felt confident about what would happen between Johnny and I. I trusted the Blue Man with my life.

Chapter fifteen

Sabrina – November 2020

I looked at the dead brown insect on my baby's changing mat. There was no doubt about it, it was a German cockroach. Jake had crushed it thanks to swift, video-game honed reflexes.

"Jake?" I craned my head in the direction of the kitchen. "Any luck finding the kitchen roll?"

"I think we've run out," Jake called. He came into the bedroom carrying a pack of anti-bacterial wipes. "These are probably even better though. Cockroaches carry all sorts of diseases."

Jake cleared up the cockroach carcass while I turned to check on Leo. Our three day old baby, born on Halloween morning, was fast asleep in his Moses basket next to my side of the bed. Such an innocent wee thing; he was oblivious to the infestation in our flat.

We had arrived home from hospital with Leo snoozing in his car seat, only to find the hallway covered in dozens of brown bugs. After a cursory search for 'rugby-ball-shaped beetles that live in houses' an image of the pests that now invaded our home had appeared and I had recognised them instantly. These weren't innocent wood-beetles, as I had thought when I had seen one or two in the kitchen cupboards. These were sinister German cockroaches. Worse still, the kitchen had swarms of them crawling all over the cupboards, sink and cooker.

Another adult roach, over an inch long, scuttled along the skirting board. I yelped, then stepped on it, crushing it with my slipper. The pest split in two, its bottom half lying immobile and the top-half with head continuing to scurry away.

"Jake! There's another, come quick. I didn't manage to kill this one," I shouted.

My poor, vermin-ridding veteran of a husband swept back into the bedroom and crushed the escaping cockroach.

I shuddered. "I cut it in half and it was still moving."

"Yeah," Jake sighed. "They're tough little bastards. Apparently they can even live without a head for a week. They eventually die of thirst, but they can keep going for seven days."

I made a mock-vomiting gesture to lighten the mood. "Great. Just what we need – zombie vermin taking over our flat."

Jake looked grim. "I think we need to badger the estate agent again. When did they say the pest control man was coming?"

"Yesterday," I said, with a resigned shrug.

Jake shook his head. "It's not good enough. They need to be smart here, the last thing they want is a newborn baby coming down with a horrible illness because of cockroaches."

"Oh Jake, don't." I rubbed my arms to ward away an imaginary chill. My eyes flittered upwards to our ceiling as a creak alerted me to the neighbour in flat five. "You know, don't you think it's a coincidence that N.J. moved in a few weeks ago and now the whole building is overrun with cockroaches? I spoke to Betty and she said they've had them in their kitchen. Not as bad as us, but still all over their cupboards."

Jake squirmed. "Yeah, David in number three said they're all over his speakers and base guitar. They've basically ruined his equipment and he's a musician, that's his livelihood. It sounds like him and his girlfriend Sarah got it the worst, for whatever reason. They're concentrated in their flat."

"Oh my God, you mean they live in electronic things?" I glanced across the hallway to the TV by the living room door.

He nodded. "They like the heat and apparently are attracted to the electromagnetic field. There's nothing they don't like though. If it's an infestation, they'll live inside furniture and clothes, you name it. We'll have to bug bomb all our things before we move out, or else chuck them in the bin."

Infestation. My gaze travelled once more to the ceiling. The only thing infesting this place was the new neighbour in number five. "I'll bet N.J. brought them in when he dropped his takeaway outside David's flat that time. I'll bet he's a dirtbird, that fella upstairs. His flat must be swarming."

The Blue Man. I didn't say my thoughts out loud, but my head was rapidly filling with all manner of connections. Was it more than mere coincidence that the mysterious N.J. – aka Norman James – aka the Blue Man, had moved in upstairs and now the whole building needed pest control to come and spray all the flats because of German cockroaches? Maybe there was a supernatural element to it; like the biblical plagues, for example. Plagues of insects. I thought back to one of my favourite horror-comedies, the Mummy. Due to an ancient Egyptian curse, when the mummy Imhotep was resurrected, he brought with him a plague of locusts. Was this similar? Had Megan and I resurrected the Blue Man, a curse that we had managed to bury for twenty years, and revive by meeting at the café a month ago? I was about to say my thoughts to Jake, but it sounded stupid even in my own head, so I suppressed the notion.

"I think he's having a hard time with them too. I heard him on his phone talking about finding them coming out of a hole in the wall in his shower room and asking for someone to come and sort it out, today. He's no better off than us, honey."

At that moment Jake dashed across the bedroom and smashed his hand against the end of the Moses basket. When he pulled his hand back I saw a brown smear, the remnants of crushed cockroach, mere inches away from our precious sleeping baby.

"That's it. I'm taking Leo out and walking over to the estate agent's office. He's not safe here, none of us are," I said.

Jake pulled a face as he cleaned his hands with a disinfecting wipe. "Alright then, I'll stay and kill as many as I can while you head over there. We can't live like this. If they don't get the pest controller in soon, they'll need to find us somewhere else to live."

I took a photo on my phone of the squashed cockroach on the end of the Moses basket, then gathered my sleeping son into my arms. Thankfully Leo was dozing so heavily, he didn't stir as I transferred him onto my chest.

I slung Leo's nappy bag over my left shoulder and balanced Leo's floppy weight against my right shoulder. The estate agent's office was only a three minute walk away along the main road and across the intersection. It would be more hassle to carry his buggy downstairs; luckily Leo was still small and light enough for me to carry him in my arms for short trips.

I left the flat door unlocked since Jake was still at home. I held the bannister as I stepped off the landing onto the stairs and my breath caught in my throat as I looked down to the ground floor. N.J. was rifling through the pile of mail on the table by the front door.

A thought to turn back crossed my head, but it was too late; N.J. had looked up. "Hello there, love. Sandra, was it?" he said in his thick Belfast-Glagow brogue.

My heart hammered in my chest. "It's Sabrina."

He pulled a wry smile. "You told me your name was Sandra."

I flushed, remembering the lie I'd told him. "Well, I prefer Sandra, so I sometimes go by that."

He shrugged, dismissing my excuse. "Have you had a problem with bugs in your flat too? Mine is overrun."

I reached the bottom of the stairs, slowing as I approached him, dreading having to pass him. "Yes. I'm going to see the estate agent now."

"I've already called them. They're sending someone round tomorrow to spray the whole building."

He spoke with a finality to his tone as though to say, *you don't need to bother going to the estate agent, I've handled it.* Or maybe that was how I interpreted it. Either way, I said nothing.

N.J. gestured to Leo, sleeping on my shoulder. "I'd get him out of this place, if I was you. I hope you aren't bottle feeding him, those bugs blew up my kettle, they were living inside it."

I shuffled Leo's soft sleeping body higher up on my shoulder and curled my arm around him protectively. My baby was breastfeeding, thank goodness; not that it was any of the nosy neighbour's business.

It was as if N.J. read my mind. He pointed at Leo. "You should breastfeed that one, if you get my drift."

Urgh. How dare that creepy stranger talk about the manner in which I fed my child. I was sure my face must have been beetroot with outrage, though still, I bit my tongue. I walked towards the front door without saying a word.

"Here love, let me help you." N.J. made a swift move towards the door, in one quick stride that surprised me. Maybe I was naive, but his slovenly dress-sense in his usual blue hoody and chequered pyjama trousers, along with his unkempt hair gave the impression of someone who would move about at sloth-like speed. His quick movement stunned me to a stop; I came to an abrupt halt a metre from the door as he blocked the exit.

I was expecting N.J. to sweep the door open for me, but instead he reached towards me with open fingers. Before I could make any sense of what was happening, N.J. had grabbed Leo off my shoulder and transferred my sweet, sleeping baby onto his own chest leaving me empty-handed and frankly, stunned.

I quickly opened the front door, wedged my foot against it to hold it open and grabbed Leo back; but not before N.J. planted a soft kiss on my child's downy head.

"Thanks," I mumbled, in a sound more akin to a startled squeak than my own voice.

"Not a problem. I have kids of my own, so I do. Three girls."

Once again, N.J. had surprised me. I hadn't expected him to be the paternal type from his gruff demeanour. "Oh really? I haven't seen them about. It would be lovely to have some other kids in the building."

"No, they're living with my ex over in Stranraer. That's where I was living until she kicked me out. But, sure, that's life." He shrugged. "It's only a ferry ride away. Here's where I grew up, like. You can't beat Belfast."

N.J. pulled a cigarette out of his pocket and followed me outside. Hearing more about his life made him seem more human to me and less – well, less – Blue Man. It helped drive away my crazy notions earlier about him being connected to the supernatural and cement the fact that he was an ordinary man, just the fella next door.

"So, what do your initials stand for anyway, your nickname N.J? Is that, like, N for Norman? You know, and J for James?"

N.J. took a puff of his cigarette and blew a long stream of smoke, careful to exhale away from Leo and I. "Something like that."

I paused, waiting for him to tell me his name. Instead, I got a cryptic smile.

A sinking feeling crept into my stomach, pushing away my sense of ease after his story relating facts about his life. It didn't add up. Why was he so willing to tell me about the fact that he had three daughters, and an ex-girlfriend, and a connection to the Scotland, only to go from being so open and candid to closed and cryptic? As Leo and I turned to walk down the street, I found myself keeping my head craned ever so slightly to my left side to keep an eye over my shoulder. It was said that the Devil sat behind your left shoulder. Only salt would ward him off. A crisp wind stung my eyes as I turned off the garden path and walked out onto the main street. I let the rivulet of salty tears flow down over my left cheek and drip onto my left shoulder. Maybe I was a superstitious fool. But wasn't it better to be safe than sorry?

Chapter sixteen

Megan – November 2020

Paddy carefully painted white over the stencil of the soon-to-be-baby's bedroom wall. Sky blue for our coming-soon-son with white letters reading: Harry. Blue and white provided a calm, neutral atmosphere that made me feel relaxed as I organised all the baby sleep-suits in the new dresser, and hopefully would help Harry to sleep once he was born.

"Our wee house is really coming together, don't you think?" I straightened one of the bumpers on the new cot, tightening the ribbons on the corner. Perfect.

Paddy panted as he set the paint brush for a break. "Aye, not bad. Are you sure you want to stay in here though, while I'm doing this? Not sure breathing paint fumes is best for the baby."

I shuffled across to him and hugged my arms around his middle. "Nice try. You can't get rid of me that easily."

He kissed the top of my head. "I'm serious though, babe. It would make me feel better if you went and relaxed. Why don't you have a cuppa on the new sofa? Put your feet up for a bit? I'm nearly done here anyway."

I raised and eyebrow at him, and fixed a smirk on my face for added measure, but acquiesced. "Fine then. But I'm going to eat the rest of the red velvet cake, just so you know."

I waddled out of the baby's room and held the bannister as I walked downstairs. The new carpet felt so fluffy underfoot and I felt acutely aware of the new house smell in every part of our semi-detached home. Not sure if pregnancy hormones were heightening my sense of smell, or that I was enjoying the experience of being a homeowner at last, but it was as though brand-new everything was seeping into my very pores. If I could have bottled the brand-new everything smell and sold it as a holistic cure for anxiety, I definitely would have done so.

I set my tea and cake onto the new glass coffee table, then lowered myself onto the leather L-shaped sofa that had been delivered last week and lay back on the plush cushions. This was the life. Nothing to do except watch daytime TV and scroll through Facebook.

A picture of a wrinkly newborn in a mint green baby-gro popped up on the homepage. He was lying on a double bed, his eyes shut against a strip of sunlight cast across the duvet. It was another photo of Sabrina's new baby Leo; lately she had put a stream of them up in an album titled *Two becomes three*. She had written a caption under the snapshot: *Leo is a sun worshipper, just like his mummy.*

It was hard not to respond to such a cute photo. My fingers scurried across the keypad. *Awk, look at that. Like mother like son. I wonder if he'll get ur lovely tanned complexion when he's older?*

A few minutes later, Sabrina wrote back. *I know, you wouldn't think he's my son to see him, he's so pale. Takes it after his dad, I think.*

I read her message, then re-read it. Too late now, but I hoped she wasn't offended. I hadn't meant to imply that Leo was white, even though Sabrina was so swarthy. In truth, I was jealous that she had always turned a deep brown colour in the summer, thanks to her Spanish side I suppose, whereas I had to use bronzer over my skin that only went red even in mild sun. Best to change the topic after such awkwardness; it wasn't as though we were close anymore. Our friendship was just reigniting. Was that the right word: reigniting? It seemed appropriate at any rate; our relationship had burned brightly back in our schooldays, and though the flame had never been completely extinguished, now it needed fuel to get the fire going again. Suggesting that Sabrina's baby didn't look like her would be a major dampener on such a fire.

Well, he's a gorgeous baby anyway, he looks the spitting image of u, I typed. I'd already hit send when more doubts surfaced: had I inadvertently insulted her husband now? What was his name again: Jack? No; Jake. Had I implied that Jake was ugly, by commenting that the baby looked like her?

Flip sake, this whole friendship-rekindling malarkey was turning out to be hard work. I really knew so little about Sabrina, it was amazing. How had we ever been besties for three years?

Sabrina replied: *Thanks. He got his good looks from his dad, but he got my hair.*

I closed my eyes. Shit; she had taken it the wrong way, as I'd thought. Best try to fix the damage with another compliment that hopefully wouldn't come across badly. I looked at the sparse brown curls on top of baby Leo's head. "He's lucky then, as you have the most gorgeous dark hair." I sent the message. Nope, no way to take any offense to that comment. I took a big bite of cake, in need of comfort food after a brief chat with my old chum.

My hands rested on my bump. My stomach was definitely protruding these days, but most of my colleagues and family said that I my bump was 'neat', although I felt as big as a house. Sabrina had been massive when I'd seen her and she had only been around thirty-two weeks or so when we'd had our café catch-up. Hope I wouldn't get as huge as she had. Mind you, it looked like she had put on a *hefty* amount of weight and apart from the odd bit of cake here and there, I hadn't indulged myself too much, so I could still fit into most of my pre-pregnancy trousers.

I was lost in my thoughts when another comment came through in the same thread from Sabrina. It's nice that we're both having boys. They can be playmates as they'll only be a few months apart in age too.

My eyes skimmed the first sentence, and then as I read it again, my blood must have dropped one degree Celsius with each word. I typed a response: *How did you know I'm having a boy?*

Sabrina's reply: *Didn't you share that you were?*

No I most definitely didn't. Not that I wrote that, though. Once again, as on that day at my twenty-week scan a month ago, a sense of dread set in. Sabrina could really be *creepy*. I hated feeling like she knew everything about me. She had never said outright that she had gypsy fortune teller abilities, but I was a hundred percent certain that she did. It wasn't a comforting thought.

I shivered. It wasn't my imagination, but the living room seemed to have become frigid. Even though it was only November, not yet winter, I was sure that if I exhaled deeply I would have been able to see a cloud of my own breath. It was as though the room was aligning with my thoughts; the last time Sabrina had shown a creepy insight into my life, a supernatural event had occurred soon after: that day at the hospital, a sinister face had appeared on the ultrasound image behind my unborn baby's left shoulder. The Blue Man, right there, in the womb with my innocent child.

My heart began to pound in my chest in anticipation. The same thing was happening again. Sabrina had made an eerie comment, saying things about my business that she couldn't possibly have known, leaving me afraid. I wanted to shut my eyes, scared of what I might see. But what was the point? Closing out whatever unseen force there was wouldn't make it go away.

My shoulders stiffened, the hairs on the back of my neck rising, like miniature radio masts tuning into a different frequency. Millimetre by millimetre I began to twist my head to the left until I was looking behind my left shoulder.

I was right; there was a bulge in the long, blue curtain. The shape gave the appearance that a tall person was standing behind it; an adult at least Paddy's height by the looks of it, about six feet tall. The fabric curved near the top giving the impression of a rounded forehead and jutted where a sharp nose poked forward, pointing in my direction.

I yelped. My feet scurried on the leather sofa, propelling me away from the threat. I heard a flurry of feet as Paddy rushed into the room. He stood in front of the curtain, blocking me from the bulge that I was sure was the Blue Man, right there, in our living room.

"What's wrong babe, I heard you scream?"

My hand shook as I pointed to the curtain behind him. "Check behind you, right there. I saw something."

Paddy swivelled around and swept the curtain aside. Nothing. He fumbled with the metal handle and pulled it shut.

"The window was open," Paddy said, looking confused. "Did a bug get in?"

I shook my head. "Don't you feel the temperature? It's like a morgue in here."

Paddy chortled. "I wouldn't go that far, but yes it's a wee bit chilly alright. That's an Irish autumn for you."

I rubbed my forehead, composing my thoughts. It was time to tell Paddy, whether he thought I was crazy or not. "Paddy listen. You're going to think I'm mad, but I know what I saw. There was a person behind that curtain just then. I'm not imagining it. It was the Blue Man."

Paddy stared at me. He didn't smile, or frown, or react. His round blue eyes were serious. "Were you asleep? I must have woken you up?"

"I was chatting with Sabrina, on Facebook, I hadn't dozed off." I took a sip of tea. It was cold. "You must have seen the shape in the curtain when you came in."

Paddy looked behind to the curtain, then back to me. "Well, yeah. It was ruffled because the window was open. A bit of wind was blowing it. Did you leave the catch undone?"

"I never touched it." I rubbed my arms to warm myself, then linked my hands around my legs for protection. "This isn't the first time something weird has happened."

The words spilled out of my mouth, telling Paddy all about what I had seen during the twenty-week scan and Sabrina's creepy foresight about the gender of our unborn child. He listened without speaking, only blinking as I talked.

"Can I have a look at the messages you two wrote today?" Paddy said.

I handed over my phone, glad that he was going to read the chat with Sabrina. After a few minutes, Paddy gave my phone back. He had opened my profile page. Instead of the photo of Sabrina's Leo, a picture I had uploaded a fortnight ago showed. It was a photo I had taken of our baby's room. We had been in the midst of painting the walls blue. A large tin of blue paint sat next to the unassembled cot. A toy chest decorated with rocketships and planets sat by the window. I had written the caption, *Getting ready for baby*, under the photo.

"That's how she knew we're having a boy," said Paddy.

I swallowed to wet my parched throat. "Yeah, but it's not like I spelled it out. Isn't it still a bit creepy that she read between the lines?"

"Not really. You said she was strong at English when you were at school. She's a reader, makes sense she'd read into it."

I tapped to exit the Facebook app with a sniff. "I still think it's creepy. I mean, like how much attention is she paying to my photos? Every wee detail, I mean, it's just – weird."

I was flailing and I knew it. Paddy had called me out with cold, hard logic. Okay, fine. So Sabrina had put two and two together to figure out we were having a boy, not using her psychic powers. It still didn't mean there was nothing supernatural going on.

"If it's making you so uncomfortable, then defriend her. You don't have to be in touch."

I sighed. "I can't. It's like I told you before, between the two of us – Sabrina and me – we've dug up something from the past that was buried. And now that it's out in the open, we need to deal with it. I need her – to move on from this. I think we got rid of it – him – the wrong way before and that's why he's back. But I'll make sure that Sabrina and I – together – that we do it right this time."

Paddy stooped to pick up my teacup and plate; I caught the look on his face. Scorn was written all over it. I hated that expression on my husband's face. Of all the people who should have supported me, believed me, he was my biggest sceptic.

"You seem very conflicted, that's all. One minute you seem to be terrified of this old school chum of yours and the next, you need her like she's as close as a sister, or something."

"Or something is right." I sat up, fuming. There was only one way I was going to get Paddy to understand.

"Why is it that you believe your own mother when she talks about the supernatural, but not your own wife?"

Paddy's face flooded scarlet. He cocked his head in an offhand way. "Well, now, it's not exactly the same thing, is it?"

"It is – entirely. It was so important to you, clearly, that you even took me to the ruined abbey after one of our dates, and told me the story."

I let my annoyance internalise, the hot fumes of my own simmering anger boiling the memory in my mind. Paddy had told me all about the Grey Lady, a noble woman who had once had an illicit affair with a monk. She had got pregnant – out of wedlock. When the other monks at the abbey and the local villagers had found out, they had flogged both of them to death for their sacrilege. The Grey Lady had held onto a wooden doll as she had died, a present that had been intended for her child.

"How is the Grey Lady any different from the Blue Man?" I snapped.

"The Grey Lady is an ancient folktale that people from my village on the outskirts of Derry know. The Blue Man is a ghost story that Sabrina made up to frighten you – I'm sure of it." Paddy's eyes were wide, defeated.

I bit my lip before I continued. "The Blue Man is an urban legend based on a real person who lived in Mersey Street and worked in Harland and Wolff shipyard and died on the mudflats of the Connsy, near where Vicky Park is today. The people of Sydenham know about him – that's how Sabrina knew the story."

"My mother saw the Grey Lady, when I was a child. She was out walking the dog–"

"And I saw the Blue Man," I shouted, cutting him off, "But you believe your mother and not me!"

Paddy's face fell. "What can I say–"

"You told me how your mother had found a doll near the abbey and put it on top of the ruins one day and that when she came back the next day, it had moved and was looking out through one of the higher window frames. You believed her when she said the Grey Lady's ghost had done it. But when we were at Vicky Park a few weeks ago and I found a thistle, and said it was a symbol of the Blue Man, you told me it was just a weed and that it meant nothing. You believe in ghosts when it's about your mother, but you act like I'm crazy when it suits you!"

He hung his head. "I'm sorry, babe. I shouldn't have doubted you. It's just that, what with our child coming, and my job and all. Well, the stress got to me. I'll try to be more supportive."

I glared at him, hoping my eyes boring into him would put the finishing touches on his remorse. "Apology accepted. The only way to deal with a ghost is to confront it and then send it back to where it came from. I'm glad you're on my side, because if the past is anything to go by, this is going to be quite the task. I have to rid myself of the Blue Man properly, for once and for all. But the time isn't right yet – he has only half-materialised. The more I see Sabrina, the stronger his power will be. Then I can draw him out and act on it."

Chapter seventeen

Sabrina – May 2000

Why the hell were we at Holywood Seafront? We always went over to Vicky Park on Saturdays, not Holywood. I clenched my jaw. It was because of Johnny. Megan and her obsession with Johnny.

"I'm telling you, he must be further along the beach. He told me he'd be down here." Megan's voice had a note of desperation. She walked ahead of us, swinging her carrier bag with a two litre bottle of White Lightning.

"Maybe he's still at his Da's house," said Louisa-Mae. "Did you know his auld man lives in Holywood?"

Megan stopped dead in her tracks and Lauren, behind, crashed into her. "Who told you that? Johnny never said to me that his dad lives here?"

Louisa-Mae's nostrils flared as she sucked in air, her chest swelling. "He doesn't want people to know his parents have split. He lives with his Ma in Cairnburn on weekdays and stays with his Da at weekends."

Megan's eyes narrowed. "How do you know so much about Johnny?"

"We played together as kids. Mum was friends with his Ma." Louisa-Mae jutted her chin.

Convenient how Louisa-Mae always referred to her own mother as 'Mum', but other people had a 'Ma'. It always seemed like she was demeaning other people when she spoke like that; not that I'd ever say that to anyone. Not even Megan.

Speaking of Megan. She seemed to have accepted Louisa-Mae's explanation, for she started walking again and swinging her carryout. Megan was probably thinking what I was: that if Louisa-Mae and Johnny had been childhood friends, that ruled her out as a competitor for him, romantically-speaking. Well, at least, that's how I saw it. My heart sank a bit as I watched Megan walking ahead though. Normally in our foursome, she would have walked with me, letting Louisa-Mae and Lauren trail behind us with their arms linked while they gossiped. But not now. After Tech class the other day, she seemed to have got it into her head that I wanted to take Johnny off her. Yes, Johnny was a screw, but I'd never nick a boy off my best friend. Friends before men, always.

Megan would never listen to that, though. My heart sank further as I watched Louisa-Mae speed up and slip her arm through Megan's. Blonde and redhead walked together like they were two peas in a pod, as my Nanny would say. Louisa-Mae had her head close to Megan's, whispering in her ear. Wonder what she was saying?

I was jolted from my thoughts as Lauren sauntered alongside me. "Give me your wing there."

I offered my elbow to her and she linked her arm around mine. "Has Megan said anything to you about me?"

Lauren gave me a sugary-sweet smile. "No. Why, would she have? You two are besties, I thought?"

Better to drop it. I had a feeling Lauren *did* know something that Megan had said behind my back, but would never betray Louisa-Mae's confidence. "What boys are going to be down here tonight, do you think?"

Lauren's sugary-sweet smile became sly. "Not Johnny, anyway. That's the bad news that Louisa-Mae is telling to Megan, right now. Aww, it's going to break her wee heart. She'll have to find someone else to buck tonight."

I looked from Lauren to Megan then rounded on Lauren again. "Did you and Louisa-Mae have something to do with this?"

Lauren let her mouth drop open theatrically and let go off my arm, shoving me away in faux outrage. "We would never do that! How could you think that?"

My cheeks prickled. "Well then, why isn't he coming tonight?"

She grabbed my elbow and pulled me close, hooking her arm through mine again. "Maybe it's because he got what he wanted from her last night, so he's going to find another wee girl to spread the legs for him tonight instead."

What was I meant to say to that? It was up to Megan who she wanted to buck and none of anyone else's business to interfere with that. Maybe once the A-levels were over, and I went off to university, I'd find new friends. Louisa-Mae and Lauren were getting too bitchy these days; more like enemies than friends. University was the natural transition I needed to disguise breaking up with my toxic friends; a gradual fade out of our friendship rather than a quick dissociation. I dreaded to think what Louisa-Mae and Lauren would do if they caught on to an obvious betrayal. They were fun, sure; I would miss the parties and the craic, but not the nastiness and gossip – or worse if I openly chose to leave our foursome.

As we reached the wind tunnel leading up to the High Street, Daz and Rab came bounding out of it.

"Have you seen Johnny?" said Megan. *God*, I wished she hadn't said that. It made her seem a wee bit too desperate. My mum's words were always in my head: girls should play hard to get.

Daz stuck his hands in his pockets, an awkward grin on his face. No wonder; the bendy knob jibes were probably still fresh in his mind.

Rab smirked. "He's not well. He's come down with a nasty case of crabs. They're crawling all over his cheesy baps. Dunno where he might've got them." He turned to Daz, who was sniggering behind him. "Do you know who might've given him crabs? They say it was someone boggin', some stinking slutbag."

Daz guffawed behind him. "Aye, I had some cheesy baps myself a few weeks ago, but some dir-ty wee girl licked them all clean for me."

My eyes went wide at what happened next; Megan swung her leg up between Daz's legs and kicked him right in the ghoulies. Daz grabbed his privates as he keeled sideways howling in agony. Rab backed up against the wind tunnel wall with his hands held up in surrender as Megan rounded on him, pointing her finger right in his face.

"Don't make up lies. You watch your dick or someone might hack it off you!"

Megan stormed off through the wind tunnel. I'd never seen her so angry. Louisa-Mae's jaw was slack as she exchanged a wicked grin with Lauren, loving the drama, then rushed to follow Megan.

No beach tonight then; Lauren, Louisa-Mae and I had no choice but to follow Megan as she hurried up towards the High Street.

"Where does Johnny's dad live?" Megan looked over her shoulder at Louisa-Mae.

Louisa-Mae grabbed her sleeve and pulled ahead, leading Megan. "C'mon, I'll show you."

Johnny's Da's house. This was going to be bad. This was going to be *so* bad.

We turned off the High Street and trailed after Louisa-Mae as she lead us to a corner duplex, tucked in a cul-de-sac. She nodded her head towards the bottom flat.

Megan said nothing. She marched up the short garden path and rang the buzzer for Flat A. When there was no answer, she rapped on the small glass pane on the door: one-two-three-four-five angry bangs. Still no response. Megan walked to the front window and ducked low, pressing her face against the glass. A net curtain hid the living room inside. As she banged on the glass, my feet made an ever-so-slight turn away from Johnny's Da's house. Megan's anger was unnerving; or maybe it was the anticipation of what might happen. Knowing Louisa-Mae and Lauren, nothing good.

"He's not here." I rubbed my arms against the early evening chill. "Let's go back to the High Street, I want to get chips."

Megan didn't look at me or say anything. She followed the paved path around the side of the duplex to the back.

Lauren and Louisa-Mae exchanged *sleekit* grins and dashed after her.

The sound of a heavy door scraping open and the rustle of a draft excluder dragging on carpet signalled that we weren't going anywhere; except inside the flat.

My heart sped up in sync with my legs as I hurried after my friends. When I got to the back of the flat I saw that the kitchen door lay open and all three of them were crammed behind the open fridge. I hesitated on the back step. This was wrong.

"Oh my God, what are you lot doing? Johnny's not here. Let's go and get chips, I'm starving."

"You can eat something here," said Louisa-Mae. She frisbee-threw a pack of ham at me; it bounced off my chest and fell at my feet. "Have that."

"This is trespassing. What if one of the neighbours sees? Let's go now, you lot. Come on!" My voice sounded desperate in my own ears.

"This is trespassing," said Lauren in a mock-nasally whine. "Ooh!"

"Go home then, feardy-cat," said Louisa-Mae. She opened a tub of cooked chicken drumsticks and bit a chunk off.

My gaze dropped downwards to the doormat under my feet. Yep, that was me pretty much. Or was it? It was time to make a decision; be a sheep following my friends, or be a lone wolf.

My stomach rumbled. Lone wolf it was. "I'm away here to get some gravy chips. Who's coming with me?"

"Get me a curry chip." Lauren popped across to the back doorstep where I stood and pushed a pound coin into my hand. Then she joined the other two again at the fridge.

Before I left I watched my mates in disbelief as they devoured Johnny's dad's food. Megan stuffed her face with Dairylea cheese triangles. "This must be where Johnny gets his cheesy dick."

I watched her grab a pack of sausages next and hold them aloft. "If he's so proud to throw around his big, fat, sausage to every wee girl in sight, let's see what he makes of these squashed in his bed."

Every wee girl in sight. So, Megan still didn't believe me when I told her the truth – that I hadn't bucked Johnny at Louisa-Mae's party? She seemed oblivious to me watching and listening outside. I was a nobody in her world now, a hanger-on. Megan swept out of the kitchen and vanished somewhere inside the flat. My once best friend thought I was a liar, and how she was acting tonight was out of character too. Megan was not the type to break and enter into somebody's home, for revenge or for kicks. Maybe I didn't know her at all. The person I thought I had been close to for three years was a stranger.

"I'm going now," I called, but no-one answered.

"I'll see you guys later," I added. But they had gone, into the depths of Johnny's dad's flat. Trespassing on private property. I wouldn't be an accomplice to breaking and entering. I turned and left the garden and hurried away from the street. If I were a better, tougher human being; the kind who wasn't afraid of standing up to her mates, I would have been able to convince them that what they were doing was wrong. But I wasn't a hero. I was a loser.

***

"Sabrina, where's my chips?"

I turned and saw Lauren hurrying towards me, her frizzy perm bouncing as she ran.

Her chips were probably stone-cold. How long had it been? My gravy chip was long gone and after that I'd wandered the streets wondering what shenanigans those lot had been up to. Lauren snatched the polystyrene box and started devouring her chips, even though they stuck together like rocks. As she ate, Louisa-Mae and Megan caught up. I shot a smile in Megan's direction, but she avoided my eyes so I dropped my head.

"There you are, feardy-ba. We wondered where you'd gone off to." Louisa-Mae wrinkled her nose at me.

I folded my arms. "I didn't run off, I told youse, I was away getting chips."

"I'm just raking about." Louisa-Mae dug her elbow in my ribs. "You missed all the fun though. Tell her what you did, Megan."

Megan affected a sly smile that she was happy, this time, to share with me. I found myself smiling back, her grin infectious.

"What did you do?"

"I'll show you." Megan reached into her coat pocket and pulled out a wad of polaroid photos. "Nice wee mementos here, all thanks to Johnny's camera, which I broke too for good measure."

I took the photos and started leafing through. "Oh my God."

The photos had all been taken in Johnny's bedroom. Sausage meat had been spread across the walls, leaving pink smears on his Manchester United wallpaper. More sausages had been squashed on his pillow and under his duvet. His underwear drawer hung open, his boxers covered in chunks of raw meat. In another photo, Johnny's bedroom mirror had been defaced in blue permanent marker.

"The Blue Man woz ere," I read aloud.

"That was me." Louisa-Mae jabbed a finger at the picture.

"I thought you and Johnny were friends?"

She smirked. "We are – sort of. But I'm friends with Megan more, and if he hurts one of us, he hurts us all."

I flipped the photo to the back of the pile to look at the next one. Louisa-Mae claimed to be a childhood friend of Johnny's, but seeing what she had done in his room made me think; would she do it to my house? Would any of them do it to my house, if I did something to annoy them? In Louisa-Mae's case, she didn't have loyalty to anyone. She purely thrived on chaos. Chaos and hurting people, for kicks. Now I was convinced.

"You're not going to tout on us, are you?" Lauren stood with her hand on one hip, fixing me with a stare. I blinked at her, feeling my forehead flush. Had she read my mind?

"What do you take me for?" I screwed up my face, exaggerating my incredulity for effect. "I don't slabber about my friends to no wee lads."

Lauren gave a satisfied smile and I relaxed. If she approved, then Louisa-Mae would too and I didn't want them doing something worse to me – or my house. "Turn over to the bits I did," said Lauren.

I flicked ahead, my eyes scouring the polaroids. Johnny's clothes had been ripped and scattered all over the room. Designer labels: Tommy Hilfiger, Fila,

Redtrap; they were all torn and covered in muddy footprints.

"Brown sauce," Lauren boasted, lowering her chin over my shoulder to look at the trophies of her handiwork. "We spat in his cider too."

"Eew, youse are boggin'." The words spilled out of my mouth before I could think to censor them. "Johnny is going to come after all you lot for this, you know."

Megan shrugged. "He can try. Who says it was us anyway?"

"The Blue Man woz ere. He'll know it was *youse* lot. He'll think it was me too," I said.

It hadn't been my intention, but my eyes stayed on Megan. Megan's widened in horror as she stared back at me. "Don't look at me, I didn't write it."

"But you were the first to say the catchphrase – remember that day in class when you said it to Mrs Miller? Johnny and all the rest thought it was a right *geg* at Louisa-Mae's party."

Megan's brow furrowed. "I'm not talking about Johnny, I'm talking about Norman."

Louisa-Mae, Lauren and I paused as we processed what Megan was saying and their faces reflected how I felt: completely lost.

"Who's Norman?" said Lauren, one eyebrow raised. "Is he a screw?"

"Norman James, dum-dum," said Megan. "From the Ouija board."

"Oh... right." Louisa-Mae's eyes lit up with a devious glint. She turned to Lauren and made a circle with her finger at her temple. Megan hadn't seen it, but I did. "Don't worry, babe, Norman loves you. He'd never hate you. You're his special girl," said Louisa-

Mae. She grabbed Lauren's arm and the pair of them walked away, their heads together as they sniggered.

Megan didn't seem to notice – or care. That was the whole point though; Megan was preoccupied. Lately she had really been hanging on to all this business of Norman James McMurray. What was with her obsession? Was it my fault? I had started the whole thing by telling her the urban legend in the first place. Guilt nipped at me. Megan hadn't started acting weird until she'd heard my story, that night in Vicky Park. Megan wouldn't even have heard of the Blue Man if it weren't for me. As the cool evening wind funnelled along the High Street from Belfast Lough, an ominous sensation settled deep in my stomach. Trouble was brewing and I had a horrible feeling that Megan would bear the brunt of it.

Chapter eighteen

Megan – May 2000

The doctor's waiting room was so boring. The magazines were all for old women and the radio was on a classical music channel. I had half a mind to request Cool FM, but kept my mouth shut. It wasn't a good idea to annoy my mum any more than she already was. I slid a sideways glance at her on the seat next to me. Her lips were pressed tightly together and she was staring defiantly ahead; or anywhere but at me, really.

Maybe I had enough time to read through the two letters I had written. I felt the folded paper in my school blazer pocket and pulled them out. Both had been rumpled from the number of times I had read them and tucked them away. When I got into school at lunchtime I would slip the letter for Sabrina in her bag, as I always did. It was our secret way of saying the things we wanted to talk about but felt too embarrassed to bring up face to face. The other letter had no physical recipient, though I knew he was out there listening and watching.

My eyes rested on the first letter and started reading:
Hi Sabrina,

I'm sure you've been waiting a while for my next letter. Well, here it is. Things have been funny between us for a few months now and we both know it. I don't really know why Johnny has come between us, but he has. I also don't know how we can fix this mess in our friendship. It really hurt me on Saturday when you said that the Blue Man would be angry at me. It seems like first you were jealous of me and Johnny and now you're jealous of me and Norman and you want to wreck that relationship too. I know Johnny stuck the lips on you first at Louisa-Mae's party, but then he moved onto me and we went much further than that and you got jealous, of course you did. Who wouldn't? And that likewise, you knew about the Blue Man first, but now he's closer to me – he's been telling me so much through the Ouija board. And I think you're jealous of that fact too. Maybe you're even jealous of how close me and Louisa-Mae have been getting. The thing is, friendships change and move on, and maybe after three years, maybe we're just drifting apart. But, since we used to be best mates, I thought I'd at least write you one last letter. I still want us to be friends, and we still have two months of school left so we have to see each other in class – I don't want to make things weird, OK? Ta amities, Megan.

I clicked the top of my pen and scratched out the last line. Did I really want to stay friends with Sabrina? I wasn't sure anymore. Better to not commit to that. I folded up the letter again and wrote Sabrina's name in bubble writing on the top.

I switched my attention to the second, more important letter.

Dear Norman,

I can't wait to speak to you tonight. Sometimes I wonder if I should bring the Ouija board to school and do it in the toilets at break time, but the smokers always go in there and the prefects on duty do my head in. I wish I could talk to you more often. You're my best friend these days – my real best friend – not the fake bunch of millies who I hang around with. Louisa-Mae is really pretty and she has great hair. She's a geg too and always gets the boys to come to parties. But she can be a right nasty piece of work, plus she's not as hard to get as she likes to pretend. One night she got really bleutered in the bandstand and ran around in her bra. She said she did it accidentally, but really it's cause she's desperate for attention and wanted to show off her diddies, which in fairness are really huge and make me so jealous. Then there's her sidekick Lauren. She's kind of a skinny scarecrow with a frizzy black perm. I'd be scundered if I had no tits like she does and a wee lad got the leg over me. She must stuff her trainer bra with toilet roll. And last, there's Sabrina. My so called best friend. The only good thing I can say for her is that she's pretty with her dark Spanish features, although she doesn't know it and thinks the boys don't fancy her. It's only because they know she's so frigid it's mortifying. In reality though, she's just a tag along. She's Little Miss goody two shoes. I don't know why her virginity is so sacred to her other than she's a boring, stuck up snob.

If only you could be here with me in real life. If only I'd known you when you were alive. I feel like I can tell you anything and you understand me. Nobody else does, only you. I wish you could be here with me now. I'm about to go into the doctor's office and I'm shitting bricks. You see...

The receptionist called my name, jolting me back to reality. I folded both letters and tucked them into their envelopes, then shoved both quickly back in my blazer pocket. I stood, took a deep breath and smoothed down my school skirt with sweaty palms. The short walk to the doctor's office felt like a march to death row, my mum a prison guard behind me. I might as well have been receiving a death sentence; the mood was all the same anyway.

"Hello Megan," said Dr Rutherford. "Have a seat. What can I do for you today?"

I sat down on the empty patient seat beside the doctor's desk and lowered my eyes. How could I look Dr Rutherford, my family doctor since I had been a baby, in the eye?

"My daughter here will be needing the Morning after pill, Doctor."

"I see." Dr Rutherford wheeled his chair closer to his computer and began typing. I let my face fall behind a shower of hair. Why couldn't the ground swallow me up? "How many days has it been since the need for emergency contraception happened? I ask because it's only really effective for seventy-two hours afterwards." Dr Rutherford spoke to his computer screen, making the shameful burn in my cheeks even hotter.

"Friday night and it's now Monday morning, so that would be within three days, wouldn't it? Is she OK to take it?" My mum's voice had a note of panic.

"Yes, it should still work." Dr Rutherford finally looked at me above the rim of his glasses, fixing me with a blank, stern gaze. "But you'll need to take it straight away as soon as you get it."

"Thank you doctor." My mum's grovelling made it so much worse. "Thank you for giving her an appointment so quickly and for being so understanding."

He printed off a prescription and handed it to my mum then returned his attention to me. I might as well have had herpes and crabs and syphilis all at once; my family doctor couldn't have given me a worse look. "Take care of yourself now, Megan. You're doing your A-levels this year, aren't you?"

I nodded, unable to say anything, shame burning my lips shut.

"Then I'd focus on studying. Young men can wait until you're at university." With that, Doctor Rutherford swivelled his chair around and faced his computer.

Outside the doctor's office, my mum grabbed my arm and squeezed, her fingernails digging into my skin even through my school blazer. "See you, wee girl? If you ever embarrass me like that again, you'll find yourself out on your ear."

"Aye sure, go ahead and try it. You know I'd be happy to go and smoke weed with Aunt Tracey. She's got a spare room in her flat, she'd have me."

Mum shut up then; she knew I was right. I knew she was simmering, wondering if Aunt Tracey had already allowed me to smoke some of her dope. Or maybe more accurately, since she knew her sister well, *how much* Aunt Tracey had *already* allowed me to smoke.

"Aren't you glad your second child is a boy?" I shot a sideways sneer at her, just to goad her further.

"Pity he wasn't the only child I had. Stuart doesn't give me half the nonsense you've been giving me lately. Suspended from school for damaging school property and now letting the wee lads go at you like you're the town bike." She shook her head, her greying-blonde hair falling over her face. "Shameful hussy you are, a scarlet woman."

I sniggered to myself. Mum always failed to offend me, but never failed to amuse me. "No wonder Dad beat the shit out of you and left, you're so pathetic you can't even raise a good Christian girl. You're shit at everything you do, parenting included. You're the worst mother ever."

I actually got Mum to gasp that time as her feet hit the pavement outside the Doctor's surgery. She pressed her lips together like she wanted to say something, but was struggling to formulate her thoughts, then finally let them fly. "You're the most ignorant wee shite I've ever had the misery to say is my daughter. After school today, pack your clothes in a bag and go to Aunt Tracey's. If you want to get high with her, so be it. Wreck your life. You're eighteen now, big enough and ugly enough to take care of yourself."

With that she was gone, leaving me reeling. For once she had followed through on a threat. So many times she had told me to get out and now I'd been turfed out – on my ear.

***

"Mum? Are you in?" The brief echo of my voice floated across the hallway.

Stuart's mousy head appeared over the bannister on the landing. "She's not home yet, dummy."

"Good." I dumped my school bag by the door and started upstairs. "I'm hoping to be gone by the time she's back."

That seemed to have piqued my wee brother's attention, for the flippin' numpty stood waiting for me at the top of the stairs. "So she finally kicked you out then? About friggin' time. I wondered when she was going to turf you out."

"Fuck off, spastic." I shoved Stuart aside as I reached the top and he fell against the hot-press door. Not long till he was too big for me to push around, and the wee shite was only twelve.

"Go and see the present I left for you. Go on then – have a good look." Stuart pointed into my room and laughed as he bounded down the stairs.

My eyes scanned the room as I walked inside and straightaway landed on my Ouija board. Stuart had scrawled all over it in biro. There was a picture of a dick with balls and a caption reading: *The Blue Man is a cocksucker*. Other mindless taunts included: *Megan and Sabrina are lezzers, Louisa-Mae has a fat fanny* and *Johnny has crabs*.

"Very funny." I forced my voice to sound like I wasn't bothered, but my heart hammered. Stuart had almost sabotaged my sole means of communicating with Norman. Would Norman be angry? It would serve Stuart right if he was and decided to take revenge on him.

In the meantime, revenge was up to me. I grabbed a box of tacks off my bedroom window sill and dashed to Stuart's room, all thoughts of packing abandoned. I pulled up the carpet at his bedroom door and pushed the tacks under it, the sharp ends sticking through though disguised by the fabric. My fingers worked quickly until, one by one, all the tacks had been pushed through. I hastily flattened the carpet back into place. A row of painful spikes would be waiting for the wee shite when he came back upstairs.

With my horrible revenge in place, I dashed into my room and dived onto the bed. Soon the thud of Stuart's feet sounded on the stairs. I held my breath and stifled a giggle.

Thud, thud, thud across the landing. Such a heavy wee git for a twelve year old.

A piercing shriek filled the whole upstairs. I jumped off my bed in time to see Stuart, red-faced, howling and hobbling backwards, his bleeding feet staining Mum's new cream carpet. A plate of cheese on toast toppled sideways and landed face down, adding to the growing assortment of colourful stains on the landing floor.

"What did you do, you evil bitch?" Stuart massaged one foot then the other, tears pouring over his cheeks.

I folded my arms and laughed down my nose at him. "That's what you get for graffiti-ing my Ouija board."

Though his tears, Stuart grimaced. "It wasn't me, it was the Blue Man."

"Yeah, as if writing 'the Blue Man is a cocksucker' is something that Norman would do."

"Norman?" Stuart's face, crumpled with confusion, smoothed into plain fear. "Is that who you've been talking to in your room?"

Stuart's words hit me like a tonne of bricks. "Were you listening in on my private conversations, you nosy wee shite?"

My annoying brother waggled a threatening finger at me. "I'm going to tell Mum. Megan's got a boyfriend, Megan's got a boyfriend!"

"Norman isn't my boyfriend, he's my best friend."

'Yeah, he's a boy and he's a friend – so he's your boyfriend!"

I fumed. "For your information, whether he's my boyfriend or not is none of your business."

Stuart shook his finger back and forth. "But he isn't even a boy – the dirty secrets continue! I've heard him – he's a man. You've been talking to a man on the phone."

For a moment I was confused; I hadn't been talking to Norman on the phone, only through the Ouija board. So whose voice was Stuart hearing?

"How can you have heard Norman's voice? When I've been in my room playing the Ouija board, it's only been me talking to ask the questions, and the board spelling out the answers." I fetched the Ouija board from my room and showed him the letters.

"Liar, liar, pants on fire. I've heard you asking questions and then a man's voice answering." Stuart made his voice deep, his chest protruding. "He spoke – like – this."

I paused, blinking at my brother, not knowing what to say. With words failing me, instead I brought the Ouija board down on Stuart's head. "You're one to talk, don't call me a liar."

I turned back to my bedroom to pack, making sure to slam the door from the unwanted intrusion of my brother. Stuart's words gnawed at me. Had Stuart really heard Norman speaking? If so, if Norman had really been answering my questions verbally then why hadn't I heard him? Why had I been getting answers spelled letter by letter and Stuart had been getting the real deal; the Blue Man speaking from beyond the grave?

Chapter nineteen

Sabrina – November 2020

Leo slept peacefully in his Moses basket on the bed while I scrubbed. Babies had it so easy; eat, sleep, grow. My job was much harder. Jake and I were busy cleaning and unpacking all our belongings after the exterminator had bug-bombed our roach-infested flat. At least the nightmare was over; the main thing was our flat was now a clean, safe place to raise a child in. At the end of the day Leo's health, and ours, was all that mattered.

Mental health too.

My sanity had been on the fritz what with all the sleepless nights, filled with the torturous beat of N.J's music from above in Flat five. *Dah-dum-tish-dum-dum-dum.* At least the incessant beat had abated while N.J. had been in the thick of the roaches infesting our building. Now that the biblical plague was over, would the insanity-inducing music start up again?

Black mould growing on the wall by the window distracted me from sweeping up dead cockroach carcasses and wiping down surfaces with antibacterial wipes. Why was it that anything associated with N.J. involved disease harbouring flora or fauna; mould spores or cockroaches?

I beat my chest then brandished my cleaning sponge to the heavens. "And the great Lord, O'Man O'Blue says, 'stretch out thy rod and smite the dust of the flat, so that it may become vermin throughout all the land'. And after that, let the darkness spread, mould so black it can be felt!"

"What's that you said, honey?" Jake shouted from the bathroom.

"Nothing sweetie, just ignore me. I'm cracking up. Maybe the cleaning spray has gone to my head," I called back.

Jake puffed and panted as he struggled past the bedroom door hauling a large box. "I'm going to take these outside and check them for any live roaches."

"I guess that's a good idea after Steve in number three said he had some living in his musical equipment," I added with a sigh.

"I'm a bit worried that some might have survived even after the whole building got sprayed. I might put our TV and other electronics in a big plastic box with a bug bomb and duct-tape it shut for two weeks. Don't think any roaches could survive that."

I snorted. "Yeah, they won't survive and neither will we without TV."

Jake swept into the room and kissed me. "We'll manage. There's other things we can do to occupy ourselves."

"Like sleep." I linked my hands in the small of his back. "Between these cockroaches, mould and weirdo neighbour, I could do with forty winks."

"Looks like Leo beat you to it." Jake smiled at our sweet, snoozing son. "Do you want me to take him out for a walk in the pram while you go to the laundromat later?"

"Yeah, actually that would help a lot. It'll give me time to wash all our clothes and bedsheets and put them through the drier on high heat." An involuntary shudder overcame me. "As hot as possible to kill any vermin that our eyes might have missed."

"Okay honey, let me get all our electronics bug-bombed and then I'll take him off your hands." Out he went, leaving me, and the baby, and the pests, and the mould. And the phantom from above.

Leo's soft breathing calmed me as I continued scrubbing. It wasn't long before Jake swept back into the bedroom and took our baby off my hands. I shoved clothing and bedding into a giant laundry bag, as much as I could stuff, and dragged it out onto the landing. Normally having to go to the laundromat was a chore that I despised, but compared to cockroaches, I relished the thought of doing the laundry. The white noise might even send me off to sleep; for a cat-nap, at least.

I was locking up the flat, when the silence of the building was punctuated by a sudden blast of music. The familiar *dah-dum-tish dum-dum-dum* boomed across the communal space so loudly that I felt our wooden front door vibrate. I left the laundry bag on the landing and crossed the threshold to the stairs leading upwards to flats five and six.

As I turned onto the landing, the door of Flat five opened. N.J. appeared wearing yellow rubber gloves and carrying two large bin bags, one in each hand. No longer muffled, the music blared out clear as day behind him and finally I recognised the one, incessant song that he had been playing, on a constant loop, for the past month: *Willow's Song* from *The Wicker Man*.

If my knowledge of horror movies hadn't been extensive, through my love of the genre, I never would have recognised that fact. In spite of my love of all-things-horror, I couldn't help feeling disturbed. Here was yet another Scottish connection between N.J. and the Blue Man. The Wicker Man had been set in, and filmed on location in Scotland. The film added another common thread between N.J. and the Blue Man; an occult connection. Or was I reading into it a bit much?

"Alright there, love?" said N.J.

I had been so preoccupied by recognising Willow's Song that I hadn't noticed how N.J. was shirtless. He wore a pair of blue Levis and nothing else, barefoot and shirtless as he was. My eyes were drawn to his bare chest; he had the sinewy, athletic frame of a bare-knuckle boxer and his chest, shoulders and arms were covered with blue snaking tattoos in Pictish designs. Another Scottish connection between N.J. and the Blue Man. I swallowed a lump in my parched throat.

"Oh – hello," I mumbled.

N.J. jabbed his thumb behind him to indicate his open doorway. "Were you on your way up to see me?"

The answer of course was yes, but what could I say? My feet had been bolder than my brain, marching me up to his flat without allowing me time to prepare what to say.

"Was the music too loud? You know, if it is, just bang on your ceiling and I'll turn it down," he said, without even so much as an apology.

An image of either Jake or I banging on the ceiling with a broom handle flashed into my mind; like I would ever do that. Even the notion seemed antisocial and un-neighbourly.

If N.J. wasn't going to be direct, neither was I. "Is it the Wicker Man soundtrack?"

He shrugged. "Dunno. Just like the sound of it, is all. You like horror films?"

Before I had a chance to answer, a woman appeared in the doorway of flat five and slumped one shoulder against the doorframe. She had short, black, dishevelled hair and wore a leopard-print bathrobe. "Who're you talking to, Johnny?"

Johnny. Not N.J. His name was Johnny. So, he had lied to me as I had lied to him? Had he sensed that my real name hadn't been Sandra when I had introduced myself?

No; I was reading into the situation too much, giving N.J. powers of telepathy that he didn't have, all in the name of the Blue Man. There wasn't anything supernatural about the situation. I chided myself and focused my thoughts.

"N.J meets Sandra," I said, tilting one corner of my mouth up into what I hoped was a sarcastic grin. "Or is it Johnny meets Sabrina?"

"Neil John is my name. Or N.J. to you. Johnny to my friends and family." Johnny smirked as he jabbed a finger over his left shoulder, indicating the woman standing in the open doorway of his flat.

It couldn't be the same Johnny, could it? No, that would be far too much of a coincidence. Not the blonde-haired pretty-boy from my school days, the one who all the girls fancied? Johnny that I had known in my school days had hazel-brown eyes, whereas N.J. who stood before me had one hazel-brown eye and one ice blue; heterochromatic, as I had observed before with knowledge from watching too many films about demonic possession.

Demonic possession; I gulped, if only to wet my fear-dried throat with saliva. What if N.J. was possessed by the Blue Man? The Blue Man, with ice-blue eyes; one half of N.J. as Neil John governing the right side of his body with the hazel eye and the other half possessed by Norman James on the left side. The Devil's side. Evidence of the evil, satanic possession as shown by an ice-blue eye. My heart began to speed up, catching up to my racing thoughts.

Could it be? Could it be more than coincidence?

Back in our sixth form days, Megan had insisted that there was a connection between Norman James McMurray and Johnny Montgomery. Could this be the same Johnny Montgomery, my new neighbour, who happened to have moved into the flat above me two months before; around the time I had met up with Megan again after twenty years? If it was, it would be proof that my meeting up with Megan was ill-fated and that supernatural forces were, indeed, at play.

I felt sick. A wave of nausea coursed the nerves of my stomach. I clenched my abdomen, trying to quell the urge to vomit. In spite of my queasiness, I had to know.

"Johnny? Not Johnny Montgomery? Who used to hang around with Rab and Daz back in school?"

I studied N.J.'s face; behind the lines that had been carved in the last two decades lay familiarity. Yes, despite his different coloured eyes, I saw the same cheeky teenager that I had known in 2000. This was Johnny, the boy I had kissed, the boy who Megan had slept with. Johnny who had been at the centre of all the trouble throughout the summer full of the Blue Man. As his eyes widened in surprise, a boyish innocence overcame his face and I was certain; this was Johnny from my school days, no doubt about it. Before he even had a chance to answer me, I already knew.

A boyish grin spread across his face, crinkling his eyes. "Am I that well known, like?"

"Who's this you're *talking* to?" said the woman again, her voice filled this time with urgency.

Now I was convinced; my catch-up with Megan had caused a mysterious, dare I say it, supernatural convergence in all of our life paths. Belfast wasn't that big a place that faces from the past could stumble upon each other through happenstance. Yet there I found myself, the second time in as many months, where a face from a summer I would rather forget had appeared. What an unfortunate fact.

The Blue Man was making sure we – Megan and I – were aware of another unfortunate fact; that he was back. If events were to unfold as they had the first time, it was only a matter of time before his presence became stronger. The Blue Man had escaped the void into which Megan and I had sent him. Dread filled me, flooding my veins, pooling in every muscle. The Blue Man was back, and after what we had done to him, he would be after revenge.

Chapter twenty

Megan – November 2020

Why did Sabrina's text disturb me so much?

Guess who my new neighbour is? Johnny Montgomery. Believe it or not.

I'd rather not believe it.

Johnny, another figure from a shady past who had drifted into the present. It had only been in recent months that I had seen Louisa-Mae's fat carcass dandering around Belmont and Lauren, in all her *millbag* glory with five kids round her knees outside the Housing Association, and now in more recent weeks Sabrina had come back into my life.

The coincidences were becoming too frequent now; maybe it was time for me to take action while I had control of the situation, before a sinister event would be forced onto me. If I was in charge, surely nothing bad would happen to me?

I knew where the box was straight away; luckily I hadn't yet packed everything away and all the extraneous junk had been shoved into the attic. Paddy hadn't seen me pack it, didn't even know I had it. Why I had decided to keep it for all these years was beyond me. Or maybe that was precisely it: beyond. The beyond was influencing everything around me. I hadn't played with the Ouija board since I was eighteen, but I was ready to ask all that I needed to ask. I wasn't an insecure teenage girl anymore, Paddy was right. I was a confident, mature, mother-to-be.

I set the Ouija board on the kitchen counter. The kitchen seemed the best place to communicate with the dead; it was full of light, the brightest room in the house. Nothing dark or scary could possibly happen to me here. I made a cup of tea and put some chocolate digestives on a plate; a sweet treat to repel any sinister forces, even if nothing more than a placebo.

I pushed the pointer around the board a few times, making figure eights as I had two decades before, to get a feel for the board and let my fingers find their rhythm. I took a deep breath and let the questions flow from my head, down my board and spill onto the board.

"Is anyone there?"

No answer; only figure eights that I made myself.

"Have I made contact with anyone?"

Yes. My heart skipped a beat as my brain worked to streamline the questions I had planned.

"Am I speaking to Norman James McMurray?"

Yes.

"Did you have any influence on Johnny Montgomery moving into the flat above Sabrina McCann?"

Yes.

My head was spinning. "But why?"

The pointer landed on the letter Q followed by U-E-S-T-I-O-N-S.

"Questions? What questions?"

Johnny. I wanted to throw the pointer in frustration against the wall, but I kept my hands planted firmly on it. If I was going to be in control, and to get to the bottom of all the weird happenings lately, I needed to ask the right questions – and stay logical. Why was Johnny, a boy I'd been associated with only briefly in my late-teens, so important?

Unless–

"Are you related to Johnny?"

Yes.

I gasped, but didn't dare take my hands off the board. I did the calculations quickly in my head: if the Blue Man lived in the Edwardian period, somewhere around the turn of the century, that would make him–

"Is Johnny your great-grandson, or something?"

Yes.

Why didn't I see that earlier? Norman had always shown so much interest in me and Johnny having a relationship. But now I was married, soon to be a mother. What was the purpose in bringing Johnny back into my life?

"Am I related to you or to Johnny?"

No.

Phew. My relief dissipated as I began to think of other connections – and the right questions to ask.

I gulped before speaking. "Why am I so important to you?"

The pointer landed on the letter M followed by A-U-R-E-E-N. Maureen.

The name floated back to the forefront of my mind from a dusty corner of my subconscious. "Maureen Ann Boyd. That was your true love, wasn't it?"

Yes.

"She was pregnant with your child, wasn't she?"

Yes.

My brain worked at lightning speed, adding up the information. So, if Johnny was the child of the child of Maureen Ann Boyd's baby, then what was my connection to Maureen? As my mind skidded to a halt on a possibility, an unearthly coldness filled me.

"Am I the reincarnation of Maureen Ann Boyd?"

Yes. Oh. My. God.

No wonder Norman had designs for Johnny and I; he wanted his descendant to be reunited with the woman he had loved while he had been alive on earth. The more I discovered, the more I struggled to contain the rising bile in my throat. But I needed more answers. Not all the dots had been connected, yet.

"You want me and Johnny to be – together?"

Yes.

"But that can't be. It's too late. I'm married to another man in this life. I'm not the woman you once knew when you were alive before. Maureen is gone." I stopped speaking. Dead air hung between us. I knew it wasn't what Norman wanted to hear.

An image of Sabrina calling to her neighbour's house to complain about noise, only to find out it was Johnny flitted into my mind. Sabrina. There were still more answers I needed.

"What has Sabrina got to do with all of this?"

The pointer weaved figure eights on the board, but didn't spell out any words.

"Sorry, that was too complicated a question." I cleared my throat. "Is Sabrina related to you or to Johnny?"

No.

"Is Sabrina related to Maureen Ann Boyd?"

No.

"Then why is Sabrina involved?"

The pointer landed on C followed by O-N-D-U-I-T.

"Conduit? Does that mean, Sabrina is a channel for all the psychic energy?"

Yes.

"Without Sabrina, I wouldn't have made contact with you?"

Yes.

"But if I can't be with Johnny in this lifetime, then what is your purpose?"

The pointer landed on B followed by A-B-Y.

"You want to be born again?"

No.

My eyes wandered away from the Ouija board and landed on my own baby bump. I shook my head; no, it couldn't be. Not my innocent child.

"Do you want to have a baby?" I gulped.

Yes.

I swallowed a lump in my throat. "But how can you have a baby if you're dead?"

The board spelled out Johnny's name.

Was he saying that Johnny was his baby? It was true in a sense; Johnny was his baby's-baby's baby, his great-grandchild. But we had already established that. So where was the conversation going? I had to think of the right questions to ask.

"If you don't want to be born again, is that because you're already reincarnated?"

Yes.

"Then – it couldn't be, could it?" My mind skidded to a halt at the possibility. "Are you reincarnated in the body of your great-grandson, Johnny?"

Yes.

"And you talk to me – or move about outside of his body – when Johnny is asleep?"

Yes.

It was mind-blowing, but I had to find out more. Johnny was the reincarnation of the Blue Man and I was the reincarnation of Maureen Ann Boyd, his true love. They couldn't be together in his lifetime at the turn of the century, so–

"You want me and Johnny to get back as a couple so that we can have a baby together to continue your family line?"

Yes.

Oh – my – God.

I hung my head. "Sorry that can't be the case. It just didn't work out between me and Johnny when we were eighteen. I really tried. Are you sad?"

No.

"Why not?" The question tumbled out of my mouth; too quick or else I would have taken it back. It felt like meddling now, to torment the Blue Man any further.

The pointer landed on B then proceeded to spell out three words. I read aloud. "Bide my time? You're going to bide your time in the hope that Johnny and I will get together? I've already said it's too late, Norman. I'm a happily married woman, a mother to be."

Yes.

Yes that he agreed I was a happily married woman, or yes that he was going to bide his time? Poor Norman; he was going to be disappointed, if the latter was the case.

The pointer landed on F followed by A, T and E. Fate.

I took my hands off the pointer and under its own control, it landed on D followed by E-S-T-I-N-Y. Destiny.

"Norman, you need to let this go. It wasn't your fate to be with Maureen when you were alive and it isn't my destiny to be with Johnny now. You need to accept that. Go back to Johnny's body and do both of you a favour – find a woman who wants to be with your great-grandson and settle with her."

No.

As I stood up from the Ouija board, it continued to spell out one last word: power.

"Power? Whose power? The Devil? I don't think so. You can't have what you want. Don't get any closer to me. If you appear to me like you did before then I'll make sure you're banished – properly this time. Consider that a warning, Norman."

I grabbed the board and pointer, one in each hand to keep them apart. The Blue Man would be sorry if he thought he could mess with me, and my family.

Chapter twenty-one

Sabrina – May 2000

Nobody was in the toilets, thank goodness. I hurried into the end cubicle and closed the door, my heart pounding. The unopened envelope was in my hand. Megan hadn't written me a note in about eight weeks; it had been her turn and she knew I had been waiting for her reply to my last letter. As with all her other notes, she had written my name in bubble letters with a triangular segment at the top left corner of each, giving the impression that the bubble was shiny. Megan was quite the artist. One day, she'd be a famous entrepreneur and I would be there to go to the opening of her business, applauding with all the other customers waiting to buy a custom made product.

I ripped the envelope open with my thumb and sat down on the toilet seat to read it. Instead of 'Hi Sabrina' my eyes were met with 'Dear Norman'.

Dear Norman? Who was that? Some new boy Megan was seeing? Had she mixed up a private letter for a wee lad with her letter for me? As I wracked my brain to think of what boys we knew called Norman, a chill ran through me as my brain registered her words. Norman James, a.k.a. the Blue Man.

Megan had written a letter to a ghost; the spirit she had been contacting through the Ouija board. My fingers started to fold the letter shut, but my curiosity was stronger. What did she have to say to a long dead person that she couldn't say to me, supposedly her best friend?

My eyes devoured the letter, travelling further down the page, dissolving her words into a vocabulary-soup that flooded my brain. I couldn't see any reason why she would lie in a private letter, but these thoughts were harsh, unfair. Megan thought that I was boring and a stuck-up, frigid, snob. Not that she let on any of that to my face.

Tears swam in front of my face, washing the words away, falling onto the page. I heaved with sobs. I had always thought that me and Megan, we would be best friends for life. We'd be there to watch each other graduate and would be the maid of honour at each other's wedding. None of that was plausible now. How long had she hated me? Just recently since Johnny had come between us or all along, from the beginning?

"Sabrina? Are you in there?"

Louisa-Mae's voice jolted me away from Megan's letter. I sniffed tears away and opened the toilet cubicle door.

"I was looking everywhere for you, you weren't in Form group." Her gaze dropped to Megan's letter. "What's that? Are you alright?"

She reached for the letter and I loosened my grip, letting her take it. I watched Louisa-Mae's eyes race from left to right and zigzag lower down the page, her lip curling the further she read. Her jaw hardened as she finished reading, her lips taut.

"Can you believe that?" I hiccupped with sobs and Louisa-Mae pulled my head onto her shoulder in a gesture that felt more as one of solidarity in commiseration than true consolation.

"I'm going to take this. I need to show this to Lauren." Louisa-Mae's stoic expression broke into her usual devious smirk. "Did you read the last part?"

I shook my head, flinging tears onto my blazer sleeves. "I stopped reading after that bit about me."

"Here, listen to this." Louisa-Mae adopted Megan's higher-pitched, nasally voice and read the last paragraph.

If only you could be here with me in real life. If only I'd known you when you were alive. I feel like I can tell you anything and you understand me. Nobody else does, only you. I wish you could be here with me now. I'm about to go into the doctor's office and I'm shitting bricks. You see, Johnny bucked me on Friday night and we didn't use a jube or nothing, and now I have to get the morning after pill. Mum was raging when I told her, but I had to. I'm only eighteen, it's not the right time to get knocked up the duff.

Louisa-Mae's eyes crinkled as she grinned. "Well? What about that, then?"

I sniffed tears away. "How can you be happy? You read what she wrote about all three of us there."

"Not that bit, the part about her being pregnant!"

I pointed at the letter. "She isn't pregnant, she got the morning after pill."

"Yeah, but nobody else knows that." Louisa-Mae crumpled the note into her blazer pocket. "I'm taking this to show Lauren."

Without another word, Louisa-Mae turned, showering me in a curtain of red-gold hair. I blinked as the curly tresses stung my eyes and watched as she swept out of the toilets. What was she going to do to Megan? Nothing good, it seemed.

***

Or maybe I was wrong. Megan had snuck the letter into my bag on Monday. It was now Friday and nothing much had happened over the past few days, other than I had avoided talking to, or looking at Megan at all. What was worse was the fact that she had tried to talk to me, only succeeding in forcing an awkward conversation between us.

Sabrina, I'm so sorry about that letter. I wasn't myself. I was high when I wrote it.

Well that makes it even worse then, as you're more honest when you're doped-up.

I didn't mean any of it. You didn't say anything to Louisa-Mae, did you?

That had only made the awkward silence between us even more tense; but at least she'd had the good sense not to try and talk to me any further.

Thank God I had a reason to be leaving school as the tension between Megan and I was unbearable. My dental appointment was at half eleven. The bell rang, signalling the end of break-time just as I finished signing out at reception. I exited the front doors and walked out to the bus stop in front of the school. A few boys loitering at the garage nearby caught my eye, particularly the bright blonde head in the midst of the group.

"Sabrina!"

Johnny strode across the driveway of the garage in my direction. Daz and Rab trailed behind him like two bouncers flanking him. My heart jumped into my throat as he strode towards me; though in the absence of his sexy grin, his mouth was taut and angry.

"Johnny? What's up?"

Johnny's eyes were narrowed under an angry brow. "Did you and your mates break into my Dad's flat and wreck up my room?"

I blinked at him, my mouth gawping.

"And don't say it was the Blue Man," he added, before I had even spoken.

I shook my head. "It wasn't me."

"Aye right, who was it then?"

My mouth closed then opened like a fish out of water. Disembodied words, that couldn't possibly have come from my brain, floated into the air. "It was Megan, not me."

I had never touted on a friend before, never betrayed a girl, especially for a user like Johnny. Then again, Megan was no longer my friend; at least if her letter was anything to go by.

"Megan." Johnny's mouth curled into a sneer as he spat the words. "I find it hard to believe she did it alone."

"Well, I wasn't there. So what's it to me?" Even as I said it, the guilt nipped at me, a phantom piranha eating at my conscience. Even if Megan was no longer my best mate, I still shouldn't have slabbered about her behind her back.

"How would you know she did it if you weren't there?" He stuck his hands in his blazer pockets and I tried not to think of what a screw he was. "See if I find out you were involved too, I'll come to your house and put in your windows. I'll come for all of you and wreck up *your* houses."

I inhaled through my nose, my chest swelling with indignation. "You try it and I'll kick your head in."

Johnny glared at me, his eyes blazing. "We'll see about that. You can tell Megan I'm coming for her first."

Megan. As Johnny and Daz left, a wave of guilt finally crashed down on me. Megan had a lot coming for her, knowing Louisa-Mae and Johnny. I had betrayed my ex-best friend. Norman, the supernatural new best friend she had found in the Blue Man, wouldn't be able to save her from what would surely happen to her now.

Chapter twenty-two

Megan – May 2000

The Blue Man was in pieces.

The pieces of balsa wood were scattered all over the Technology room floor.

Someone had snuck into the classroom and had smashed my A-level Tech and Design project on the floor. I had an idea who that someone was; and their accomplices.

There wasn't anything else I could do about my broken Technology project, except gather the bits and try to put it back together again. I got on my knees and swept the scraps of splintered wood into a pile. The clock face and all the mechanical components inside it were smashed into smithereens. Nothing much I could do about that. Instead, I started piecing the fragments of the Blue Man's face together, rebuilding his jaw and left side of the face up to his cheekbone. Bit by bit the larger sections slotted into place like a jigsaw. Once I had got his face and head aligned, I worked to stick the fragments together with PVA glue. I gathered up the pencils and pens that were scattered across the floor and pushed them into the holes I had drilled all over the Blue Man's head.

Before it had been vandalised my Blue Man desk companion, the centre-piece of my A-level Technology coursework, had shown a perfect face complete with mouth-clock and day and date eyes. Now I stood back and surveyed my salvaged project. The cracks actually *improved* my design; or at least how the A-level examiners would assess it. It implied imperfection, a human who had been damaged, but had tried to piece himself back together. He had a crazed look now, together with the pens and pencils sticking out of his head at wild angles.

Had Sabrina done this? Sabrina didn't have a vindictive streak in her, but she had been moping for the past few days at school since she had read my letter intended for Norman. She had avoided meeting my eyes in the form room and in the classes we had together. But there was no maliciousness behind her sadness. No; it was unlikely that Sabrina had sabotaged my work. It was most likely the usual culprits: Louisa-Mae and Lauren.

Break time was nearly over, and next we had form time. All three of them: Louisa-Mae, Lauren and Sabrina would be in form class. Soon I would confront Louisa-Mae and Lauren about sabotaging my project and take pleasure in seeing their disappointment when I could break the news that not only had I put my balsa wood pen holder of the Blue Man back together again, but their vandalism had improved it. Those two losers would be laughed at for the failures they were.

Why did Mr Bell have to leave the Technology classroom open? I mean, I understood that it was practical for him to allow his GCSE and A-Level students come in at break and lunchtime to finish off their work; but why couldn't there be another way to do it? Like, couldn't he give us all keys to the classroom? If that had been the case then Louisa-Mae and Lauren wouldn't have been able to get into the room to smash my design project in the first place.

I still had time to log onto the computer in Mr Bell's office to print off my design brief analysis for my Blue Man Desk Companion and glue it onto the drawings alongside my A3 sketch. When the computer booted up, I clicked on the My Documents folder followed by Technology and opened it up.

Only one word document showed up. Instead of being labelled 'The Blue Man desk companion' it had been relabelled, 'The Blue Man did it'.

My heart jumped into my throat. I clicked on the Word document and waited for it to open. Only one sentence repeated for an entire A4 page: 'The Blue Man did it'.

There had to be a mistake. I restarted my computer and clicked into the relevant folders again. Nope; this was no accident. My Technology folder on the computer had been changed and the document had been relabelled.

My mouth was dry and my eyeballs numb as I stared at the page full of 'The Blue Man did it' over and over, boring into my brain. Whoever had done this was more vindictive and calculating than a person taking revenge in the heat of the moment by simply throwing my design project onto the floor and smashing it. There was nothing in the computer recycle bin either, so I had no way to recover my documents. I looked across at the plastic box of floppy discs labelled 'A-level Tech and Design' and rifled through until I found mine. Lucky for me, Mr Bell had made us all do backups of our work.

I pushed my floppy disc into the slot and opened the icon when it popped up on the screen. Into Classwork, then into Design projects.

Same as before: A Word document titled 'The Blue Man did it' followed by an A4 page with the same one sentence repeated over and over, filling the entire page.

The Blue Man did it.

Tears prickled my eyes and I pressed my thumbs into the corners to try and stop the flow, but they wouldn't be hindered. My nostrils burned and mucus ran down over my lips. This wasn't happening; there was no way this could be real. Someone would have had to know my password details and logged on pretending to be me. Not only that, but have had knowledge of where the coursework floppy discs were kept.

I switched off the computer and left the Technology room, my head spinning. Louisa-Mae and Lauren had gone too far this time. Would they really have done it? Neither of them took A-level Tech. What about Norman's advice when I had done the Ouija board, on the night of my date with Johnny? Norman had said that Louisa-Mae was my true friend and that Sabrina was the one to watch out for. Could Sabrina have done it? Sabrina took Technology with me, so she would know which project was mine and where the floppy discs were kept. It was possible that she could have seen me type in my computer password too. But was she malicious enough to have done something like that? Sabrina was a follower, not a leader. More likely she was in on it with Louisa-Mae and Lauren, even if not the main instigator. My mind was made up. I would confront all three of those horrible bitches and get to the bottom of it.

I stormed round to the Maths room and saw all of my classmates sitting around in the corridor, waiting for Miss Wright to come. Louisa-Mae's red hair stood out like a fiery beacon with Lauren's black fuzzy ponytail bobbing around as she laughed at some wick joke that Louisa-Mae had made. Hopefully not one at my expense.

All heads turned as I approached the pair of them. Everyone knew, then? So be it; that was enough to confirm the truth for me. Sabrina, the *sleekit* bitch, was nowhere about but I'd see to it later that she got her comeuppance too.

I strode across to Louisa-Mae and grabbed her by her collar, shoving her against the wall. Her mouth fell open as she banged against the plasterboard, an indignant look on her arrogant face.

"Did you think I wouldn't find out it was you, huh? What's your problem?" I shouted in her face.

Louisa-Mae tore my hands off her collar. "I don't know what you're talking about."

"My Technology project? My design of the Blue Man? And what about my coursework, eh? All changed to say 'The Blue Man did it'? Did you think that was funny? That's my A-level work you bitch, my actual Technology grade is on the line."

Now it was Louisa-Mae's turn to shove me. I gasped as the air was knocked from my lungs as I hit the corridor wall. "Why don't you get your facts right before you start accusing people of things they didn't do," she said.

"If it wasn't you, or you." I pointed at Louisa-Mae and Lauren in turn. "Then who did it?"

Lauren stood shoulder to shoulder with Louisa-Mae, the pair of them making an imposing duo, both with their arms folded. "Maybe it was your precious Norman. Were you thinking of him when you let Johnny get you knocked up?" said Lauren.

Gasps resonated along the corridor from my nosy classmates listening in.

"Oh my God, Megan's pregnant," said one of them.

"Megan, are you up the duff?" asked another.

"She is. She pretends to be pure but she's a slutbag who bucks a different wee lad every weekend – she spreads the legs smoother than butter." Louisa-Mae pointed at the cold-sore on my lip. "Look, see? She even has herpes from sucking Daz Neilly's big bendy dick!"

My anger surged as a wave of laughter erupted from my classmates. I grabbed a handful of Louisa-Mae's precious long, orange hair in each hand and slammed her face down into my knee, which I brought upwards to meet her nose. Blood spurted over my tights. Louisa-Mae recoiled holding her bloody face with her left hand. After a comical second in which I watched her stagger backwards, blinking pained tears from her eyes, Louisa-Mae swung her right fist. I saw it coming towards my left cheek a moment too late; her knuckles connected with my cheekbone and I fell backwards.

Louisa-Mae threw herself down on top of me raining punches into my stomach, chest and face. I shielded myself with both arms as best I could, but she was stronger than she looked; and heavier. I felt my hands pulled away from my face and held to either side; Lauren looked down on me. Without being able to defend myself, Louisa-Mae grabbed my tie and pulled. A choked scream rattled out of my throat and my forehead pounded as all the blood rushed to my face.

"Kick her head in!"

"Beat the shit out of the pregnant slutbag!"

"Knock the shit out of the dirty tart!"

And then there were fat arses, and legs, and blazer-clad backs, and the breath was squashed out of me until only blackness was my escape.

***

As I sank back onto my Aunt Tracey's sofa, I watched my cousin Natasha light up a spliff. She took a drag and passed the joint to me. I sucked the smoke into my lungs and let it soothe my body from the inside out. I needed a wee something to perk me up after school earlier. More than a *wee* something actually; I had washed down the last five tabs Johnny had given me with cider in my bedroom, but that had only been ten minutes ago. They hadn't had time to work their magic yet. Neither Natasha nor my Aunt Tracey knew about those. Aunt Tracey and Natasha liked the odd spliff and were into their hash cakes and shroom tea, but I guessed they would draw the line at having anything harder in their flat. I'd have to find someone else who I could buy some from on the sly, now that Johnny and I weren't on speaking terms. At least not if he found out who wrecked up his Dad's flat.

Johnny. Such a nasty wee user, spreading rumours about me and all, but here I was with my head done in over him. It made no sense. Why couldn't he have liked me as much as I liked him and maybe none of it all would've happened: Sabrina and I would still be friends, Louisa-Mae and Lauren and I wouldn't have done criminal damage to someone's property and my A-level Technology wouldn't have been wrecked. I would've been enjoying my last few weeks at school with my friends living in my own house instead of kicked out and living with my Aunt and avoiding school like I was a gutless coward.

Norman would know what to do. I needed him to give me some good advice. Norman was like a big brother to me, or a father figure; the Da I didn't have. I'd talk to him later and see if he could help me map out my next few months. It certainly was a mess to be fixed; Norman had said that Louisa-Mae was my true friend and that Sabrina was the one to watch, as she would try to steal Johnny off me. Neither of those things had been right. Life had gone off the rails over the past few months in a way that didn't make any sense in such a quick timeframe that even Norman, a supernatural person, didn't foresee.

A thud against the living room window jolted me from my thoughts. Natasha and Aunt Tracey turned to look too. I had been expecting to see a bird sliding dead down the pane, but instead saw a yellow slime waterfall. Cracked eggshell littered the outside window sill. Another egg smashed against the window leaving a smear on the glass next to the other one.

I pushed off the arm rest and got to my feet, feeling off-balance as my head was so heavy. My feet struggled to walk to the window as my legs were obstacles that kept getting in the way, tripping me up. Adrenaline coursed through my body; this had to be Louisa-Mae. How did she find where I was living?

I pressed my face against the glass and saw Johnny's blonde head among others; Daz with his hood up and Rab skulking further along the street. Daz was on the balls of his feet, ready to run but Johnny stood squarely looking at my Aunt's flat. I gritted my teeth and staggered to the front door.

As I pulled the door back another egg exploded against it, narrowly missing my head. I ducked as yolk splashed my hair.

"That's so you know it's me. I don't sneak into people's houses, I come right to their face," Johnny shouted. He had another egg in his hand and tossed it from one palm to the other, but didn't throw it.

"Did Louisa-Mae put you up to this?" My words were slurred. I cleared my throat. "You know she was in on it too, right? She was with me. So was Lauren. She was the one that touted to you, wasn't she?"

"Never you mind who touted. It wasn't who you think," said Johnny.

At risk of getting an egg in my face, I stepped out onto my garden path. "You shouldn't have slabbered about me to all your mates, Johnny."

"Away back inside. Look at you, you're so steamin' you can barely speak." Johnny pulled his arm back with the egg raised high in his fist, ready to launch it at me.

"Look at her face, someone's given her a right steaker," Daz laughed.

My hand flew to my sore, swollen eye socket. The bruise must have been black if they were able to see it even in the growing darkness.

"Louisa-Mae beat the shit out of her because she slabbered about her to the Blue Man." Johnny didn't take his eyes off me although he spoke over his shoulder to Daz. "But she doesn't know something that I know, about her precious *Norman*."

An invisible boa constrictor squeezed the air out of my lungs at the sound of the Blue Man's name.

"How do you know the Blue Man? You're nothing. You're nobody." Spit flew out of my mouth landing on the garden path. I wiped saliva off my chin with the back of my hand.

"Leave her, she's having a whitey, she's off her face," said Rab.

Johnny shook his head. "Norman is raging at her for having an abortion. That baby was special."

Abortion? I didn't have an abortion. So that was the rumour Louisa-Mae and Lauren were spreading about me, was it? I looked at Johnny's hard set brow, his clenched jaw. Was he angry at me for taking the morning after pill and not letting myself get up the duff? That couldn't be right. What boy would want to become a schoolboy Dad?

Johnny's voice shifted into a lower, more menacing tone. "Norman is going to come after you now, not me. You think us egging your Aunt's flat is bad? Wait till you see what the Blue Man does to you now."

I shook my head. "Shut your trap, you don't know anything."

"He knows everything about you. He watches you all the time. How do you think I found out your Ma kicked you out?"

"No he didn't, you're wrong. You're lying. You don't know anything!" My whole body shook, including my finger as I pointed it at him. "Louisa-Mae told you I was staying here, or Lauren, or Sabrina."

He grinned and I saw the devilry in his eyes as he ignored me and went on. "He told me you were staying here, with your aunt."

I put my hands over my ears. "You're a liar! Stop telling lies!"

I turned then and ran back inside Aunt Tracey's flat and slammed the door, shutting out the chorus of laughter behind me. My head was spinning, the whole world falling in on me in a blue, swirling haze. Norman wasn't, couldn't, be angry at me. Could he?

Chapter twenty-three

Sabrina – April 2021

Leo loved the noisy whirr as my old faithful car chugged along the Albertbridge Road. His blue eyes were wide at the incessant hum of the engine. Of course, didn't all babies love motion; that was why veteran parents always recommended taking colicky babies on long car rides to settle asleep. In a way I appreciated the journey too: Northern Ireland had been in another lockdown from just after Christmas until the end of March. I hadn't relished spending a good chunk of my maternity leave stuck at home. April brought with it both spring and a new sense of hope to the country.

As we approached the Holywood Arches near the CS Lewis Centre in East Belfast, my happy thoughts faded. All I could imagine was what Megan would think of my car. I still hadn't managed to admit to her the shameful truth of having had everything in Liverpool repossessed after losing the traffic accident court case. Jake was right that I should have been honest with her, but to me, the truth stank of 'failure' and having bad credit, no matter how noble the fight had been in court, reeked of 'poor' – two truths that I found hard to admit; especially to a boastful, materialistic friend.

As we turned into a side street near the Health Centre, I saw Megan waiting in front of the Holywood Arches Library. Her two month old baby son, Harry, was in a fancy, rainbow-coloured three-in-one: car-seat, carrycot and pram. My stomach lurched; my red and black buggy was only thirty pounds, the most I could afford. I had duct-taped the front wheels so that they didn't fall off on kerbs. Her travel system had to be five hundred quid, at least – more than my secondhand car. I could feel her eyes boring into Leo's buggy already, judging it.

"Sabrina." Megan threw her arms around me. "You're looking well."

"And you," I said, patting her back, my chin on her shoulder.

"Wow, Leo is looking blonder than I thought he would be from your profile photos." Megan stretched the kiss-curl on his forehead and let it go; it sprung back into place. "He's got such incredible eyes too, so blue."

She looked at me; her eyes flitting between mine, studying the colour. I knew what she was thinking, she didn't have to say it. How did I manage to have such an *Aryan* looking child when my colouring was so Mediterranean?

"Harry is getting so big," I said, changing the topic.

"I know, I can't believe he's ten weeks old already. Can you believe he arrived on Valentine's Day? How old is Leo?"

"What a coincidence, Leo came on a holiday date too. He was born on Halloween. He'll be six months next week."

Megan gave a bland smile. "Well, how about we get caught up over brunch? My favourite restaurant is near Connswater and they have seating outside, if you're worried about Covid. You do like seafood?"

"Anything is fine by me, I'm not picky."

We walked side by side across the traffic lights and up Bloomfield Avenue. Megan's eyes drifted once more to Leo's buggy. "I'll really have to get one of those soon, Harry is getting so big he's outgrowing this car seat." She tapped his fancy carrycot with a bemused smirk.

"Aye, it's a handy wee buggy, very light weight." I turned my face ahead to avoid her expression, though my imagination betrayed me, picturing her face as politely dismissive of my child's transport.

"In fact, Harry is getting so big that I had to sell my old car and get a new family-sized car." Megan jabbed her finger towards a dark grey Toyota Yaris parked further along Bloomfield Avenue. I glanced, but didn't let my eyes linger; I wasn't sure why she had to overindulge her materialistic side by showing off her fancy travel system and brand new car. What did that car cost anyway, like, £16,000? Even my Mondeo that I had in Liverpool, before it got repossessed, hadn't cost as much as that. As if I wasn't insecure enough already about money. Or maybe; maybe that was it. Maybe *she* was the one who felt insecure. Maybe she wanted to prove that she had made an exceptional comeback after wasting her later teen years as a drugged-up dropout who had scraped two Cs in her A-level Tech and Geography and a pass in her B-Tech Business by the time she had left school. Who knew? I certainly wasn't close enough to her to ask and didn't care to psychoanalyse her, based off my own musings. Nevertheless, my cheeks burned; if she had seen my old Skoda, she certainly wasn't letting on about it.

Megan led the way into her favourite cosy bistro. Harry's travel system and Leo's buggy dominated the space near the door, drawing the attention of disgruntled looking middle-aged, middle-class diners. No doubt they were wondering whether the two babies would make a racket loud enough to put them off their brunch. Not that I cared. All I could think about was how much of a suburbanite Megan, the once hard-partying club-hopping teen had become. We ordered our food as the babies slept, allowing me a cautious glance towards the cynical, baby-hating diners.

"I had a difficult birth with Harry," said Megan, over a bite of salted chilli squid. "My hips were too narrow, so he got stuck coming down. His oxygen started to drop, so they had to rush me to get a C-section. The doctor said it left my womb so paper thin, it might be hard for me to carry another child. Guess that doesn't bother me anyway. We're happy with one."

I looked down at my fish pie. Such an unsavoury topic swept away my appetite quicker than she could have said difficult labour.

"Did you have a natural birth?" she went on.

I nodded. "Water birth, no drugs. I'll never forget the pain though, that was the downside of having no epidural. I remember everything. But at least Leo wasn't drugged up when he came out. He had an Apgar score of nine. The midwives said that usually natural birth babies have lower scores because of the strain they go through being pushed out."

Megan glanced down at Harry, asleep in his carrycot. "Harry had a low Apgar, I think because of the drop in oxygen. He was a rather frail baby at first, but he's been putting on weight and getting bigger just this last couple of weeks. He's still being monitored as he had a small hole at birth, but they said it should close before he's a year old. Anyway, my mum is chuffed at having a baby in the family. She doesn't think Stuart will ever give her a grandchild, what with his mental health problems – the schizophrenia and all."

"That's nice then that she's got something to keep her so happy," I said.

"So, have you seen – you know – Johnny around much? Is he still your neighbour?"

I pushed my fish pie around my plate with my fork, making a potato smear across the china dish. Honestly I'd been expecting the topic to come up earlier. Halfway through our meal was a record, considering.

I gave a one-shouldered shrug. "Aye, he's still there. I see him from time to time. He still plays loud music every weekend, living up the bachelor lifestyle I suppose but neither Jake nor I have bothered complaining about the noise. We'd rather keep to ourselves."

A slow smile twitched at her lips. "Does he realise who you are?"

"No, I don't think so. It might've come up, but then his girlfriend interrupted us as she seemed suspicious of him talking to me. To be honest, I'd rather not talk to him at all." Leo roused from sleep, blinking his huge blue eyes open and looking at me. He must have sensed my tension as we were so in sync with each other. I lifted him out of his buggy and put him to my breast.

Megan watched us and stroked Harry's cheek as he slept. "Aww, that's so sweet. I'm feeding Harry myself too, though I'm planning to give it up in a couple of weeks once he's twelve weeks old."

"How come? Is he having difficulty latching?" I tore my eyes away from Leo's contented face as he nursed and looked at my old chum.

"It's not that. It's just so sore for me. My nipple cracked and I needed a course of antibiotics. My skin is just so sensitive, you see. You make it look so easy." She smiled as she watched Leo nursing, though it didn't reach her eyes. "I suppose your skin must be naturally tougher, what with your swarthy complexion and all, so it mustn't hurt as much for you. I'm so fair skinned, you remember how easily I burned in the summer when we were at school?"

Was Megan for real? What had my olive-skinned Mediterranean appearance got to do with how easily I could breastfeed? "Well, I – it hurt for me too at first, but I just struggled through it. Leo's Health Visitor has been so good though, showing me other nursing positions to help with his latch. You'll get there, if you stick at it."

My head was still swimming with Megan's assumptions about me, and Leo, and how little we really knew each other despite having been best friends at school; but I was grateful that we had steered onto a different topic away from Johnny, or the past. Especially not the topic that hadn't yet come up-

"I need to tell you something else."

Or not; speak of the Devil. Megan swallowed the last bite of her food, the pause in conversation filled with invisible knives that could have cut the psychic strings between us.

"You remember how I used the Ouija board, a couple of times, back when we were in sixth form?"

Several times a week, if my memory served me right; though I didn't say it to her. I didn't answer. Why couldn't the conversation just fade away? I cupped my hand around Leo's ear with the pretence of soothing him while he fed, but really to protect him from hearing topics that I didn't want him to know.

"I've been back in touch with the Blue Man. You remember Norman?"

This was going too far; either I had to cut the lunch short or intervene. Options were Maypole ribbons trailing through my brain. "Megan, maybe it's best to forget all that stuff. It's in the past. We've moved on."

"Have we?" There was a sharpness to her question that surprised me.

"We have Leo and Harry now. It's time to let the past fade away now."

She shook her head. "See that's the problem though. I don't think it can. In the past year, you and I have been drawn back together. I've seen more and more of Lauren and Louisa-Mae knocking about after I hadn't seen them in decades. Then mysteriously Johnny moves into the flat above you over in Cregagh. Of all the people who could have moved in, you ended up neighbours with Johnny Montgomery. Don't you think these are signs that something supernatural is influencing what we do?"

I couldn't deny that I'd had – for want of a better word – suffered a case of the heebee-jeebees since I'd met up with Megan the previous summer. The connections between Neil John, better known as Johnny, and Norman James, aka the Blue Man, had left me spooked. But since Leo had been born and many months had passed since I'd last seen Megan, I had tried to put all that behind me as nothing more than post-traumatic stress, a mere hangover from the sinister summer during which we had sat our A-level exams. Seeing Megan had stirred up bad memories, that was all. Nothing ghostly had taken place; only my overactive imagination and love of horror movies wreaking havoc on my head.

"If you want to know my opinion, I'm sorry that the Blue Man ever became a part of our lives. It started as just an urban legend I'd heard round my way in Sydenham growing up." I hung my head, looking down at my baby's small form curled around my stomach. "If I'd known what a mess it was going to cause in our lives, I wouldn't have told you. I wish I hadn't told you."

"It's fine, Sabrina. I'm fine. At least I know what I'm dealing with. And you're right. It's something that needs to be properly buried in the past, but it has to be done in the right way. I've been looking into something – doing some research, if you get what I mean." Megan paused, watching me with wide, pleading eyes. "If I asked you to do something for me, would you?"

I gulped, swallowing bitter saliva down my tightened throat. "Depends what it is. What is it?"

"Well, you see, it's to do with Johnny. It's a long story. Would I be able to come over and visit you at your flat?" Megan's gaze dropped to the table. Why was she suddenly so coy?

"Is that so you can meet up with Johnny?"

"Kind of." Megan took a rattling breath. "You'll think I'm crazy, but I'm going to tell you anyway. Norman has been talking to me again through the Ouija board and it turns out that he is reincarnated in the body of–"

"Let me guess, Johnny." Leo unlatched from my breast and I put him back in his buggy fast asleep, glad that he wouldn't hear the conversation.

"Right." Her eyes bulged with anger momentarily; so she hadn't missed my sarcasm. "We communicate when Johnny is asleep, or high off his face, blocked out of his skull, or so on, you get it."

I scoffed. "With the number of parties that fella has, I can understand how you're able to talk to the Blue Man so much. He's pretty much bleutered most of the time."

"Not only is Johnny the reincarnation of Norman James McMurray, he's his great-grandson too," said Megan matter-of-factly.

A chill skimmed the back of my neck as more customers swept in off the street; at least, I hoped that was why I suddenly shivered.

"I want Norman to leave me alone and I think I've found a way to keep his spirit sealed inside Johnny," Megan continued.

I rubbed my arms against the chill. "It's not going to hurt Johnny, is it?"

She shook her head. "He doesn't even know Norman's spirit resides in him, so no."

"No, I mean the ritual – or thing – you're planning to do to trap the Blue Man inside him," I said.

"It won't hurt at all. I just need to meet him and give him something. But it needs to be done while he's awake so that Norman will be inside him. Think of it as like sticking a cork in the lamp that holds a genie. I just want to seal Norman inside Johnny's body so that he can't haunt me – or us – anymore."

If all Megan wanted to do was come over and visit Jake, Leo and I at our house and then pop next door to become reacquainted with Johnny, then it didn't seem like a bother at all. I nodded my consent. "Do you think it'll work?"

"It should do. You remember the ritual you did with me that summer in the back garden of my Mum's house, to trap the Blue Man in the first place – don't you?"

Against my will, memories seeped out of the marshland of my mind: an ancient ritual that dated back to pre-Christian Ireland. "Yeah, I think so. You had that funny statue made out of yew wood – and that special rock."

Megan nodded with a sudden fervour. "Amber gemstone from Lough Neagh. It can banish spirits and ward off evil. Besides, just like you were there before, I'll have you there supporting me again with your energy."

Supporting me with your energy? What did that mean? It was a weird way to ask me to emotionally support her, if that was what she was trying to do. Of course, if this was going to help her to move on past the Blue Man and let the entity go from our lives for once and for all, then it was worth it.

I sighed. "After all this is done, can we agree we'll never mention the Blue Man – Norman – again, ever?"

"Never. I swear it," she said. Her face was so composed, determined that I found myself answering, against my better instincts.

"Alrighty. Just tell me when you want to come over and I'll see to it that Jake and Leo are out of the flat. I don't want them mixed up in all this – drama."

I had almost said craziness, but stopped myself in time. Megan was deadly serious. I didn't know what I made of it all myself, but Megan certainly believed there was a malign supernatural force at work and I wanted our friendship to work. We just had to get past this one issue from our past. If we were to become close again, we had to deal with the trauma from our shared past. That was worth it for me.

Chapter twenty-four

Megan – April 2021

As my head drooped forward onto my chest, my body was simultaneously stolen away on a tide of sleep and freed of the spirit shackling its body. I was no longer Megan, a modern day millennial. I was transported back in time to 1918, free floating to a life I had lived a century before in Belfast.

My name was Maureen Ann Boyd. I was in the prime of my life, eighteen years old; young, slim and beautiful. My long, blonde hair glistened like gold thread when I gave it a hundred strokes of the brush. Until recently I had been living like a normal woman in her prime, going to the Hippodrome on Saturdays, even despite the restrictions, whenever I could scrape together a ha'penny. But not anymore. One thing had stopped me. Not the Great War; that was thankfully over, nor the Spanish Flu that was on the wane. Instead, there was a wee bulge in my belly. An irreversibly life changing bulge.

I would soon have to give up my job at the Ropework Factory and what would I do then? Ma and Da didn't have any money. Sure, didn't I know that well enough? I'd been selling flowers or hawking sticks on the streets since I was a wean to bring in money and had barely made it through national school, never mind secondary. My wee brother sold newspapers for a few shillings, but where did that get us? A run-down house in Dee Street. But it got me him too.

He passed by every day on his way to work. Norman. He was a welder and boys-a-dear, he was a sight for sore eyes! He was tall with black hair and piercing blue eyes; soulful, deep-set eyes. He was Scottish originally, from Glasgow, exotic to us girls at the Ropeworks. Sure, wasn't I the envy of all the girls as we crafted our ropes, sang songs and talked about who was courting who?

Norman and I had been courting for a few months. I first realised I was in love with him when I saw him, so dashing in his kilt for Hogmanay. I fell head over heels for him that night, and we had taken our love further, out under the open stars and the full moon. But now it had been the second time I hadn't been on my moon and there was no denying my belly had changed shape.

No denying that there wasn't a ring on my finger either.

Norman had asked me to elope with him over to Gretna Green. I wanted to say yes, but I had told him no. It wasn't because of the money. Yes, granted we were both poor, but poverty wasn't what stopped me.

Not even my parents could have stopped me – though they were against it too. The problem was, I was to be betrothed to another.

Oh, the shame! My intended, dear Martin, dear sweet Martin, was the eldest of a farming family of five. I had been visiting my cousin in Tyrone when we had met purely by chance. I knew I had nothing to offer him, other than my looks. But he had fallen heads over heels for me, thanks to Lady Luck, and after three months of courting, we had got engaged last year. That had been one month before I had met Norman. Martin hadn't been blessed with good looks as Norman or I had, but he was strong and worked hard. We were due to be married in another quart. Of course, that wouldn't happen now; my hand fell to the curve of my stomach. Soon everyone would know.

Ack, Martin was a good man, so he was. There was no denying that. He was kind to me when he visited, which wasn't that often what with him being in Tyrone and me being in Belfast. Dear knows how long it took him on a horse and cart coming over to pay me visits, but I appreciated it all the same. It showed his devotion to our soon-to-be union. Ill-fated union. For you see, we had never lain together, Martin and me. So, there could be no way he would think the baby was his.

Norman knew about the baby. Sure, wasn't he the doting father-to-be! But I had told him – oh, how I had told him – that we couldn't be together. It just wouldn't – couldn't – work out for us, no matter which way you looked at it.

Ah, poor pitiful child of mine. What would you do when you realised what a stupid article of a mother you had, getting herself in trouble and out of wedlock too? Ack, poor silly girl, thinking herself a woman. Doing womanly things beyond her years, falling for the charms of a silly poor boy and his charming white smile. Where was it all going to lead to? A silly spinster on the shelf, jilted by the man with money and torn from the one she loves. Everyone to laugh at her then. Ah, foolish girl. Away on, they would say, a scarlet woman.

My poor Ma and Da. It's not how they raised me. It would be better if I worked for as long as a shawl could cover my indiscretion, and then run away and put the child up for adoption. Better than ending up in a mother and baby home, oh no. Time was not on my side. If I was lucky, I would have six, maybe seven months to work out a plan.

My dear, beloved Norman. Hopefully you would understand one day. Whatever decision I made would be for the best. It would be for us both. But I knew that one day, maybe even in another lifetime, we would be together as love, not life, had intended.

***

There he was and there I was. It hadn't been my idea to lure him there. I had been forced to write the letter, enticing him there to his doom, on the banks of the Connswater River where it flowed into Belfast Lough. Though it hadn't been my words it had been my hand that had brought him there, on a moonlit night, thinking we were to elope to Gretna Green. They told me that they wouldn't kill him if I did what they made me do, but how stupid of me to believe them.

Oh, my poor, sweet, naïve love! How vain and foolish we had both been to believe in a dream that couldn't last.

Martin and his brothers had dictated the letter to me and had stood over me, by candlelight, as I had written it, with a knife at my back. My hand still trembled at the thought of my hollow words and how they would lead him to his doom. *Dear Norman, Tonight is the night. Our night. The night that the three of us; you, me and the baby, will elope to Gretna Green. I have arranged a boat and a boatman. Meet me at the curve of the Connswater River, where it flows into the lough. We shall soon begin a new chapter on our next adventure.*

I hated myself for playing any part in such skulduggery, tricking my love by my own handwriting, even though I had been forced to. My Norman, my beloved. The pain of my forced betrayal stung even more to see how dashing he looked in his blue tartan kilt and blue Balmoral, wearing a travelling cloak, all ready to elope in the night. He looked dashing, a wonderful sight that I had fallen for on that Hogmanay night, mere months ago though a lifetime before, when we were untarnished and in the throes of first love. Now he stood on the mudflats, waiting for me. He stood looking for the boat that I had promised would ferry us out of Belfast and across the sea, a boat that would never come.

Martin's younger brother, the middle one, held a hand over my mouth while the other hand secured my arms behind my back as we stood in the bushes. I was as helpless as a flailing fish on the riverbank, watching as Martin and his third brother, the youngest, set upon Norman on that cool, moonlit night.

Norman, my love, had spoken first. *Who are you?*

I'm the intended of Maureen Ann Boyd, though tainted as she is, Martin my fiancé had replied.

But that can't be. Maureen is to be married to myself. We are to be a family.

Not anymore. She didn't tell you, did she? The child isn't yours. It's mine. Conceived on a trip to Tyrone in January. Would you be cuckolded by a lying, sneaking harlot?

Lies. Tears had sprung from my eyes at the sight of my Norman's shocked, heartbroken face as he digested those words, those lies.

Why am I to believe you? Where is Maureen? What have you done to her?

Not nearly as much as what I'm going to do to you.

I had watched helplessly as they beat him to a pulp, two on one, cowards as they were, lynching my Norman and dragging him through the mud. A silent scream had struggled in vain to escape my throat, suppressed under the tightening grasp of the middle brother. All I could do was watch as my love was killed, and listen to his final, haunting words.

If you think that death will be the end of me, then you are mistaken. If God will not allow a true union between my beloved and I, then I will make sure you cannot have her, body and spirit either. I give my soul to the Devil willingly that you may take her as your wife, but she will never bear your seed. For that child in her stomach is mine as she has only been true to me. And now death may have me, but my eternally damned soul will be waiting to see that my curse upon you succeeds. I will be back again.

With that, my love had lost his fight for life in the mudflats while the noose around his neck had tightened and the breath had been expunged from his body under the watchful eye of a round, full moon. His face had turned purple under the strain, but in the waning hours afterwards as I had cried over his corpse, it had paled into a macabre shade of ice blue. His teeth had been pulled back in a grimace as he had gritted them in a final struggle and there his face would stay; wincing, grimacing, forever captured in the agony of death.

But he had been true as his word. It had not been the last of him.

Chapter twenty-five

Sabrina – May 2000

Somebody had pelted Megan's aunt's flat with eggs. I had arrived too late. Guilt stabbed every part of me; my heart most of all. Whatever Megan had written about me in that letter to Norman, she had still been my best friend for the past three years. I felt awful about betraying her to Johnny. Who the hell was Johnny anyway, apart from some meaningless boy who would have tried to buck all four of us – Louisa-Mae, Lauren, Megan and I – if he could have got away with it.

I rapped the front door and waited. A mousy-haired woman in her fifties answered. She wore a long purple shawl over a tie-dye dress with a red beaded necklace hanging low on her chest, an archetypal middle-aged hippy.

"What is it? You're not one of those wicky-bickies who egged the windows, are you? I'll call the police on all of you." Her eyes were half-shut and I smelled a strong odour of hash wafting out from her hallway. Her threat seemed only half-assed, considering.

A tall, pretty girl with long brown hair peered out from behind the woman. Apart from her hair colour, she looked like a younger version of Megan's Aunt. "It's okay, Mum, Megan said it's her friend. You can let her in."

Friend. Megan still liked me, despite all that had happened. I came into the hallway. "Is Megan here?"

"She's in the kitchen having a strong drink – some wee lads came by and egged the place, so she's a bit upset. I think she was keen on one of them. I'm her Aunt Tracey. This is her cousin Natasha."

"I wanted to see her after what had happened in school today – and clearly just now too. Is she okay?"

"She got beat up pretty badly by that bitch Louisa-Mae, but she was mostly just shaken up. Thankfully nothing was broken," said Aunt Tracey.

"I know. See if I get my hands on that wee girl, I'll kill her. Don't know why Megan ever hung about with her in the first place, she sounded like a right nasty piece of work from the very start. You're not friends with her, are you?" said Natasha.

I shook my head so much it probably made me seem defensive. "Not anymore after how she jumped Megan. You'll be glad to know she got suspended over it. So did the other one, Lauren. Both of them got two weeks' suspension for beating up Megan and sabotaging her Tech project work."

"Hmph. Should've been expelled." Natasha's lip curled.

I nodded. "Well, that's what I think too, but apparently Louisa-Mae's Dad is on the Board of Governors at the school. If it's any consolation, it'll be on their permanent records too, so at least that'll affect them applying for Uni – or jobs."

We went through into the living room of Aunt Tracey's flat. Megan was slumped in an armchair staring into space. Her face was white and her hands were cupped around a tumbler of brown fizzy drink, knowing Megan, vodka and coke. She looked up when I sat on the sofa and offered a weak smile, though her eyes stayed sad.

"Sabrina, you came over. I didn't think I'd see you again," she said. She pushed herself up from her armchair. "Let's go and talk in my room."

Natasha and Aunt Tracey didn't say anything, though by the looks on their faces, they understood. Megan and I had a lot to discuss.

As I followed her down the short corridor to her room, I couldn't help but notice that her usual slim frame had whittled away so that she wasn't much more than a bag of skin and bones. Not that I'd ever say that to her. I hadn't noticed as she had hid her body well under her heavy blazer at school and under baggy shirts on weekends. Must have been all the drugs. Back at Louisa-Mae's party a few months ago that now seemed a lifetime ago, she had tried poppers, then moved on to regular joints and now, who knew what? Johnny had introduced her to E's and acid; who knew whatever the hell else she was taking? Booze was enough for me, or the odd joint, though I wasn't even fussed on that. Did I even know my former best friend of the past three years at all?

Megan sat on the end of her bed and I sat on a swivel chair by a desk near the window. The air in the room pulsated with the tension between us. It wasn't cold, but my arms erupted in goose-bumps. I pulled the sleeves of my cardigan down and rubbed them.

A loud sob jolted me back to the moment. Megan's head drooped and her chest heaved as she cried. It caught me by surprise; I sat, frozen in my chair unsure of whether to console her or not.

"Why me?" Megan looked up, her cheeks streaked with black rivulets of mascara. "At this point in my life too."

I twisted my hands in my lap. "I'm sorry it got so out of hand. I know you had been counting on an A."

Megan's forehead wrinkled. "Not about my A-level Tech work, about Johnny."

Far from abating, the goose-bumps on my arms prickled as the hairs stood on end. If there was any more static electricity in the room, I swear there would've been forks of lightning between us.

"It should've worked with me and him. I mean, I really thought he liked me. I wanted to make it work." I watched the lump in her throat move like a sinusoidal wave as she swallowed tears. "The problem is, I love him."

Movement to the left drew my eye. Megan's bedroom door opened several inches. Both of us straightened up. Hadn't Aunt Tracey and Natasha understood that we wanted to talk in private? At least they had given me that impression a few minutes before in the living room.

In the minutes that followed, I wasn't sure of what had happened; almost like watching a film play first in slow motion, then at double speed. At first, Megan had stood rooted, her eyes fixed on the door motionless. Maybe my mind had played tricks on me, for the room seemed to darken as a shadow raced across through the open bedroom door to Megan's bed. It put me in mind of how a cloud passing in front of the sun would make everything darken. I glanced out the bedroom window. A cloud had indeed passed in front of the full moon; a moment later the bedroom was illuminated as the moon reappeared. Just my imagination; only my imagination. As the shadow traversed the room, a rancid smell filled the air, coming from Megan's direction. It was a sour smell, a stench like rotten meat mixed with earth. Or maybe spilled blood; ferrous and rank. My brain struggled in those moments to place the sensations; of smell and sight – and sound.

An ear-splitting scream filled the room. I jumped in my chair and clapped my hand against my chest to steady my nerves. Megan threw herself into her bed, the duvet a whirlpool around her. Her hands and legs kicked out in all directions. Was she having a seizure? How many Es had she taken? My mind spun through the options. I didn't know how to do CPR. If she had taken an overdose, I would need to call 999 and tell them what she had taken. Ecstasy? LSD? She might die if I didn't find out exactly what was in her system. The way her limbs flailed didn't strike me as indicative of a seizure, though. It seemed more like she was fighting an invisible assailant. Her eyes and mouth were wide, her face locked in a silent scream. The haunted look on her face terrified me; I found myself unable to move either to help her or to get help. A metallic tang flooded my mouth, my own sour saliva pooling under my tongue.

"Megan!"

Aunt Tracey and Natasha burst into Megan's room and dashed across to her bed. That seemed to jolt her from the seizure; rather than her body continuing to spasm until her movements subsided into a sleeping heap as I had expected, she sat bolt upright panting. I knew she was lucid, because she looked at each of us in turn and blinked, still wide-eyed as she took in her surroundings. She skittered backwards until her she was upright against the wall and pointed a shaking finger at the window.

"He went out the window. He's still in the garden!"

Aunt Tracey and Natasha looked at Megan, then each other and frowned. I wasn't confused; I knew who Megan was talking about. I stood up from the swivel chair and peered out the window. In the semi-darkness the details of the garden were hard to see. A small square of grass not more than ten by ten feet was surrounded by a bricked wall about eight feet tall. A chrysanthemum bush in the far left corner cast a deep shadow that stretched into the middle of the lawn. Potted plants around the perimeter cast further shadows, though none of the dark pools were big enough that they could have concealed a man, even if he crouched.

"Nobody is out there," I said.

"I can see him, he's right there. Go and get rid of him, call the police!"

"Megan, love, no-one is out there." Aunt Tracey slid a comforting arm around Megan's shoulders and hugged her close. She addressed Natasha. "She's just having a whitey. How much hash did she smoke?"

"None. She was only drinking vodka – at least as far as I know," said Natasha.

"You're not listening to me!" Megan tried to push herself up off the bed, but Aunt Tracey held a tight grip on her shoulders. "He went straight out the window in front of all of you. Don't mess me around, I know you all saw him."

The window was indeed open, but only by about six inches. If the Blue Man, or anyone for that matter wanted to climb out, they would've had to open the window wide, which wasn't the case.

"Go and get her some coffee, Natasha love. She needs to sober up." Aunt Tracey pulled Megan's head onto her chest and hushed her.

Megan pushed Aunt Tracey off and sprang up from the bed. She bounded out of the room with her hair flying behind her. The wild look in her eyes, together with how coordinated she was made me think she had taken E's, speed or LSD. Did Aunt Tracey know about the harder drugs Megan was taking? I doubted it; and I sure as shit wasn't going to be the one to have that conversation with her relatives.

Natasha flew out of the room behind Megan, while Aunt Tracey stared at me with a deer-in-headlights look on her face. "What's going on? Who's this boy she's talking about that's in the garden?"

"It's not a boy. Has she told you about the Blue Man?"

Aunt Tracey had a haunted look on her face. "Not that folk tale about the Scotsman who haunts down near the shipyard?"

I nodded. "She's been spooked by the ghost story ever since I told her it a couple of months ago. I think she just hallucinated that he was here."

We hurried out of Megan's room together and joined her and Natasha in the garden. Under any other circumstances I would have laughed at the sight; Natasha struggled to restrain Megan's arms as she flung potted plants, stones and even clumps of grass over the wall at the far left corner. But it was no laughing matter. Either Megan was suffering from temporary insanity through her ever increasing drug dependency or there were more supernatural influences at work. As though influenced by an invisible force I turned to look behind my left shoulder and my gaze fell on Megan's bedroom window. Could the rushing darkness I had seen be something more than a shadow thrown across the room by a cloud in front of the moon? The hairs on the back of my neck rose at the growing realisation in my mind.

Yes.

Yes, it was my belief that an influence beyond the realms of human understanding was affecting Megan. Why she could see it and not anybody else was another matter.

Chapter twenty-six

Megan – May 2000

My bedroom seemed to collapse in on me, swallowing me into the darkening maw of a giant, unknown beast. Sabrina, sitting by the window melted away. All the furniture melted away. It was just me, all about me. Alone.

Why me? With Johnny. Why me, not anyone else? Addicted to Johnny. But his Dad's flat. Sausages. Aunt Tracey's flat. Eggs. Sausages and eggs. Apples and oranges. We weren't a good match. Why not?

Fuck the A-levels. Fuck Sabrina. I would've given up my life if only I could have Johnny.

What would I give up, if only I could have Johnny.

I'd sell my soul to the Devil, if only for it to be me and Johnny. Johnny and I.

"Me...gan."

A masculine voice, hoarse and guttural.

"Megan."

Again, floating to my ear. From the doorway. Nothing else existed in my room except me and the open doorway.

There he was. He'd come for me. At first it was his face, peering through the open gap. His skin was glacial blue; an unnatural colour, devoid of life. His ice-cold eyes pierced deep, enveloping me in a coldness that penetrated my soul. His wicked smile caused wrinkles to spread across his decayed skin, streaking across his hollow cheeks and over his bony temples, up and across his withered forehead. Dark pools of shadow filled both skeletal eye sockets. His mouth was wide, the lips thin and desiccated, the corners of his smile curved up into a crescent moon of pearly white teeth. He wore the blue Balmoral and navy tartan kilt of local legend, though far from being a handsome man as I had imagined he would have been in life, death made his smile a grimace. Death gave his once attractive features an angry intensity, every sinew twisted in hatred.

Hatred of what? Me?

The Blue Man had sold his soul to the Devil – and now he had come for me.

"Megan." Norman's voice was a rasp that grated inside my ears. "Why did you betray me?"

Time had slowed down. Not only was my body frozen, but my mouth remained sealed. In my head I spoke: *I didn't betray you. I've always been your faithful friend.*

He waggled his bony index finger, reprimanding me. "It wasn't your life to forfeit."

What was he talking about? I willed him to hear my thoughts. *I don't understand. I didn't forfeit my life. Do you mean when I wished just now that I could sell my soul to the Devil if I could be with Johnny?*

"No. The life that should have come of you from Johnny. It wasn't yours to forfeit."

Unprotected sex. He had to be talking about conception. If I hadn't taken the morning after pill, maybe Johnny would have got me pregnant.

I wasn't pregnant. I didn't kill anything – there was nothing inside me to start with.

"You interfered with fate. You controlled destiny. What you did interfered with the natural order."

I watched his ice blue face twist into a sneer as he glided through the gap into my room, now mere feet away from me.

I shook my head; or at least, in my mind I did. My body didn't seem capable of moving. *The only thing that interferes with the natural order is you.*

"Oh, so that's what you think? Then you don't know anything. You – are supposed to be with Johnny – and it's up to you to fix that."

I can't, it's too late now. I'm moving on. I'll find a man who loves me and respects me.

In one smooth movement like a panther leaping at its prey, the Blue Man lunged at me from door to bed, springing from his spot without moving either feet or legs. He moved at an unnatural speed that only a demon, not of this world, could have mustered. At that moment, an energy in my own body was freed, releasing me from where I sat petrified. I dashed under my duvet and curled into a ball, instinct taking over me.

The Blue Man tore my cover back and flipped me over, so that I lay sprawled on my back. He threw himself on top of me and though there was no weight at all to his body, a cold weight of death shrouded me, pressing at my throat, bearing down on my chest. I closed my eyes, willing him to let me go.

If you won't be with Johnny, then I'll kill you now and take your soul for another lifetime. You can be reborn into a body that will co-operate with what you should rightly be doing with this lifetime.

In that moment I understood. Norman wanted me to be with Johnny; and if I couldn't then he would take my soul and force it into reincarnation, to be with Johnny's soul in another life.

No, wait. My telepathic voice pleaded. *Give me time, I'll do what you want. Don't kill me. Don't give up on me. I like my life as Megan, I'll find a way to do what you want.*

The Blue Man released his grip on my physical body and my spirit self was sucked back into its earthly husk, quick as running water. He cast me one last jeering smile, then dived towards the window. His spectral body flowed like smoke out through the six inch opening at the bottom of the frame. He sprang across the lawn on all fours, more panther than man, and launched himself up onto the wall at the end of the garden. There he sat in a squatting position as though he were about to leap frog off into the darkness at any point; though his corpse-blue face remained inclined towards my window, mocking me with his moon-white grimace.

How long had Aunt Tracey and Natasha been in my room? Together with Sabrina, the three of them stood there looking confused. What was confusing about the Blue Man assaulting me in my bedroom and escaping, scot-free?

"He went out the window. He's still in the garden!"

Sabrina rumpled her face in a way that made me want to punch her. "Nobody is out there."

Was that dozy bitch for real? "I can see him, he's right there. Go and get rid of him, call the police!"

"Megan, love, no-one is out there." Aunt Tracey pulled me against her in a motherly hug; not what I needed. Either she was a dozy bitch too, or I was crazy. "She's just having a whitey. How much hash did she smoke?"

She was looking at Natasha, not me. My cousin answered her. "None. She was only drinking vodka – at least as far as I know."

Fuck them all; they all thought I was ready for the funny farm. "You're not listening to me!" I started to get up, but Aunt Tracey's spidery fingers held my shoulders tight. "He went straight out the window in front of all of you. Don't mess me around, I know you all saw him."

"Go and get her some coffee, Natasha love. She needs to sober up." Aunt Tracey's voice had an annoying edge to it; a patronising tone. That confirmed it for me right there; she thought I was a loon.

Enough of all of them. If no-one was going to help me, then I would get rid of Norman James McMurray by myself. Me versus the Blue Man. If I could see him in the first place, then I had more psychic energy than I thought. Maybe Sabrina had rubbed off on me; or at least shared some of her great-grandmother's gypsy fortune-telling energy.

Unlike the Blue Man, my new-found psychic powers drew the line at being able to flow out of window gaps like smoke. I ran out into the back garden and found the fiend still sitting on top of the back wall. He towered over me by about four feet from his squatting position up high, balanced on the edge of the brickwork.

Go away! I forced the words by telepathy. *I've made an agreement with you, so leave me alone to find a way!*

And live my life in peace. It floated in as an afterthought, though I didn't know if he heard it. Probably not, any of it; for he kept sitting there grimacing at me.

I grabbed the nearest thing I could reach, one of Aunt Tracey's beloved potted petunias, and flung it at the monster. The plant either missed him, or sailed through him, for I watched it arc over the wall into the garden behind. What better plan of action did I have to rid myself of the Devil blighting me? I grabbed another potted plant, and another, and a clump of grass followed by another. But the more I threw, the brighter his eyes seemed to glow, the intensity fuelled by my fury – I guessed.

Then, eyes over there, to my left. Eyes among the branches of the neighbour's chestnut tree. Eyes peering between the strands of grass. He was watching me from here, there. Everywhere.

Please leave me alone, why are you doing this?

My arms wind-milled powering fists that attacked all around me. My legs struck in every direction. I could sense my body and mind drawing closer, the line between life and death blurring. Did it even matter? Did my life matter if the rest of it were to be haunted by the malevolent apparition that was now attached to it?

When I paused for a breath, he was gone. Just as quick as he had arrived, I was free of my tormentor. I rested my head on a nearby shoulder and let my body collapse as it filled itself with life-giving air, let light from the moon restore goodness where there had only been darkness, let hope chase fear away. It was enough for me, for now.

Chapter twenty-seven

Sabrina – April 2021

"So, is this, like you know about the loud music, and all?"

Johnny ran his index finger around the rim of his coffee mug, his eyes following me. The fact that he wouldn't look me in the eye for more than half a second wasn't what made our meeting awkward; it was the fact that there I was, sitting across my kitchen table with a fella who had been less than a footnote in my life for the past twenty years and now, much like Megan's ghost of Norman, had floated back into my present. Fingers crossed he wouldn't be part of my present – or future – for too much longer.

I slurped my own coffee, maybe a tad too loud, perhaps a notch too forcefully, and wiped the froth off my upper lip. "No, actually it isn't." I scratched my neck. "It's about another matter."

"If it's about my girlfriend getting down to the laundry room before you do – listen, I'll talk to her about that." He scratched the back of his neck and winced at me, by way of apology. "She gets a bit competitive, you know? Fuck all else to do around here, so there's not. She's looking for work, she'll be out of your hair soon."

Had that really been an issue? Johnny's confession stumped me, even if only momentarily. Come to think of it, there *had* been one or two times when I had been bumbling about making a lot of noise as I hauled the laundry basket out onto the landing – only to hear Johnny's girlfriend hurrying down the stairs from the floor above, her arms laden with a shopping carrier bag full of laundry.

I'd save that matter for another occasion; this time I had to get to the *real* issue. I raised my hands in front of my face. "No, no, it's not that either. Listen, I don't know if I introduced myself when we talked before on the stairwell, a few weeks ago. My name is Sabrina, formerly McCann."

Johnny's eyes were wide as saucers as he stared at me. He gawked across the table, his mouth agape. "You're not, no kidding?"

I gave a solemn nod and closed my eyes as he digested the news.

"Sabrina McCann?" Johnny's wide-eyed shock morphed into a knowing smile. "As in, the one who used to live in Sydenham and knocked about with those headers—"

"Louisa-Mae, Lauren and," I paused, her name struggling to fall off my lips. "Megan."

I nodded and offered a weak smile. Johnny's face also broke into a wide grin. He waggled a finger at me. "I knew it. I thought you were familiar. But your burgundy hair fooled me. Away on, you're Sabrina McCann." He ran a hand through his hair. "How long has it been? We go way back. What've you been up to?"

Any number of answers that I could've given raced through my head, though I didn't say them. Living and working in Liverpool, being married to my lovely English husband Jake, our gorgeous son Leo, my whole life since school. I didn't know Johnny at all, didn't feel comfortable telling him all the details of my personal life.

"Not much, just getting on with things."

"Aye well, you're looking good." Johnny shot me a boyish smile. "But then, you always were."

I cleared my throat and averted my eyes from his. Was he for real? He knew I was a happily married wife and mother, apart from the fact that he had a girlfriend himself. A change of topic was in order. "How's things been with you?"

He took a swig of coffee and wiped his mouth on the back of his hand. "I'm getting by. I'm on a zero hours contract doing deliveries, so lockdown was hard cause I had no work. But I've been busy since everything opened back up. Can't complain."

Time to get right to the point so that I could ask him to leave my flat as soon as my coffee was done. "Do you remember my best mate when we were at school? Megan?"

"Megan." Johnny's forehead wrinkled. "Aye, wasn't she the skinny one with the bleached blonde hair? I think so, yeah."

"We've been back in touch recently. We hadn't heard from each other in *yonks*."

He recoiled in surprise, though it struck me as forced. "Seriously? You two were so tight I never thought youse would've lost touch."

I sighed. "Awk, well you know. I was living in Liverpool and she moved to Derry. She left just after the A-levels were over, went to uni in Londonderry and then got a job – and a husband – and stayed up there."

His surprised expression was legitimate then. "Away on, Megan at university? I never would've thought it, she was an E-head."

"She cleaned herself up after that summer. Do you remember all that talk about The Blue Man?"

It was an abrupt way for me to bring up the topic, but I had to throw it in there; had to see how Johnny would react. Rather than his face morphing into one of fear, or even confusion, it became blank. "Aye, I remember something. She made up this ghost story about the Blue Man so she could blame him on all the crazy shit that she did. Really it was cause she was a header and went off the rails."

I sat for a moment and digested Johnny's blunt assessment of the most haunting summer of my life. From one point of view, he was right; Megan had indeed blamed a few misdemeanours on the Blue Man. But was that really how other people saw her, as crazy?

Was that how I saw her? What else would have allowed me to invite Johnny into my kitchen, to sit across from a shady figure from mine and Megan's past – and to warn him about my former best friend, no less?

I tucked my hair behind my ear. "Sort of. The thing is, Megan didn't make up the Blue Man. She really believed in him. In fact, she still does."

Johnny smirked, his eyes crumpling into slits. "Aye right, you're having me on. Are you trying to tell me that a ghost wrote 'the Blue Man woz ere' on my bedroom mirror that time at my Dad's flat?"

So Johnny *did* in fact remember all the events of that summer, more than he had been letting on? I shook my head. "No, Louisa-Mae was the one who did that. Megan didn't make up the story either – I was the one who told all of them the urban legend of the dead Scotsman. It was the night we were in Vicky Park. You, Daz and Rab came and found us there, right after I told them all the story."

"Oh yeah, I think I remember that." Johnny's face broke into a wicked grin. "That was the night Louisa-Mae went down on me in the bushes. And she threw Megan's wallet into the mudflats and told her the Blue Man was going to get her, or something."

"Louisa-Mae, I knew it! I always suspected she had a thing for you, but she never admitted it."

Johnny wriggled in his seat, the playful smirk still in place. "We played together when we were kids. But we started bucking each other from we were about thirteen."

"I never knew." I snorted to myself. Louisa-Mae and Johnny, sleeping together, when all along she had been calling everyone else – particularly Megan – a slutbag.

"Aye, well that was the whole fun of it. No-one knew. Not even Daz or Rab, though I think Rab suspected since he had a thing for her."

Memories of Louisa-Mae with him in the bushes at Vicky Park and a few weeks later when he was having sex with Megan popped into my head. I opened my mouth to ask him if Louisa-Mae had been shagging him all that time too even when he had been seeing Megan, but stopped. It didn't really matter. That was a long time ago now relegated to history. I didn't care, even if Louisa-Mae had bucked him till the cows came home. It was irrelevant to me or my life today. Not only that it was distracting me from why I had invited would-be lothario Johnny Montgomery into my flat in the first place, especially since it was at the inconvenience of my husband and son who'd had to go out for a walk. I needed to warn him about Megan.

"Listen, it's to do with the Blue Man why I asked you to come here today. Megan seems to think that the Blue Man has come back into her life again. She's been bumping into lots of people from her past recently. You know, like me, and Louisa-Mae. And now that she knows we're neighbours, she's got it into her head that it's all an omen for something more sinister."

Johnny beamed a flirtatious smile at me. "You were talking about me with Megan?"

I wanted to roll my eyes, but didn't. "Well, I only mentioned it in passing since we were catching up with people we knew from school."

"Hope you were saying nice things?" He winked at me.

Was this idiot for real? Maybe my best tack was to steer the subject back on course. "Megan is under the impression that you are related to Norman James McMurray, that he's your great-grandfather."

Johnny frowned. "Who?"

I leaned forward. "Norman James McMurray is what Megan believes is the Blue Man's real name."

Johnny's face was blank as he processed what I was saying. "My great-grandfather wasn't called Norman James McMurray. He was called Martin Roberts."

A warm blanket of relief washed over me. Could it be that Megan's fears about the Blue Man were all nothing more than a figment of her imagination? That the unnerving terror I had felt in our teens as I had watched an invisible assailant attack her had been nothing more than mass hysteria that we all had created?

"People knew him as Marty, not the Blue Man." Johnny's cocky smile was back in place.

I drained the rest of my coffee in one long gulp. "Well, even if that is the case, Megan believes you're related to the Blue Man. She wants to meet you to–"

What was I going to say? That Megan wanted to do a ritual on him? That she believed Johnny was also a reincarnation of the Blue Man, as well as being one of his descendants? It all sounded nuts, like Megan was unstable. Was she unstable? I had to find out more information and see if it could prove either way if Megan had hallucinated the whole thing about the sinister ghostly Scotsman of our past.

"Was your great-grandmother called Maureen by any chance?"

"Wait, what were you going to say then? What does Megan want to meet me for? She doesn't still fancy me, does she?" Johnny stretched his arms behind his head, smug as the cat who got the cream.

Johnny could be so frustrating. I tapped my fingers on the table. "Was she Maureen Ann Boyd?"

He shook his head. "No. Her name was Maggie Galbraith, before she married my great-grandfather and became Maggie Roberts. What does Megan want to meet me for?"

I stood up and walked to the kitchen sink, setting my finished coffee mug in it. It was all a waste of time. I had wasted my time – and Johnny's – over a fantasy cooked up by my high school best friend, a person I didn't really know, who now seemed of unsound mind. "It was nice to see you Johnny, but I think I've kept you long enough. Don't worry about Megan. She doesn't want to meet up with you for anything important."

Johnny took the hint that I wanted him to leave and stood up too. The Blue Man had been a malevolent presence in our lives for so long, it hadn't occurred to me that there could be a more rational explanation for all the events. But if I wanted to check – to be sure – I would have to see how Megan reacted when I told her that Johnny wasn't related to Norman, as she believed.

Chapter twenty-eight

Megan – May 2021

As far as May days went, it was a lovely one; the sun beat down on us as we sat on a bench overlooking the Holywood Seafront. Belfast Lough stretched ahead of us, no longer home to the great ships that Norman would have worked on when he was alive. I shook thoughts of the Blue Man out of my head and looked down at Harry sleeping in his pram. The roof shielded him from the strong spring sunshine and protected him from the keen sea air. After checking on Harry I turned to a glimpse of Leo sitting on Sabrina's knee as he played with a plush lion.

"Won't it be nice to have a barbecue down here over the summer? Your Leo will be nine months and my Harry will be five months. They might even be able to play together a wee bit by then," I said.

Sabrina offered a pursed smile. "Leo might even be walking by then."

"And Harry crawling," I added.

"That'll be grand. I'm sure Jake and Paddy will hit it off too," she said with a contented sigh.

At least, I think it was a contented sigh. Really, what did I know about Sabrina other than she had a tendency to spook me out sometimes with her perceptiveness about life events. I suppose that was the whole point in getting to know each other again; after twenty years, and all.

"Our lives are so different now than how they used to be. Look at us now, married women with kids. Me and Paddy. Quite a bit different to me down here shagging Johnny Montgomery." I looked out across the sand, picturing Johnny as he had been at eighteen in his denim jacket with blonde curtains hanging around his face. "That was nice though."

Sabrina's mouth twitched into a smile that fell as fast as it formed. "Yeah, well I've heard that you never really get over your first love. Though Johnny's quite a bit different to how you remember him."

"I'll have to be the judge of that myself. Have you thought any more about when I could come up to your flat for a visit to maybe, you know, stop by and pay Johnny a visit too?"

Sabrina's expression sobered. "I saw him last week actually. I invited him over for a kind of, like, catch-up. I told him who I was."

I nudged Sabrina's arm. "Get away, you didn't? How did he react when you told him that? Did he remember you?"

There was a tiredness in her eyes as she nodded conformation. "He was sort of flirty, actually. Putting on the old school boy charm."

I rocked Harry's pram back and forth, even though he wasn't stirring in his sleep. Sabrina's words had the power to make me jittery, though I didn't know why. If I were being honest with myself, maybe it made me jealous. Why should I envy the idea of Johnny fancying Sabrina? We were no longer eighteen year old girls in competition for boys.

"Did he ask after me?" I said.

She cocked her head in an off-hand way. "Not really. He remembered who you were after I mentioned you."

What did Sabrina have to say to get Johnny to remember who I was? If I asked, she might think I still had a thing for him. Paddy was the only man for me; and the polar opposite of Johnny. Paddy was dark, where Johnny was fair. Paddy worked as a solicitor, whereas Johnny was, what? A layabout?

"What work is he doing these days?" I asked.

Sabrina sniffed. "Said he does food deliveries on a zero hours contract."

"Did you talk about anything to do with – you know – Norman?"

She nodded. "I asked him if his great-grandfather was called Norman James McMurray. He said that he wasn't."

A cold, sinking feeling pooled in my stomach. It was the way Sabrina looked at me. There was a cynicism in her eyes, but it wasn't what hurt. What hurt was the patronising expression she had as though she felt sorry for me. There was an element of fear too, like she was afraid of me for being crazy.

"Actually, he's right. Norman wasn't the man who raised Johnny's great-grandfather. Norman James McMurray died out on the mudflats where the Connswater River flows into Belfast Lough. He was murdered by the man who raised his child as his own and married his true love Maureen Ann Boyd, making her his wife. It was the final insult to Norman. That's why the Blue Man has come back. To make a wrong a right."

Snippets of the real-life events flickered through my mind, like watching a montage from an old-fashioned cinema reel. I saw Maureen Ann Boyd with her belly swollen, ready to give birth. Maureen with a babe in her arms and the murderer, who became her husband, glowering down at the child over his wife's shoulder. The child growing up to become a man; Johnny's grandfather. Now he had a wife and daughter of his own. Another image; his daughter being wed to a man and taking on the family name Montgomery. Now Johnny's Dad as a grown man, passing on the new family name to his son.

Sabrina shook her head. "Johnny's great-grandmother wasn't called Maureen Ann Boyd either. Johnny hadn't heard of either of those names – Norman James McMurray or Maureen Ann Boyd."

I clenched my teeth together, digesting what Sabrina was implying, before answering. "The man who raised Norman's child – the man who became Maureen's husband – was the eldest of three farming sons called Martin Roberts. Known to friends and the wider community as Marty."

Sabrina's mouth fell open, then shut.

"When he married Maureen, he forced her to change her name – both first and second – to avoid the stigma of the rumours surrounding her affair with Norman. She became legally known as Margaret, her grandmother's name, and adopted the moniker of Galbraith, which was her mother's maiden name. Maggie Galbraith married Martin Roberts and became Maggie Roberts."

Sabrina's face whitened.

"Before you ask, the reason I know is because Norman helped me to find out the information I needed to know."

I looked the opposite way from Sabrina, out across the angry grey expanse of crests and troughs in Belfast Lough.

"I – I didn't know. I don't think Johnny knew."

"Yeah, well, nobody knew. The dead are very good at keeping their secrets." I huffed, then exhaled more slowly to calm myself. "Don't worry if you would rather not have me come over to meet up with Johnny. I know where he lives now. I might just pay him a visit myself. Like you say, it's better to put all this stuff with the Blue Man to rest now properly – before more relationships are damaged."

Sabrina. Such a sceptic. I wanted to be angry at her, but then again, I couldn't blame her. It all sounded so insane that to anyone looking in from outside, it might have seemed like the whole thing was made up. In twenty years, my life had moved on much further than Sabrina McCann and Johnny Montgomery, but both of them were like two ends of an elastic band, pulling me back the further I wanted to escape.

Sabrina flapped her hands, her face red and flustered. "Listen, I didn't mean to doubt you or anything. It's just that Johnny insisted and I thought, who better than him to know who his great-grandparents were. You can come over to my flat whenever it suits. But here, this ritual or whatever it is. You're sure it won't hurt him?"

I grabbed her forearm and gave a reassuring squeeze. "I promise you, it's no big deal. In fact, do you know what it is? Do you remember the ceremony that we did in the back garden of my house to exorcise the Blue Man in 2000? Do you remember the Amber gemstone? What I need to do with Johnny involves the Amber gemstone."

Sabrina's puzzled face became serene; it was clear she remembered the healing power of the Amber gemstone. Lucky for me it was still right there, in the back garden of the house I had grown up in. My brother Stuart lived in my mum's house now, but he wouldn't mind if I came and took the gemstone. It had a greater purpose now.

Chapter twenty-nine

Sabrina – May 2000

"She's at Sydenham Youth Club. They both are." Megan's cousin Natasha's chin jutted out with pride as she showed us the message on her phone. She flipped it shut and pulled on her shoes. "Are you up for it?"

Megan jumped up off the armchair like she had been stung by a bee. "I'm game if you are. It's payback time for those two bitches."

I didn't move, still processing what they planned to do. Louisa-Mae and Lauren both deserved comeuppance for what they had done to Megan's A-Level Technology project, but revenge wasn't the best payback if you asked me. Let the school deal with them both. Then again, no-one had asked my opinion.

"Well? Are you in, or not?" Natasha glared at me. Her mascara-clumped eyelashes looked like two hairy house-spiders. I lingered on the thought to amuse myself; what else would lighten the mood?

"She's not up for it," said Megan, her mouth a hard line. "She chickened out of Johnny's flat and now she's chickening out of this too."

"If you aren't in, then you can go home. And don't tout to anyone or you're next," said Natasha, as she slung on her puffer jacket.

I stood up, feeling defiant. "I never said I wasn't in on it. It's about time Louisa-Mae got a good diggin'."

Only problem was, I didn't really feel that way. Violence didn't solve anything, not even if it was inflicted on a bitch like Louisa-Mae. I glanced at Natasha as she hurried out the door, her long brown hair flying behind her. Out of the frying pan and into the fire; had Megan and I left the clutches of troublemakers like Lauren and Louisa-Mae only to fall under the control of an even bigger bully? I looked at Megan. She followed her cousin out the front door of Aunt Tracey's flat like she was a demigoddess, a smile on her face showing the awe she felt for Natasha.

Natasha's phone buzzed and she checked another message. "My mate Arlene's just said they're trying to chat up some up some wee fellas outside the club to blagg their way in. C'mon, let's get the train down there now."

"They'll not get let into Sydenham Youth Club. Only people from the estate go there, they run it. I can't even go, cause I live off Connsbrook. You have to be from Inverary to get in there, and if you aren't and you try, they'll kill you."

Megan rounded on me, a sour look on her face. "Let's hope they leave some for us to finish off then."

I fell silent and marched in line behind them, watching Megan's blonde hair bounce as she walked. Did I even know her at all? She was unrecognisable, different in the space of three months than she had been in the whole of the three years that I had known her. What had changed?

The Blue Man. Norman James McMurray had entered our lives. Whether real or imagined, his presence was a malign addition to the past quarter of a year.

Question was, had Megan really seen the Blue Man? Her whitey must have been a bad one if she'd hallucinated a full-blown figure as real and flesh and blood as any of the rest of us. Guilt nagged at me, biting at the clenching muscles of my stomach. In the hours that had followed the episode in Megan's bedroom that had seen her screaming and fighting an apparition that the rest of us couldn't see, Aunt Tracey, Natasha and I had given her a few vodkas to calm down and we had all smoked one or two joints. I couldn't speak for the others, but I was definitely buzzed. Not blocked enough to get into a fight with my former friends; not even tipsy enough to pretend. But what choice did I have? All I could do would be to go along and hope that the commotion was bad enough that Megan and Natasha wouldn't notice if I slipped away and went home.

We got the twenty-five bus from the Albertbridge to the Garage at the top of Palmerston Road. As the bus chugged along on the short journey, sickness welled in the pit of my stomach while Megan and Natasha lounged across the seats at the back, feet up and mouths wide as they cackled over what they were going to do to our former friends.

"Here, Sabrina, are you going to pile on too when we stick the boot in Louisa-Mae's head?" said Megan.

I forced the corners of my mouth upwards into a smile. "Course I am, I'll get the first dig in."

Such a gutless yellow-belly, so I was. I hated myself for going along with it; but what else could I do? Better Louisa-Mae getting a diggin' than me.

We got off the bus and started down Palmerston Road. The downhill slope towards Sydenham Youth Club felt symbolic of my journey through the last few months of my school life: my friendships on a downward descent into a bleak unknown; my uncertain future with or without Megan in it; with or without the Blue Man.

I stumbled over a pebble, twisting my ankle. With or without the Blue Man. Preferably without. But if Megan never let go of the sinister entity in our lives, would he ever be gone?

As if to taunt me, I watched the giant, looming Harland and Wolff cranes reflect the last dying rays of sunlight as twilight spread across Belfast. That was where he had worked, Norman James McMurray. That was near where he had died. A hundred years ago, on the mudflats where the Connswater River flowed into Belfast Lough, that was where he had met his fate. A man had died and a devil was born.

I stumbled again, this time as I crashed into Megan, who had stopped walking ahead of me. We were at the youth club.

"There they are." Natasha pointed along Station Road. Two retreating figures: one red-headed, the other black-haired and bushy, walked towards Sydenham Station. Both Louisa-Mae and Lauren were oblivious to us behind them, unaware of what was to come.

"Hang back, they'll see us. If we jump them here, some nosy auld bastard in one of these houses will call the pigs on us. Let's get them at the station," said Natasha, her voice cold with authority.

We were panthers, stalking them in the darkness, dark creatures biding our time to devour them in the night. Night creatures, closing the gap. We zig-zagged up the ramp into Sydenham station, and still they didn't see us. We turned to follow them up the concrete flight of stairs of Sydenham bridge over the bypass. We were mere metres behind them when Lauren turned saw us, and did a double take. She nudged Louisa-Mae and they both stopped on top of the bridge and turned.

"Awk, alright there, Sabrina?" Lauren looked past Megan and Natasha to me at the back. The awkwardness of her gesture struck an invisible fishing line of tension that hooked us all, five girls, and reeled us in together. "What are you doing down here?"

"She lives here in Sydenham, you fuckwit," said Natasha.

Lauren clenched her jaw. "Who was talking to you, gobshite?"

Louisa-Mae pushed between them, a buttery smooth smile on her face. "Are youse wanting to come over to Vicky Park with us? We have a carryout."

She held up a plastic *Winemark* bag. The tops of a couple of two-litre bottles of White Lightning poked out.

"What fucking planet do you live on? Do you not realise we have unfinished business?" Natasha rolled up the sleeves of her bomber jacket and bared her fists.

Louisa-Mae looked at her clenched fists and the buttery smile dropped into a sneer. "And who the fuck are you, when you call home?"

Natasha cranked her neck, first left, then right, like a boxer warming up for a fight. "I'm Megan's cousin. And I'm not happy with what you did to her at school earlier today. In fact, I'm so raging, I'm here to rearrange your ugly fucking *bake*."

The chorus of whoops behind us alerted me to the gathering bystanders who had come to watch the fight. Must've been Natasha's mate Arlene and her cronies, the tout who had texted us about where Louisa-Mae and Lauren would be.

Wind howled across Sydenham bridge. Was it my imagination, or did a dark shape, a shadow in the form of a six-foot man, rush along the bridge from the direction of Vicky Park and the shipyard beyond? A rancid smell, like rotten meat and the ferrous tinge of blood and earth filled the air.

Instinct compelled me to turn to Megan. A shadow lingered under her eyes, dark semi-circles making her sockets look hollow, giving her face a skull-like quality. I shivered, urging myself to look away but couldn't. I was frozen, transfixed, locked on the image of my former best friend as though possessed by a devil.

What happened next seemed to take place in slow motion; or maybe my brain struggled to process the flurry of violence, dropping the pace to a comprehensible speed. Natasha threw a cross at Louisa-Mae. Louisa-Mae jabbed her left ear. Lauren grabbed Natasha's hair from behind and yanked her head back, allowing Louisa-Mae to kick her in the stomach. Megan swung a backhand that connected with Lauren's jaw, sending her staggering backwards.

Natasha elbowed Lauren in the ribs and she crumpled, clutching her stomach.

"Grab the bitch!"

Arlene's voice, goading Megan and Natasha in their game of revenge. Natasha grabbed Louisa-Mae's arms and yanked them behind her back, pinning her. Louisa-Mae was heavier, but Natasha had a sinewy, drug-fuelled rage that gave her strength. Natasha pushed Louisa-Mae forward until she was on her knees.

"Do it now," Natasha urged.

Megan brought her knee upwards and smashed it into Louisa-Mae's nose. Blood sprayed in all directions, splattering onto the concrete bridge, staining her chin and teeth red. Louisa-Mae gave a grotesque grin and cackled, her whole mouth dripping with blood.

Megan's knee smashed into her face again. Louisa-Mae cackled, loud and brash though to my ear it was exaggerated; she didn't want to show fear.

Arlene and her friends held Lauren back from retaliating, though there was no need. This wasn't Megan. This was an impostor; a devil infesting her body. But the devil inside her gave her a supernatural rage.

Megan grabbed Louisa-Mae by her hair and dragged her to her feet. Louisa-Mae stumbled along as Megan hauled her to the concrete stairs leading downwards to the platform.

"Do it! Kill the bitch," said Natasha.

The devil that possessed Megan raised its left foot and kicked. Louisa-Mae's eyes widened as she fell backwards, arms and legs outstretched like a starfish. She rolled down the concrete stairs, a tumbleweed of red hair and flailing limbs smearing a red path in her wake. When she hit the bottom, nothing flailed anymore.

Chapter thirty

Megan – May 2000

She's a bitch. She deserves it.

I jerked my head a bit, just a fraction, and looked over my left shoulder. He was there behind me, goading me on.

I'd be lying if I said I wasn't afraid. Only a numpty wouldn't be afraid of the Devil behind your left shoulder. His cold, dead breath whispered close to my ear sending an icy air from beyond the grave that raised the fine hairs on my cheek, each one standing as a warning signal. A warning that I had to do whatever it would take to get the sinister presence out of my life.

I had to get Louisa-Mae out of my life too, though this wasn't how I had planned on going about it.

"Is she dead?" Natasha spoke with a note of fear in her voice. She spoke again, a hint of nervous laughter now clear. "Someone check her."

Lauren hobbled down the stairs, each clumsy step propped up by the metal railing as she pushed ahead of us to check her friend. Lauren fell to her knees, hunched over Louisa-Mae.

"Call 999," she cried. "Please!"

In that moment, as Lauren's desperate plea rang out, we all scattered. I followed Natasha, my feet flying across the pavement. The cold night air seared my lungs and adrenaline stung my heart. Everyone who had come to watch took off in different directions; some up Station Road, some hurtling along Larkfield Drive. Natasha ran towards Sydenham estate, turning up Inverary Avenue.

"C'mon, keep up." She gestured at me to hurry and I panted along behind her.

"I think I killed her," I shouted.

"Why do you think we're going this way? There's a party, we can say we've been at it all evening."

The open doorway of the party house gaped like a black maw ready to swallow us in. Better that than what lay behind us; Louisa-Mae's crumpled, bloodied body lying at the foot of Sydenham Bridge flashed in my mind's eye. Was he following me too, the Blue Man?

I didn't dare look behind as I dashed into the party behind Natasha.

Inside, the house was full of loads of fellas I didn't know and some wee girls from school but not in upper sixth. I scanned the room taking in the faces: bleutered, stoned, wired-to-the-moon; and then saw him sitting on an armrest in the corner. He was chatting up a bleached-blonde tart wearing fuck-me boots with an orange line of foundation on her chin exposing her white neck underneath.

Can't say for sure what made me do it, but seeing him there looking so gorgeous, like such a screw and about to get the leg over a *millbag* well beneath his league; an unearthly bravado seized me and my common sense flew out the window. I strode across the room and grabbed his hands, pulling him up. Not sure where my strength came from either; Johnny was a fair bit taller than me and bulkier from playing football. Still, I managed to drag him to his feet and pull him out of the room, to the protests of the wee slutbag who was hoping he'd buck her.

"Let go of me, you mad bitch, what're you on?" he howled.

I ignored Johnny and put my hands on his back to push him upstairs, away from the pounding music, so that we could talk. Talk or do more. I craned my head towards my left shoulder a fraction and from the corner of my eye saw a shadow follow behind me as I frog-marched Johnny towards the landing.

One big shove and Johnny stumbled through the open door of a bedroom, falling forwards. He caught himself with outstretched arms on the end of the double bed.

"Any chance you're going to tell me what this is all about?"

"Sit." I jabbed my index finger at the bed.

Johnny ignored me and stood, arms folded.

With another surge of preternatural strength, I shoved him and he fell backwards onto the bed. As he landed flat on his back on the hard mattress, the wind was knocked from his lungs. Johnny recovered himself with a high-pitched, nervous laugh.

"Here, Megan, listen. I know you and I haven't seen eye to eye." He tried to sit up, propping himself on one elbow, but the flat palm of my left hand against his chest sent him sprawling backwards again. "But we're even. I told everyone about how you let me buck you, and you went and wrecked my Dad's flat. Let's call it quits."

He tried to get up again, but I held him; this time with my left hand on his throat.

I wasn't even left-handed; it was my weaker side. But tonight, all the reserves of power that had been pooling deep inside of me were being released through the left side of my body.

"You lie there, you shut the fuck up, and you listen." I straddled him, clamping my thighs against either side of his abdomen. "You have no idea what is going on. Something bigger than you, bigger even than me. There are forces overseeing things, the powers that be, and they are making things happen."

Johnny's brow wrinkled as he looked up at me.

"Actually, it's one force to be exact and it's a powerful one. It's making things happen."

Johnny's right eyebrow arched.

"It wants me and you to be together."

Johnny's left eyebrow shot upwards like the right one and his mouth dropped open, into a perfect O.

"Look, Megan, I don't know what you're on, but you must be either having a whitey or completely paralytic to think I'd ever–" Johnny trailed off, his hands on my shoulders as though he wanted to push me off – but couldn't. "You're fucking off your nut, is what I'm saying. I mean, I have standards, you know. I wouldn't buck a mental case. You should be in Purdysburn."

Johnny's face was flushed, a wild, almost panicked look on his face. A tiny part of me that was buried deep down felt sorry for him. The old me would've let him get up and walk out of the bedroom. But not the person that I had become.

"Well, it's not up to you!" Spit flew from my mouth as the words tumbled from my mouth in a blind hatred – of Johnny, of love. Of love that couldn't be.

Keeping my left hand on his throat, I fumbled at the fly of his jeans with my right hand. Johnny gasped and spluttered as I bore down on his neck, my weight constricting him. Veins in his forehead throbbed, his skin turning purple, his eyes becoming bloodshot. He writhed, twisting his body from side to side and I was thrown off onto the floor.

Johnny jumped to his feet, gasping. He fixed his dishevelled hair and buttoned the fly of his jeans that I had undone.

"You – you're fucking insane. You need to get help, seriously."

The gorgeous, blonde, love of my life swept out of the room leaving only an imprint in my mind of his silhouette backlit by the landing light in the open doorway for a fleeting instant before he dashed out of sight. Out of my life.

Instead of light and happiness, I sat on the bedroom floor in gloom, aware of the shadow behind my left side.

I spoke over my shoulder without looking behind. "I tried, I really did. I told you – he doesn't want me. We can't be together."

But the Blue Man was unforgiving.

"If you can't find a way to be with Johnny, then you know what will happen. Your soul will have to be released for another lifetime."

I shivered, my shoulders clenching tight to my neck in a weak attempt at self-protection. "I'll do it. Give me more time. I'll find a way."

I closed my eyes and when I opened them, the room was brighter and felt several degrees warmer. I dared to look straight over my left shoulder. He was gone.

A wailing, rasping sob cut the silence in the room. It took a split second for me to realise the sound came from my own throat. I let my body dissolve into a heap, feeling the wetness of my own tears, tasting their saltiness, revelling in the spasms of my chest as I cried. I needed to be grounded in reality, locked into the solitary pain of that moment.

The door flew open and banged, ricocheting off the wall. Natasha hurried across and scooped me under the armpits until I was standing.

"I was looking all over for you. Johnny was spouting some shit downstairs that you tried to rape him." Her face contorted with anger. "Did he hurt you?"

I shook my head, dislodging a shower of tears and snot. I wiped my face on my sleeve. "No, he's right. I tried to attack him. I choked him, I had my hand on his throat. I over-powered him, Tash. I almost had his clothes off. I would've done it if he hadn't pushed me off."

Natasha's anger gave way to confusion. "What're you talking about? You're tiny compared to Johnny. He's fit from football, and all."

"I can't explain it either." I tucked my hair behind my ear and sniffed more tears away. "But I'm telling you like it happened. I got him on the bed and was on top of him. The Blue Man made me do it. He made me do all of it – throwing Louisa-Mae down those steps too. I don't feel like myself anymore, I can't tell what's me and what's him. He has a scary hold over me."

Natasha's expression hardened. "Alright cuz, if that's what happened then I believe you. But we've got to do something about this ghost that's haunting you. I've got an idea. Mum can help us out too. Tarot cards and magic mushroom tea are not all she has up her sleeve. C'mon, let's head back to my place. I've got a plan to stop the Blue Man. Mum has these special rocks, that she got from Lough Neagh. You call them Amber gemstones. Let's go."

Chapter thirty-one

Sabrina – July 2021

"There. Do you hear that? There they go again."

I nudged Jake to get his attention, then put a finger to my lips so that he knew to be quiet. Jake inclined his ear towards the kitchen ceiling. What was Johnny up to in his flat above? What kinds of devilry were he and his guests up to?

"That's chanting, so it is. They're performing some sort of satanic ritual."

Jake raised one eyebrow, his mouth twisted with derision. "Oh, come on, honey. Megan has got your head full of paranoid delusions. She's got you thinking all sorts of irrational stuff. Ghosts. Men who sell their soul to the Devil. It's all hysteria, just nonsense. Nothing other than horror stories like the kind you like to read in–"

Jake didn't get to finish what he was saying. A loud bang sounded as the kitchen ceiling crashed down. Amidst a shower of splintered wood and plaster chunks stood a huge stone Irish High Cross that must have stood five feet high. It landed upright on our kitchen floor, cracking the tiles. Biblical scenes depicting the ten plagues of Egypt decorated the cross and around the circular capstone in the centre. As I stared at it, the High Cross began to become bluish in hue as dust and clouds from Johnny's flat above engulfed it. I coughed and spluttered on the debris, wafting it with my hand, and closing my eyes to the assault. When I opened them I saw that the High Cross now appeared to be a deep shade of evening blue. Standing beside it was an old man, who must have dropped down from Johnny's flat above.

The old man had a long, grey beard that hung to his collarbone and finished in a point and he wore a dark blue tunic that hung to his ankles. His feet were bare. A red leather satchel hung at his hip on his right side, emblazoned with an engraving of a tree and a word jumped into my mind: a yew tree. The man held a tall wooden staff that was about six feet high, slightly taller than he was. A wicker hat hung at the nape of his neck and a red cloak with gold threaded hem was fastened over his left shoulder. His dress and appearance brought to mind a Christian Pilgrim from an earlier age. Medieval? I couldn't be sure. Early Christian Ireland, perhaps.

"I have vanquished the foe for the present time, keeping him at bay with my staff of yew. But be warned, he will come back and his wrath will be a sight to behold."

"Who are you?" Jake shouted. "Get the hell out of our flat, you'll frighten the baby."

Sure enough, baby Leo began balling from the bedroom across the hallway. His voice rang out through the small flat. I started towards him, but the Christian Pilgrim swept in front of me blocking my way.

"Come, you must do what I bid you. Leave the baby. The monster has no need of your child. It is another babe's life that I fear for."

I grabbed the Pilgrim's cloak, beseeching him. "Let me past, I need to get to my child. Can't you hear him crying?"

The Pilgrim shook me off his cloak and spread it wide. Around his neck, hanging on a fine hessian thread, was an orange gemstone the size of my index finger.

I pointed at it. "That's an Amber gemstone! Are we really in that much trouble?"

Jake looked from me to the Pilgrim, then back to me, his face contorted in confusion. "What's an Amber gemstone? What's going on?"

But it was too late. Behind the Pilgrim, at his left shoulder Johnny dropped down from the flat above in a cloud of dust. He landed on his haunches, catlike then straightened up. My breath caught in my throat as I looked at him; Johnny wore a tartan kilt in midnight blue and light blue squares and had a dark blue cloak slung over his left shoulder. His chest was bare, displaying the Pictish tattoos I had seen when we first became introduced as neighbours, mere months before. His hair was tied back in a high ponytail, the shaved lower half cropped so closely to his skin that it gave him a severe look; like a Pagan warrior from a wild, pre-Christian time. A single purple thistle fastened the cloak in place at his shoulder. The symbol of Scotland, a fitting flower for the descendant of Norman James McMurray.

"Back out now Sabrina. Megan is crazy. She'll only drag you down with her," said Johnny.

"Listen to yourself, Johnny." I gestured to his strange clothes. "How can you stand there, telling me that Megan is living in a fantasy land when you're taking part in Satanic chanting and God knows what strange rituals in that flat of yours."

Even as I spoke, red plumes of smoke wafted through and the smell of a pungent herb burning.

"I'm not Johnny. I'm Abhartach," he sneered.

"You're the one who's crazy. I'm going to get my baby. I need to protect him from all this madness."

The Pilgrim was still blocking doorway leading out into the hallway. I ducked under his arm feeling like an angry bull charging a matador. Nothing would stop me from getting to my child. I stomped across to the bedroom and found Leo in his cot-bed co-sleeper where I had left him. My instinctive urge to shield him from harm was overwhelming. I swept Leo into my arms, brought him into the double bed and curled my body around his, tucking the duvet around us for comfort while I tried to gather my straying thoughts.

***

At some point, I sat bolt upright, throwing the duvet cover back with a gasp. My heart hammered in my chest. "Jake? Jake! I must have fallen asleep. Where are you?"

Leo lay splayed on his back, chubby arms and plump legs pointing in all four directions, his cherubic face untainted by any Satanic goings-on in the kitchen from Flat five above. All was silent, but a moment later I heard the familiar thump of Jake's heavy footsteps padding across the carpeted stairs. My husband opened the bedroom door and peered in, his hand still on the handle.

"Is everything okay, honey?" he said.

I panted. "Did you get rid of them? Are they out of our house?"

"Get rid of who?" Jake's brow creased.

"The Pilgrim, and Johnny."

Jake's expression relaxed. "Sounds like you were having a strange dream."

He walked to the bed, sat down on the end and bent closer to kiss me on the forehead. When he pulled back, I noticed he wiped his upper lip. My forehead was soaked with sweat.

"No, it couldn't have been a dream, it was so real. Let me see." I bounced up from the bed and strode through the open bedroom doorway, across the hallway and into the kitchen. The kitchen ceiling was intact. No broken wood or clouds of plaster dust. No Pilgrim, no Johnny. "I'm going insane."

Jake's warm hand on my left shoulder made me jump. With a gasp, I spun around. His strong arm looped around the back of my waist, catching me as I veered backwards.

"Woah, honey you scared the Bejesus out of me. You could've hurt yourself if you'd fallen backwards there." Jake held me close against his chest.

I pushed my wet hair back off my forehead. "I think I'm losing my mind. I just had the most vivid, most crazy dream I've ever had."

"Was there a Pilgrim in it?" Jake gave an interested smile.

His amusement annoyed me, but I tried not to let the niggle become a jab. "Yeah. I guess I've had some stuff at the back of my mind. Do you know the story of Abhartach, the ghost story of O'Cathain's Dolmen? It's an early Christian folk story from Derry."

He shook his head. I wasn't surprised; it was an obscure tale that I wouldn't have known if it weren't for Megan's wacko Aunt Tracey telling it to us, two decades before. It was time to come clean with Jake: the yew vessel ceremony that Megan and I had performed when we were eighteen and her talk of wanting to meet Johnny to give him an Amber gemstone. As I talked and Jake listened, his pursed lips became ever more puckered until his mouth formed a distinct O.

"Honey, you didn't tell me any of this before."

I sighed. "I know, and I'm sorry. But I've been processing all of it myself. I'm not sure what to do to help Megan."

He tossed his head mournfully from side to side. "It doesn't sound like there's much you can do, love. She seems pretty set in her ways."

"I don't think I want to invite her over so she can meet up with Johnny. My head is warped enough as it is – dreams of him being a savage monster, Abhartach, like from the folk tale – without helping her to go through with another ritual."

Jake stroked my hair as he held me. "I agree. I think you should maybe take a step back from all this. I don't mean stop all contact with her, but just cool it for a bit, you know?"

I nodded. "That's what I'd been thinking too. It's all getting pretty intense. I can't tell if I'm paranoid now, or deluded, or both. She's got me sucked back into this whole sinister world of hers revolving around the Blue Man – and I just can't go there again. I can't."

Tears fell onto my eyelashes and dropped onto my cheeks. I was surprised at their wet saltiness as the rivulets trickled over my lips.

"That dream I just had," I went on with a sniff. "There was a lot of biblical imagery in it, like my brain was trying to give me a warning. You know, the whole ten plagues of Egypt thing. Like how God was warning the Egyptians not to test Him, not to push Him too far. I mean, I'm not even religious anymore, but maybe this is my subconscious warning me not to follow Megan down this path, that it's going to lead to bad things happening. In the dream, the Medieval Christian Pilgrim told me that my baby wasn't in danger, but that another baby was. Do you think something bad might happen to Megan's newborn, Harry?"

Jake blinked at me, but said nothing.

"Maybe I should go back to church to get some advice. All this stuff with demonic ghosts and Amber gemstones, yew containers. I mean, the synergy between Megan and me, it's not good. We're attracting dark forces into our lives."

No sooner than I had finished speaking, I laughed, spluttering saliva. "Sorry honey. That sounds so absurd when I say it out loud. Of course I don't believe in ghosts. I love horror, and being scared, but I don't believe that spirits are actually real."

"Don't you?" Jake looked quizzical. "It hasn't been proved either way really, has it?"

I kissed him. He was right; my logical husband reminding me of my sensible agnostic ways, amidst all the mind-warping contact with Megan lately.

"Look, the way I see it," Jake went on. "Is that she was your best friend at school and of course you're sentimental about that. It makes sense that you want to re-establish your friendship with her so naturally, believing her – and to a degree, pleasing her – would be part of that communication."

I bristled at the idea that I was enabling Megan, but Jake was right. If Megan had mental health issues that I didn't know about, it wouldn't make me a very good friend if I was enabling her outlandish beliefs. Supposing that the whole story of Norman James McMurray – the Blue Man – was a fantasy.

Was it? Could it be?

"Megan told me when we met that her brother Stuart has paranoid schizophrenia. You don't think she could too?" I said.

Jake shrugged. "Who knows? Whatever the truth of the matter is, you'd be a better friend to her by cooling contact for a bit."

"Yeah, there's no rush anyway. The boys are so wee, it would be better to wait until they're older and could have a proper playdate." A shiver passed along my back; I shook it off and tried to compose myself. "Still, I can't help but sense that there's something ominous brewing. I have a really bad feeling and I can't say what it is. I'm worried that Megan is going to come to some into some kind of trouble, like what happened in 2000. Like history repeating itself. And that in some way, I'll be responsible."

Chapter thirty-two

Megan – July 2021

My phone buzzed beside me on the sofa. Stuart's number flashed up on the screen. I rolled my eyes. I wasn't in the mood. I had just about managed to get Harry off my breast and into his Moses basket and now talking to Stuart would result in another two hours of wailing.

On the other hand, if I didn't answer now, my annoying brother would keep ringing until I did. With a sigh, I hauled myself off the sofa and held the phone to my ear as I walked into the hallway.

"Stuart? What is it. Harry's just gone down."

"Listen, sis. You've gotta help me." A pause, following by laboured breaths. "The plants in my garden, they're all wilted. And the goldfish is dead."

I ran my hand through my hair. "Well, it's not a big deal. Look, I can get you another fish the next time I'm at the pet store."

"You're missing the point." His voice was urgent, a tad angry. "The geiger counter was clicking like mad. My garden was deliberately contaminated, I'm sure of it."

I peered into the living room to check on Harry, then turned my attention back to the phone call with Stuart. "I really think you're getting this whole thing out of context. Did you use the geiger counter near your microwave?"

"I'm not an idiot, Megan. I flatter myself I know more about ionizing radiation than you do. I'm trying to tell you that someone sabotaged my garden. In fact, I think he's in my house right now."

I covered the receiver with my hand and exhaled. How many times had Stuart given bogus calls to the police about phantom burglars, or spies who were trying to contaminate his home with radioactive poison? Countless times. It had been a major – massive – moment of embarrassment when I'd had to explain to the police that my brother was a paranoid schizophrenic who believed that menacing unknown enemies were after him.

"Megan, you need to get over here right now and get him out of my house."

I held the phone tight against my cheek. "Okay, you need to listen to me right now. I want you to go into your kitchen and eat the rest of the tomato and kelp salad that mum made you. The iodine and lycopene in that will decontaminate you. I can't come over because Harry is asleep, but I'll send Paddy to check on you. He's on his way home from work right now. I'll call him to stop by your house. Can you hang on about another half hour and he'll be there?"

The sound of Stuart taking several deep breaths filled the pause. "Alright then, I'll do that. I'll stay in the kitchen. Tell Paddy to go straight upstairs and check. I really would have preferred for you to do it, since you know who he is. The intruder in my house I mean."

I had been about to reply, when the words drained from my thoughts. I knew him? Who? I had never taken Stuart's nonsensical ramblings seriously before, but this time, his words made me stop. He couldn't be talking about The Blue Man, could he?

My pulse began to speed up. "Wait a minute. Did you say all the plants in your garden are dead?"

"Eh – earth to Megan, come on! Yes, that's what I've been saying the whole time! They're all wilted and brown."

My heart was in my throat. "Stuart, you didn't touch the wooden object and the gemstone that I'd put in the garden a long time ago, did you? You know the one surrounded by thistles?"

"Oh yeah, that ugly thing. I got rid of it last summer. I cut all those nasty weeds down and then threw the wooden statue in the shed, along with the weird glass rock."

Last summer – a year ago. All this time. No wonder the Blue Man was haunting me, he'd been let free. "It wasn't a statue, it was a powerful spiritual container made of yew and the glass rock was an Amber gemstone, a sacred talisman. Those and the thistles were all that kept him trapped. Don't you see? You released the Blue Man. You unleashed his evil energy on us!"

I held the phone at arm's length, looking at it in incredulity. No sound emanated from within; Stuart was weighing the gravity of what he had done.

"I – I don't know what to say," he said a moment later.

"You fucking numpty! How could you be so stupid?!" My voice screeched out of my dry throat.

"What can I do to get him back inside it?" Stuart whimpered.

"Nothing. You've already done too much!"

I slammed the phone down. It all made sense; Sabrina getting back in touch with me the previous summer. Sightings of Louisa-Mae and Lauren, then more recently Johnny. We had all been drawn to the heightened psychic energy that Norman James McMurray was emitting; a floodgate of malice coming from the demonic realm. I needed to get over to Stuart's house and find the yew vessel and Amber gemstone in his shed. The Blue Man resided in Johnny, his descendant and flesh-husk of reincarnation, but if I could trap him back in the yew vessel, seal it with the Amber gemstone and surround it by another ring of protective thistles, then I could set Johnny's soul free. For seven months, Johnny had been victim to the parasitic ghost of his great-grandfather – Norman James McMurray. I had to act now to save his soul, my soul, Stuart's soul – many more souls – from torment.

An unimaginable weight fell onto my shoulders; as though an astral boulder had been set on my upper back. Every part of my body ran cold as though the hallway was several degrees colder. Thoughts of Harry overwhelmed me; a strong maternal instinct to check on him seized me. I dashed into the living room, where the scene that met me chilled my body to its very core.

The Blue Man stood in the middle of my living room, towering over Harry's Moses basket that lay on the floor. In the clear light of day, I could see that a coating of soil covered the plaid cloak that draped over his left shoulder and his blue tartan kilt was frayed at the hem, rotted and worm-eaten from a century buried in the ground. His blue pallor was even more stark in broad daylight; as if I needed any reminder that he was an unnatural entity from beyond the grave. I stood in the doorway, frozen, and my body felt detached from my mind, petrified with an eerie numbness that wasn't of the physical realm.

Only my eyes could move; they rested on my baby. Harry slept well, oblivious to the supernatural threat looming over him.

This one slipped through the net. You weren't supposed to have a child with another man. Only babies born of my bloodline were to survive.

His acrid words echoed inside my head. He was going to kill my baby.

The Blue Man swooped forward over Harry with his arms outstretched, using his cloak and kilt to conceal the entire Moses basket. His sudden action released me from my petrified hold in the doorway; my legs kicked into action with a powerful maternal surge and I launched myself across the room. A dreadful roar filled the room. With a start I realised the sound came from my own lungs.

"Get away from my baby and go back to hell, where you belong!"

I tore the cloak aside. The Blue Man had his left hand over Harry's heart. His eyes were crinkled as his mouth stretched into a wide, menacing grimace and his face grew a deeper shade of blue with the effort as he concentrated. Energy surged around his hand; I could see smoky waves emanating from his dead flesh into my living child. Harry remained asleep, undisturbed by the supernatural actions being inflicted upon him. I pulled at Norman's hand, but couldn't release it.

What was he doing to my child? Unlike how he had scooped at me during his last attack on me when I had been eighteen, this was as though the Blue Man was putting something into Harry, rather than taking something away. But what? A part of his own energy?

It couldn't be. Such a thought was diabolical. Unimaginable. My poor, sweet child!

I had to act now if I were to save Harry. Behind my left shoulder, on the coffee table next to the sofa was a salt lamp, a housewarming present from Stuart. It looked like an orange ostrich egg on a wooden base. He had said that salt neutralised excess positive ionic charge in the air from electronics that he claimed made people feel ungrounded and headachy. I had been tempted to throw it away, but Aunt Tracey had imparted that it also kept ghosts at bay, as it neutralised telekinetic energy from the spirit world too.

I grabbed the lamp with my left hand and clicked the switch with my left thumb. It glowed like a mellow sunset, the warm colours chasing away the ice-blue of death in the room. Salt to kill the Devil on your left shoulder, or so the saying went.

Mustering all my strength, I swung the lamp up in an arc above my left shoulder and brought it crashing down on the Blue Man's head. The demon howled like a wounded Jackal from hell, his mouth a gaping black hole in his skeletal face. He let go of Harry and staggered backwards, his cloak swirling around him on an unearthly wind. Cloak and kilt trailed behind him as he crawled on all fours, writhing in pain. I watched him skulk across the room and pull himself up by holding onto the window frame.

"Get out of my house and get out of my life! You're not welcome here!"

I smashed the lamp against his bony cranium, knocking his blue Balmoral askew. The Blue Man howled. His body arched as he toppled backwards and with a deafening crash, he plunged through the living room window into the garden outside; both panes of the double glazed window exploded into a shower of glass.

Was the salt lamp really so powerful? Aunt Tracey should have told me that sooner. Of course, back when I had stayed with her as an eighteen year old girl kicked out of home, she had told me that she herself had never encountered a ghost or demon. I had been the only one misfortunate enough for that.

I tucked the salt lamp under my left armpit in case I needed to defend myself against the Blue Man again, and swooped down upon by baby, picking Harry up and cradling him against my chest. Tears fell onto my son.

"Oh sweetheart! Oh baby, I'll never let anyone harm you. Never!"

Harry blinked up at me with his large, blue eyes as if to say, 'what's all the fuss, Mummy?' I wanted to go to the window to check and see if the supernatural fiend was still lingering near the house, but I didn't dare risk any harm coming to my innocent baby.

Just as had happened before when I had a overwhelming urge to check on Harry in his Moses basket, my thoughts sprang back to Stuart. Panic gripped me and an unimaginable sense of fear for my brother.

"Norman? Are you out there? Don't you go near my brother, you hear me? You stay away from him!"

But my words drifted out the window unanswered. I knew it was too late. Stuart was in danger. I had interrupted the Blue Man's attack on my child, but deflected it onto my brother instead.

Chapter thirty-three

Sabrina – May 2000

"I'm sorry that you have to move back home, but I think it's the right decision. I have many objects in this flat that create an environment conducive to planes of higher vibration – my tarot cards, my quartz crystals, my Jade statues, my spider plants. The Blue Man has been attracted to the life force and energy in this home, things that he badly wants, being an intransient soul. That's why the first time he appeared to you was here, even though you'd been talking to him for many months through the witch board." Megan's Aunt Tracey's brow was heavy with the weight of her sadness. I looked at Megan. The pain radiating from her was almost its own physical force.

"I prefer living here with you and Natasha." Megan hung her head. "Did you speak to my mum? Did she say it was okay?"

"She understands. She doesn't want you to come to any harm. But I need to give you a few things to protect you when you move back home. There's a ceremony that you can do that will trap this malevolent spirit and keep him from causing further harm," said Aunt Tracey.

This sounded intriguing. "Will it banish him – you know, exorcise him back into the spirit world?"

Megan looked from me to Aunt Tracey and I could tell that she was also eager for her aunt's knowledge. The Blue Man had become a demonic force that we needed to rid ourselves off, for once and for all.

"No. Unfortunately his evil is too strong for that. By selling himself to the Devil, he has forged a strong power that is the closest to a physical body that he'll have in this world. What we can do instead is to trap him in a vessel and seal it."

"Will it work?" Megan spoke in a soft, defeated tone.

"It's the best chance you have. If you do it right, it should be effective."

"Should be?" I couldn't help jumping in. "Have you ever done a ritual like this before?"

Aunt Tracey shook her head. "I've never encountered a malevolent force of this calibre before."

Megan's gaze jumped from me across to her aunt. "Okay. What do I have to do?"

"First you need to draw him close by using the witch board. Ask him if he's there and wait for a response. That should be enough to lure him."

Aunt Tracey handed Megan a wooden statue of a man, about two feet high. It was reddish brown in colour and had curved tree rings that gave it a marbled effect. The man had a simple, elongated body and his hands were raised above his blank oval-shaped head as though carrying an invisible object. As I peered closer, I realised that the top of the statue's oval head had a hole, an inch in diameter, like a skull that had undergone trepanning. The inside of the carving was hollow. It wasn't a statue, it was a container.

"This is a vessel made of yew. Yew is a powerful spiritual wood that has been used since ancient Celtic times to ward off evil spirits. Have you heard the story of O'Cathain's Dolmen in Derry?"

"Londonderry," Natasha corrected her with a sneer.

Aunt Tracey smacked her hand. "I'm talking about pagan times, silly wee girl. It was known as Derry from pre-Christian times in Ireland until 1613 when investors from the City of London during the Ulster Plantation renamed it Londonderry. For the purpose of this story, which is Celtic, it was known as *Derry*."

Natasha fell silent, her lip downturned. Both Megan and I shook our heads at the same time. "We didn't know about the story," I said.

Aunt Tracey took a deep breath. "There was a cruel chieftain in the 5th century known as Abhartach and when he was killed by his tribe, he returned as a vampire. A neighbouring chieftain known as Cathain enlisted the help of a Holy Christian hermit living in the woods, who advised to slay the vampire using a sword made of yew and to then bury him head down, weighed by a heavy stone. After Cathain did this, the locals planted thorn bushes around the site. This was enough to seal the monster for all eternity; he didn't plague the local tribes ever since."

Megan looked inside the empty yew vessel. "How am I going to get the Blue Man inside this container?" she said.

"I've placed black Tourmaline crystals from the Sperrins and green Beryl crystals from the Mourne Mountains inside. Those will simultaneously protect you and banish him to the confines of the yew vessel," said Aunt Tracey.

"Crystals? How do they work?" I said.

"Black tourmaline diminishes fear and treats paranoia, so it is a natural repellent for negativity. It also helps to balance and restore the male-female energy in the body. Green beryl crystals work in conjunction with the tourmaline by assisting in the ascension process and carrying healing light to expand positive energy. Both of these crystals should cleanse the dark energy of the Blue Man and help to send his evil aura back to the astral world."

Yew vessels, semi-precious crystals, aura and astral and ascension. A moment of doubt popped into my mind. What if Aunt Tracey and Megan were nuts? In reality, nobody apart from Megan had seen the Blue Man and even then, she had been off her nut on E's. Was I nuts too for going along with her?

Then again, what harm did it do? If I took part in a ritual to trap the Blue Man in a vessel, like a genie in a lamp, then wouldn't that be the end of Megan's preoccupation? So, whether the ghost was real or a figment of her imagination, it would be the same outcome? That, and I'd have my best friend back. Win-win.

"Once you get him inside the vessel, you need to seal it with this."

Aunt Tracey placed what looked like a large, orange gemstone in Megan's hand, that filled her whole palm. It was as large as a medium-sized potato with red and brown swirls inside the opaque, yellowish-orange main body.

"This is an Amber gemstone. It's a type of quartz found in Lough Neagh."

I took it off Megan and held it up to the light to look inside. "There are tiny whirls running through it," I said.

"Yes. Embedded within those loops are the memories of the ancestors. Amber gemstones help to retain knowledge of the past. With this special gemstone as a seal on the yew vessel, we will remember the folk story of the tragic Scotsman who sold his soul to the Devil and became known as the Blue Man, while simultaneously trapping him within, and thereby protecting ourselves from his insidious presence."

I handed the Amber gemstone back to Megan and dusted my hands; an instinctive reaction that drew a brief furrowed brow from Aunt Tracey.

"Once you've trapped him inside the yew vessel and sealed it with the Amber gemstone, you need to plant a ring of Thistles around the burial site. Just as the local tribes of Derry and the Chieftain Cathain did when they banished the vampire Abhartach, this will stop him from ever crossing the circle."

"But didn't they use a ring of thorns?" I said. "In the ghost story you just told us."

Aunt Tracey waggled a teasing finger at me. "Yes, my keen observer. Thorn bushes for the people of ancient Ireland, but thistles to seal a Scotsman. Thistles are the national flower of Scotland."

One corner of Megan's mouth twitched into a sarcastic smile. "Haven't you seen Braveheart? Men in skirts don't do it for you?"

I felt myself blush; Megan was teasing me again for being a virgin. "No. I thought that seeing what's under a Scotsman's man's sporran would be more your thing."

"Ladies! Behave yourselves!" Aunt Tracey puckered her face into one of faux outrage, but it broke the tension; we all burst out in fits of giggles.

***

Another sip for Dutch courage, then another, followed by a swig. I handed the bottle of Buckfast to Megan and she glugged it down, a bulge in her throat as she swallowed.

"It's a full moon. It's a good sign," she slurred.

The moon swam in and out of focus as I struggled to train my eyes on it. Megan lit a spliff, took a big drag and passed it to me. I sucked in a lungful and blew it out, the moon hidden behind my dancing smoke phantoms.

She set the Ouija board on the grass and we both sat down, cross-legged on the lawn. Our fingertips touched briefly on top of the pointer and static electricity made us flinch in synchronisation.

"Norman, are you there?"

Not only was there a bitter sting to Megan's tone, but she had skipped straight over the generic question asking if anyone was there to a direct address to the

Blue Man. Megan meant business; not as high as her intoxicated speech suggested.

"Norman. If you're there, answer me."

The pointer spun across the board to indicate 'yes'. Ordinarily I would've flinched, but my head felt too sluggish to process it.

"Sabrina, gimme the statue."

It took a moment for me to register in my inebriated brain what she was asking for; the yew vessel from Aunt Tracey. Keeping one hand on the pointer, I reached behind and grabbed the vessel. I set it upright on the grass, but it toppled over straightaway.

"Oh my God, she could've given me something with a proper base. How is this thing meant to even stand?" Megan cried.

I saw her anguished face in the moonlight and hammered the top with my open palm, forcing the male figurine's legs into the turf. "Don't worry, we'll make it work."

Phew; I was sure I had saved the ritual from certain doom. If the vessel had toppled over, Megan would have worried about the Tourmaline and Beryl crystals spilling out, or worse still – letting the Blue Man escape the container instead of imprisoning him within.

Megan's eyes were glassy, the full moon reflected in each fearful iris. "How are we going to know if he's inside?"

I stared at the Ouija board, my mind running fast. "Em – is anybody there? Answer yes if you're there."

No response.

"Sabrina, you're a genius! The genie's in the bottle." Megan twisted around and grabbed the Amber gemstone, which sat on the grass behind her right hip.

She wedged the quartz gemstone in between the carved yew man's raised hands. It slotted easily in between.

"That was easier than I thought," I said, eyeing the vessel with approval. The yew container looked like it had been custom made to hold the Amber gemstone.

Megan shook her head. "No, look."

I followed her finger to the base of the gemstone. There was a tiny gap, about a millimetre, between the hole in the top of the yew man's head and the bottom of the gemstone.

"Push it a bit more," I said.

Megan pressed the top of the gemstone. It popped out sideways from between the figurine's arms and rolled on the grass.

"Fuck," spat Megan. She placed both hands on the pointer. "Norman, I demand you answer me if you're there."

No response. Lucky for Megan that must have meant he was still inside the yew vessel. I pressed my thumb over the top of the yew man's head as Megan fumbled in the grass for the Amber gemstone.

"That won't do any good, he can pass through your body like sand through a net." Megan's voice dripped with disdain. I removed my hand as though the vessel had scalded me. She slotted the gemstone in between the yew man's hands again and this time twisted it, corkscrew style, downwards. One of the wooden arms gave a small, but audible crack no louder than a matchstick splintering.

"Fuck," Megan repeated.

I tilted my head sideways. "It worked, it covers the hole."

She sighed and wiped her brow. "Yeah, the Amber seals the container, but the left arm is cracked now.

I peered around at where she indicated. A hairline fracture ran down the yew man's left forearm from thumb to elbow. "It's intact though. I'm sure it'll be fine. Your aunt said yew is powerful."

"Not that powerful – it broke," said Megan, her nose wrinkled.

"I meant in a magical sense. It must be still enough to trap him, right?"

She jerked both shoulders at once in a short, but angry shrug. "It better be fucking enough, I'm sick to death of dealing with this."

I couldn't have agreed more, though I didn't say it. Right now, Megan needed positivity. "It is enough. It's over now. He won't be bothering you anymore."

In the gathering darkness, as a cloud obscured the moon, Megan and I dug with trowels until we had scooped a shallow ring around the yew statue. We worked in silence planting thistles that Natasha had gathered from derelict land near their flat off the Beersbridge Road. We worked in opposite directions; Megan going clockwise to the left and me going anticlockwise to the right until our hands met with another static sting as electricity jumped between the pinky finger on my right hand and her left hand.

"Ouch," Megan complained. She rubbed her hand.

"Same, that was sore." I shook my hand, letting the fingers hang loose.

"Let's call it a night." She stood up.

I looked down at the inch gap between the final two thistles we had planted. "We could readjust those last two to fill that space."

Megan arched her back. "I'd say we've done enough. That's three layers of protection – the yew, the gemstone and the thistles. Besides, I take that electric shock as a sign that the powerful forces protecting us are at work, don't you?"

I stood up too. "All that matters is you're satisfied he's been trapped."

She dusted soil off her hands then wiped them on her trousers. "Good enough for me."

We smiled and nodded. As we turned to go back inside her mum's house, I was glad to be turning away from a sinister chapter in our lives.

Chapter thirty-four

Megan – May 2000

I flopped down on the grass and rolled backwards. My head swum, making the stars in the clear sky spin and blur into swirling lines. We had only completed the ceremony to trap the Blue Man in the yew vessel not an hour before, but I had needed to put as much distance between myself and that container as possible. Sabrina was such a good friend, she had followed me without so much as a word. We had walked in silence from my house in Mersey Street to Bridgeend station and taken the train to the next stop on the Bangor line: Sydenham, Sabrina's neck of the woods. Sydenham was close to where Norman James McMurray had met his fate, before his dead body had washed out into Belfast Lough and come aground close to Holywood beach. The impulse to go there had been too strong to resist; psychic forces were compelling my decisions.

I had grabbed the last few bottles of Buckfast and cider before I had left my house. Victoria Park was a fitting place to get bleutered and say a final goodbye to the Blue Man – then wipe all thoughts of the supernatural fiend into oblivion.

Sabrina sat down cross-legged on the grass beside me and glugged from her two litre bottle of cider. "Cheers."

"Goodbye Norman James McMurray," I said to the stars above.

Sabrina raised the cider bottle to take another swig, but halfway towards her mouth her hand froze. Her eyes were wide in the moonlight and locked on a point among the dark trees.

I grabbed her arm, my grip tight with fear. "What? What is it?"

"I thought I saw a face, among the tree trunks." Sabrina scampered to her feet.

"A face?" My voice cracked, more squeak than words. "It couldn't be – not him?"

Oh. My. God. My brain fizzed with all the thoughts flooding in at once. Had we been too sloppy with the ceremony? Had the crack in the yew let him escape? What about the gap in the ring of thistles? How angry would he be that I had tried to trap him; would he seek revenge? What would he do to me now that he had escaped?

In the direction Sabrina looked, my eyes rested on a dark mass among the trees. It looked darker than black, more dense, almost like a black hold of nothingness drawing us in. The black mass raised the hairs on my arm and neck as though pulling me in towards it.

"Your hair." Sabrina pointed at me.

I put my hands above my head and felt long strands of my hair standing on end, drawn upwards by static electricity.

I pointed back at her. "Yours too!"

Although the moonlight didn't reach through the thick branches to the dark mass between the tree trunks, two cat-like eyes began to appear and a crescent moon of bright, white teeth. The familiar high cheekbones and skin the colour of ice emerged as the Blue Man glided forwards into the clearing between trees.

A tidal surge of energy flowed from my head to my toes, propelling my legs forwards. My feet flew across the ground, barely touching grass. "Sabrina run, he's coming."

Megan, you can't escape me.

His baritone voice echoed across the park, smooth as poison in my ears.

You tried to trick me.

Creamy smooth poison in my ears. I vomited Buckfast back up into my mouth as I ran, but swallowed it down. I had to get away.

You reneged on your promise. You had no intention of being with Johnny.

The Blue Man's poisonous whisper was in my ear. An unearthly strength pushed me to the ground. I rolled over onto my back, helpless as he straddled me, pinning my legs with his psychic weight.

He leaned forward, his skeletal face looming over mine. I wanted to shut my eyes but couldn't. For a split second I thought he was going to choke me, but instead of constricting my throat, he reached for my stomach and scooped both hands inwards until his fingers interlocked. He lifted an invisible mass upwards and threw it over his left shoulder.

If you will not bear for Johnny, you will bear for no-one.

Again and again he dug and scooped at my stomach, much like how a dog would dig with its front paws in dirt and then remove and invisible mass, throwing it over his left shoulder. The sensation was a ticklish pain, like hitting my funny bone, only this was my abdomen. It was as though he was hollowing out my life essence, tearing the psychic umbilical cord to separate my soul from my body. I couldn't move, could barely breathe.

Amidst the psychic attack on my body, I detached from my physical self and floated free. I rose upwards, about six feet off the ground, and saw the malevolent fiend attacking my body below. My flesh and blood self on the ground fell limp like a rag doll, all the strength of its life force draining out. He was killing me.

I had to save myself. I had to act fast, or my life would be lost forever.

My spirit self couldn't move, only hover where it was in mid-air. It was clear I had no control over my ghostly form; but also clear that I still had my mind. I could think – and that was something.

Sabrina. I focused on her. She was on her knees, hunched over me. I watched her patting my face, then screaming for help, then shaking me – and all the while, the malevolent spectre of the Blue Man pinned my body as he dug and scooped at my stomach. I needed to send her a psychic message to help me.

I concentrated my telepathic mind onto my friend. *Sabrina, he's on top of me. Get him off. Move my body – sit me upright to knock him off.*

The Blue Man turned then, his head cranking round until he was looking straight upwards at me. A malign glint in his eyes caused his smile to stretch ever wider, a triangular gash in his face that mocked me, sneered at my very soul.

The Blue Man projected his thoughts at me. *I'll kill her too if you keep trying to call for help.*

I couldn't use telepathy on Sabrina if it would get her killed. I focused my attention on the Blue Man. *I tried, I really tried with Johnny. You know I love him.*

In an instant I found myself able to move; my soul was no longer trapped in stasis. The Blue Man stood up from my physical body and reached upward. He grabbed my spirit self by the throat and swept it downward until with a jolt, I was reattached to my human body.

You left me with no choice. I took all the extraneous life essence from you. Now it's Johnny or nothing — if you want to continue your bloodline. That will give you no choice but to find a way.

With that, he was gone. Like the phantom of the spirit world that he was, he swept away into the woods, his cloak flying behind him. I caught a last glimpse of his blue Balmoral disappearing among the trees before he was out of sight, leaving only pain in my retinas, as though I had been looking at the sun and not a fiend of darkness.

I forced my eyeballs away from the forest and towards Sabrina, giving her a sign that I was alive.

"Megan. Oh my God, speak to me. How many Es did you take?" Sabrina's voice cracked as she dissolved into tears.

Air filled my lungs in small, panting gasps until my breathing steadied. My mouth was dry and had a metallic taste. "None tonight. I took an acid tab way

The Blue Man

earlier and had some magic mushroom tea that Aunt Tracey made, before we left her place."

"What happened to you?" she cried.

"Didn't you see him?" I craned my neck to look for any signs of him, but he was gone. My body felt cold and numb.

"You mean, the Blue Man attacked you again?" Her eyes were wide, and wild, in the starry sky.

I nodded, moving the only part of my body that would cooperate. "Can you help me sit up? I lost the feeling in my body but it's coming back now – I have pins and needles all over. Sabrina, I had an out-of-body experience."

Sabrina pushed her hair back off her face with both hands, like she tended to do when she was nervous. "No way. Are you saying, you floated above yourself?"

"I saw you trying to wake me up and I heard you shouting for help."

She put her hands under my armpits and tried to haul me up, until I stood slumped against her. "Did he try to kill you?"

I shook my head. "He did something even stranger. He scooped at my stomach, like he was emptying all my guts out – you know, like disembowelling me."

As Sabrina's gaze fell to my midriff, my hands crisscrossed over it and I massaged it to undo some of the psychic damage that the Blue Man had done to me. Though what damage had that been?

Sabrina's face rumpled with puzzlement. "Did he think you were pregnant by Johnny, maybe? Could he have been jealous?"

It was as though a lightbulb had been switched on in my head. Sabrina's idea was on the right track, though not completely accurate. "No, it can't be."

"What? What is it?" Sabrina's voice was almost a whisper.

I gulped, swallowing a painful lump in my throat. "When I was twelve, the summer after I left primary school, I broke my leg. I was in a cast for three months. When I had to go for an X-ray to see if it had healed, the radiographer gave me a lead blanket to put over my middle – you know – to protect my privates."

Sabrina watched me as I paused, gathering my thoughts.

"He told me that the lead blanket would protect my babies." Tears swirled in my eyes and Sabrina became a blur. "I think it's too late for any babies now."

I threw myself on Sabrina's shoulder, my body shuddering with sobs that I couldn't stop.

"Are you – do you mean to say – the Blue Man took away all your eggs? That's what he was scooping out of you? Your ability to have children?" Sabrina's voice was a squeak in my ear.

I wiped my tears on my sleeve. "I think he might have left me with a few – but that they'll only work if I have a child with Johnny."

"What's so special about Johnny?" she said.

"I asked him that too, but he didn't answer. I suppose I'll have to find out for myself – once I trap him in the yew vessel for real this time. I'll make sure he never gets out. But there's one thing I've come to realise. Johnny is no good for me. I need to make sure I never see him again. In fact, I need to get as far away from him as I possibly can. The Blue Man's energy is stronger somehow the closer I am to Johnny."

Chapter thirty-five

Sabrina – July 2000

What on earth was I doing? I had to question myself as my feet marched a path along Severn Street, ready to head down Yukon and make the turn off towards Megan's house in Mersey Street. Nearly two months had passed. After the Yew vessel ritual and then study leave, I hadn't seen Megan, apart from briefly during our exams in June. Our A-level exams were behind us. It was late July. In a short few weeks, we'd be getting the results that would determine our future paths. Eighteen going on nineteen; we had our whole lives stretched ahead of us. By rights, Megan and I should have been having the summer of our lives before I left to study English and History at Liverpool.

Why was I going to call to Megan's house; we hadn't been in touch since the night the Blue Man had chased her in Vicky Park. Got to admit, the whole thing freaked me out. I felt like Megan was venturing down a path that I didn't understand – or want to follow; both physically and metaphorically. The drugs were one thing. The Blue Man was another.

Still, we had been close for three years; I had to be a good friend one last time and check up on her. I needed to know she was okay. Alright, fine; I needed to know if the Blue Man had continued to haunt her.

I turned in to Megan's street and my feet followed the familiar path to her house. I rang the doorbell then wiped my sweaty palms on my jeans and took a deep breath.

Megan's mum answered the door. "Oh, Sabrina love."

"Who is it, Mum?" Megan's younger brother Stuart peered over Megan's mum's shoulder.

"Em – I came to see if Megan was home?"

Megan's mum looked confused. "Hadn't she told you? She left for Derry early. She got given an unconditional offer for a Marketing course and she just secured a place in Halls for September, so she's heading there early to get settled into her student accommodation."

Derry. That was where the ghost story of O'Cathain's Dolmen came from.

"But I thought she was staying in Belfast to do her degree?" I said.

Megan's mum shook her head. "She didn't want to stay in Belfast after all that nasty business with Louisa-Mae and Lauren."

Or was it the Blue Man? The thought popped into my head, though I didn't say it out loud. Megan's mum faltered; had she been thinking the same idea?

"I'm glad she's going to continue doing something Artsy though, she's very talented. I'm sure she'll get a good grade in her A-level Technology, it'll help with her Marketing course." I mostly spoke to break the awkward silence, but maybe it wasn't a good idea. After all, not only had Megan's final piece – her centre-piece – been a sculpture of the Blue Man, but Louisa-Mae had smashed it. Even with it glued back together, Megan would be lucky if she scraped a C.

"Yes, she's rather good at Tech." Megan's mum's voice became melancholy and her eyes shone with tears. "Well, good luck with your own A-level results, Sabrina. I hope you get the grades to do whatever it is you're wanting to do."

Megan's mum's tone was so final that I didn't respond. It was clear she didn't want me to either. She didn't care what career prospects I had, or even whether I passed or failed. She just wanted me to go away. Did she blame me for all that had happened to Megan, or think me a bad influence on her daughter? It seemed so. I had never got the impression that she had disliked me during all of the times I had come over to see Megan throughout the past three years, but now I got the sense that I wasn't welcome.

"Thanks. Well, tell Megan that I hope she has a great time doing Marketing." I walked down the garden path before stopping and turning back. "Would it be okay if you could pass on her phone number – once she gets to Derry? I tried her mobile, but it was dead."

Megan's mum gave a pursed-lip smile. "Oh, of course I will. Just ring me in a couple of weeks once she's all settled and I'll pass it on. She got a new phone so that Louisa-Mae and Lauren don't have her new number."

She shut the door before I had a chance to answer. Now I was sure; she wanted rid of me. I'd never get Megan's number. I'd be lucky if I ever saw her again.

I rounded the corner out of Megan's street and started towards the Albertbridge Road when an idea sprang to mind. Megan's house was on the corner; I would be able to see into her back garden from the footpath. I backtracked a few steps and pressed my face against the wooden fence.

The yew vessel was still there, with the Amber gemstone wedged on top, surrounded by the ring of thistles that we had planted.

I stared hard at the vessel. The wood had different markings on it; the patterns of the tree rings were more striated rather than the looping whirls on the last vessel that had broken. This was a different container. Megan must have replaced the broken one, and most likely repeated the whole procedure again by herself to make sure the Blue Man was really trapped inside.

I turned away from the sight in Megan's back garden and continued away on down the street. If I were honest with myself, all of the events of the past few months repulsed me to my very core. The whole summer had got off on the wrong footing, starting with my regretful – and fateful – decision to share the urban legend of the Blue Man's ghost with my so-called friends. From that moment onwards, life had spiralled out of control. Whether there really was a mystical element to it – the fact that the Blue Man was born at the turn of the twentieth century and it was now the new millennium, a hundred years after his birth – or no supernatural event whatsoever, the fact of that matter was that the Blue Man had destroyed my closest friendships with the three girls I had been best friends with for the past three years and now? Now I was left with nothing. Now it was time for a fresh start.

Chapter thirty-six

Megan – July 2000

I rubbed the crick in my neck from poring over the old newspaper articles and arched my back to stretch the muscles. My eyes were tired from spending the past three hours reading through the old archives of the *Belfast Telegraph*, the *Newsletter*, the *Irish News* and the *Irish Times*. Among the dusty volumes, I had found what I was looking for: Body of shipyard worker washed ashore at in Belfast Lough. I skimmed the text, allowing key bits to jump out at me: *It is believed that foul play was behind the death/ young man aged twenty/ rope marks on the victim's neck.*

The Blue Man, aka Norman James McMurray, had been murdered. So Sabrina's version of events from when she had first told the story had been right – he had been killed out on the mudflats near the Harland

and Wolff shipyard. With a shiver, I thought of all those times we had got drunk in Vicky Park, after dark on many a moonlit night, so close to where the body of a lonely Scotsman had endured torture as his life was lynched out of him where the Connswater River met Belfast Lough.

I tucked the old newspapers into my handbag, confident in the knowledge that I had proof of Norman's death. Now for proof of his life. I pulled a brown envelope out of my bag and set it on the café table in front of me, ready to pore over the documents inside. I tore open the envelope and pulled out its contents. It was all the information I needed for closure on the whole, traumatising few months since April:

A birth certificate: Maureen Ann Boyd. Born April 3rd 1900. District of Belfast.

Another birth certificate. Martin Roberts. Born November 27th 1892. County Tyrone.

And their children. The name of their firstborn locked my eyes on the page in place:

A birth certificate: Norman Arthur Roberts.

And my eyes widened further at the name of their second child:

Another birth certificate: James Roberts.

Norman James McMurray was living on in name through Maureen Ann Boyd's children. She couldn't be with him in life, but she had found a way to make him live on in death.

It was a pity I couldn't have had the Blue Man's birth confirmed, as he had been born in Scotland a hundred years ago. Instead I pulled out his death certificate.

Record of death: Norman James McMurray.

Date of death: July 7th 1920.

Place of death: Belfast Lough by Harland and Wolff docks.

Cause of death: Strangulation by rope.

As I tucked the brown envelope and its contents back inside my bag with the old newspapers, my heart pumped blood, fast and furious around my body. I had all the evidence I needed to put my mind and heart at ease; now I could lock the Blue Man safely in the back of my mind, knowing that his energy was trapped in the yew container in my Mum's back garden, and the details of his life on earth were folded neatly in an envelope in my bag – ready for a dusty compartment in my head.

I stood up from the coffee table at the café inside Belfast Central Station and went down onto the platform. The summer breeze whipped my hair back off my face and cooled my sweaty back, which struggled with the burden of my all my possessions, ready for my new adventure in Derry.

A creeping feeling, like spiders on the back of my neck, made my shoulders clench. I turned my head towards my left side; only a fraction, enough to peer through my peripheral vision. I didn't dare turn fully around; I feared what I might see. My racing heart was enough to warn me to hurry onwards out of Belfast. Doubt slithered into my mind. I had repeated the yew vessel ceremony again with an unmarred, unbroken container – but had I done the ritual correctly? Had the Blue Man really been trapped inside? The only way I could have any real peace of mind was to get as far away as possible from the city where Norman James McMurray had sold his soul to the Devil – and died a painful and unjust death.

In the reflection of a noticeboard on the train platform, I caught sight of a blonde-haired head among the crowds near me, about ten metres behind me. The wearer's blonde hair hung in curtains, obscuring the teenage boy's face. The face was all too familiar. I spun around.

"Johnny?"

Nobody with blonde hair.

I was going mad. I swivelled around and focused on my train now pulling into Central Station, evermore sure of why I needed to get the hell away – far, far away – from Belfast, as soon as possible. Goodbye Johnny. Goodbye Sabrina. Goodbye Lauren and Louisa-Mae. Goodbye Norman James McMurray. The Blue Man was part of my past, not my present, from now on.

Chapter thirty-seven

Sabrina – July 2021

The woman yelped again. Yelped and yipped like a small terrier dog on heat. Her noises of pleasure were followed by deep male grunting that sounded muffled through the ceiling above. Johnny was, yet again, having sex with whatever insatiable woman he was currently shagging. In the past few weeks, I had seen so many different women coming and going – literally – that I had lost track of who his latest flavour of the week was.

Urgh, what an obnoxious situation. Johnny's business was his own – or at least, should have been his own. But when the sounds of his carnal lust resonated around my living room, then it was time to abandon ship – for a few hours at any rate.

Leo was hard at play batting mobiles on his baby gym, oblivious to the obscene noises coming from next door. Lucky for Jake, he was at work. The one good thing about my maternity leave ending in another month was that I wouldn't have to listen to Johnny having sex anymore, as he seemed to always fit in his marathon sex sessions during the daytime.

I changed Leo's nappy and put him in shorts and a t-shirt, ready to go out into the July sunshine. As we were coming out of the flat, Leo balanced on my left hip and the buggy under my right arm, I heard a gasp of surprise on the stairwell.

"Oh my goodness, Sabrina! I didn't realise you were home!"

I turned at the sound of Megan's voice. She tripped as she came down the stairs from Johnny's flat and caught her balance on the handrail.

"Megan? What are you doing here?"

Megan cheeks turned crimson. "I, well, I stopped by Johnny's to pay him a visit. I had to – erm, give him a present."

Johnny appeared behind Megan on the landing above and leaned over the banister. His blonde ponytail was dishevelled and he had a goofy grin on his face.

"Alright there Sabrina, love? Look at what Megan gave me." Johnny held up a gold neck chain. I looked at the object dangling at the end of it: an Amber gemstone.

I was about to reply that she had given him a whole lot more than just a gemstone, but I bit my tongue. "I thought you were going to come round and pay me a visit – I didn't realise you were going to see Johnny instead."

Megan breathed on her hands to warm them, a cloud of condensation rising. "Yeah, well, I didn't get round to sorting out a time with you and I needed to see Johnny urgently."

I shut the flat door and locked it, wondering whether my face showed the disdain I felt for what she had done. Wasn't Megan married? What about her husband Paddy and the baby, Harry? Megan seemed to have read my mind, for she started on down the stairs, breezing past me on the landing and hurrying on down towards the front door.

"What, no goodbye kiss?" Johnny shouted.

"Er, it was nice seeing you, Johnny. Thanks for today," Megan called over her shoulder.

"My pleasure," said Johnny, each word dripping with sleaze.

I followed her downstairs and unfolded Leo's buggy once we got outside.

"Sabrina, I'll walk with you, my car is parked on the main road. I've got something to tell you." Megan waited for me at the bottom of the path.

I gave a quick smile to conceal any awkwardness. "You don't have to tell me anything."

"No, I do – really, I do. My brother Stuart, died."

Megan's words stopped me dead in my tracks. I composed myself after a hesitation and caught up with her.

"What? Oh my God, I'm so sorry to hear that," I said.

"The Blue Man killed him and made it look like he hung himself," she added.

I gripped the handles of Leo's buggy tighter, channelling my frustration on them. "Listen, Megan.

I'm so sorry, I don't know what to say. The death of a loved one must be so unbearable that—"

"I know what you're getting at and you're wrong. I'm not just imagining that everything is to do with Norman. The fact of the matter is that Stuart phoned me right before he was taken from me and you know what he said?" Her eyes welled with tears. "He told me that he had released the Blue Man by accident because he got rid of the yew vessel and Amber gemstone in the garden. The Blue Man got into his house – he told me he was there right before he died!"

What an awful, horrible situation for anyone to go through. My mind raced through scenarios. Megan had said Stuart was schizophrenic; the rational explanation was that he had killed himself. I felt for Megan, I really did; to a point. Her brother's suicide wasn't enough reason to go completely off the rails though, and cheat on her husband – with a waster like Johnny Montgomery, no less.

"The Blue Man came for my baby. He tried to kill Harry. You've no idea what that feels like, Sabrina. I had to whack him away, out the window. That's why he went after Stuart instead. I deflected him off my child and onto my brother." Megan's face was a waterfall then; of tears pouring from her eyes and mucus running out of her nose. Her bottom lip trembled and she let loose a choked squeal; of pain, of self-pity. Of desperation.

My hardened heart melted and I pulled her onto my shoulder for a hug. "Baby Harry is alright, thank God, and he needs you. He needs you right now, so you have to go to him. Where is he?"

She wiped her nose on the back of her hand and dried her eyes on her sleeve. "I left him at my Mum's.

I'm heading round there now to get him. Her house isn't too far from Cregagh here – she lives over in Bloomfield now, near Connswater.

My head spun on reflex towards Leo, dozing in the buggy. From there, my gaze drifted across to Johnny. He had come down to the front door, standing in his open doorway, trying to eavesdrop. My eyes lingered on the Amber gemstone hanging around his neck that he twirled round and round, with idle fingers. Maybe things weren't as rational as I tried to convince myself they were. Leo was a strong baby, but I wasn't taking any chances. I needed to get away from Johnny. If Megan was right and Johnny was surrounded by supernatural energy, whatever that might be, then the sooner she could move on from such a shady character – and we could put him behind us – the better.

Megan cried on my shoulder and I held her head there, patting her hair with my left hand while I rocked Leo in his buggy with the other hand. Death of a family member was always horrible, but the timing was unfortunate. Megan and I had only recently reconnected; not only that, but I couldn't deny the horrible coincidence that seeing each other again had stirred up the Blue Man's energy. Whether real or imagined, Norman James McMurray had become an undeniable part of our lives. He might as well have been a real person; for all the attention we gave him. So much bad had happened in our lives the last time the Blue Man had been a part of our story back in 2000; Megan had slid down the dark path of drugs and metaphorical death through her Technology career and now literal death of her brother. It was a sorry state of affairs that our friendship back then had splintered after a traumatic break and now, could very well fracture again after it had barely restarted. Would I forever remind her of the death of her brother, Stuart? And what of her child, Harry? Megan had told me that he was a frail baby at birth, born with a hole in his chest. Now she disclosed that the Blue Man had tried to kill him. Megan's vulnerable brother, a paranoid schizophrenic, obsessed with radioactivity, was now dead. Would her vulnerable, frail child be next? Would Norman James McMurray be successful in murdering Harry next time? *Would* there be a next time?

Megan peeled herself away from my shoulder with a sniff. "I'll see you again soon, Sabrina, I'll be in touch."

I watched her hurry away towards her Toyota Yaris, parked further along and across the street. It was as if she had read my thoughts. I no longer worried that I would forever remind her of her brother's death; now I worried that I was responsible in some way, on a more supernatural level. There seemed to be a triangle between Megan, Johnny and I; a connection that I was desperate to sever. Maybe Megan had been right to distance herself from me when we were eighteen, after we had left school in 2000. I couldn't say how, but I felt responsible for Stuart's death, and for bringing the Blue Man into our lives. Megan had been right to distance herself from me. Maybe I was trouble. On a metaphysical level perhaps, I was responsible.

Chapter thirty-eight

Megan – July 2021

The little boy in the blue rain-mackintosh ran ahead of me, among the undergrowth and hid behind a tree.

"Ready or not, here I come!" I hollered.

Baby Harry was no longer a baby. Now he was a lively toddler. His hair was dark like his Dad's, but his blue eyes were large and round like mine.

Before I could get to the tree, a blue hand at the end of a blue sleeve appeared. The hand was raised, palm towards me in a 'stop' gesture. But I didn't pause.

"No. Get the hell away from my baby. You stay away from him!" I screamed.

My ears filled with Harry's shrieks. The Blue Man stepped out from behind the tree and grabbed Harry by the hood of his rain-mackintosh, ripping it off him. I watched as though my feet were rooted to the ground, unable to help my vulnerable child. The Blue Man reached into Harry's chest with a balled-fist and spread his fingers wide, releasing whatever he had inside his hand.

"What did you put in him? You take it out. Get it out of him!" I screamed until my throat was raw.

"Too late," said the Blue Man, his mouth curled upwards in a sneer. "You tried to stop me before when he was a babe in the cradle. I'm back to check that my present to him is still intact. Consider this a warning of what is to come."

I woke up in a sweat, Harry's dream cries still echoing in my mind. Damn temazepam; the doctor said it would put me asleep and keep me asleep. But thank God, thank heavens above, it was only a dream.

I glanced across at Harry, his tiny chest rising and falling in the midst of his own peaceful dream – unlike mine. He wasn't a lively toddler, he was five months old. My cherub, my angel, sending me soothing energy to chase away the darkness of sleep.

A dream, only a dream. Only a dream? The Blue Man had said it was a warning. A warning of what was to come.

Is that why Harry was a toddler in the dream, because the Blue Man would come back to haunt him – and terrorise us both?

"Harry," I whispered. I kissed his cherubic cheek. "I thought I stopped him. I gave Johnny an Amber gemstone to trap Norman inside. I even gave Norman what he wanted, by sleeping with Johnny. I sacrificed a lot to keep you safe."

I stroked Harry's dark, wispy curls with my left hand, then lowered the same hand and let it rest on my stomach.

"You let that thing put his evil spawn inside you. You're pathetic."

I spun in the direction of the voice; a familiar voice, but full of menace, filled with loathing. My eyes could barely believe what they were seeing. In the corner of the bedroom, my recently deceased brother Stuart sat in the armchair that I used to breastfeed Harry. Stuart wasn't transparent as a ghost, but as solid and real-looking as he had been in life. The only reminder that he was dead was his pale pallor; his skin looked the colour of wallpaper paste and he had purplish-black half circles under his eyes.

"You're dead," I hissed. I scrambled into a sitting position, pulling the duvet around me for comfort; baby Harry sighed as I disturbed his sleep, but didn't wake at the commotion.

"How could you do it? You cheated on Paddy. You let that *thing's* great-grandson buck you, as if you were nothing more than a common whore. You betrayed your husband and son – and me," Stuart shouted.

"Ssh!" I hissed. "Harry's asleep, what's wrong with you?"

Stuart put both hands on the armrests and pushed himself up. I flinched as he walked closer to the end of the bed and waggled an accusing finger at me. "You got yourself impregnated by the descendant of a devil. Did Paddy never mean anything to you? Were you pining for your first teenage love all these years later? You sicken me."

I shook my head. "You're wrong. What do you know? I had to give Norman what he wanted – a descendant of his and Maureen's. Didn't you get the message in the afterlife? I'm the reincarnation of

The Blue Man

Norman's eternal romance – the spirit of Maureen Ann Boyd is inside me. She *is* me."

Stuart's face twisted into a snarl. "All you think about is yourself. You saved your child by knocking the Blue Man off him with the salt lamp – but what about me? When he left Harry, he came after me. You knew he was in my house and yet you left me with him and now look what has happened. I'm dead!"

"Stuart please shush – Harry's asleep!"

Stuart reached behind and extracted a long coil of rope from the back pocket of his jeans. "I didn't kill myself. He strung me up and then made it look like I'd hung myself."

He walked around the edge of the bed until he towered over me and put the frayed end of the rope in my hand. It had been sliced in half, where the police, no doubt, had cut down his body. I let go of the rope and recoiled, rubbing my hand against my pyjama trousers to clean it.

"I didn't know he was going to come after you, I swear it. I had a sixth sense that Harry was in danger – I had to do what I could to save him."

Stuart pointed at his neck. The skin on his throat had been rubbed red raw, the rope marks leaving the flesh serrated. "Don't pretend you ever cared about me. You even forgot to send Paddy round to check on me, like you said you were going to do. You just left me hanging there over the stairs. The Blue Man did it to me and it's all your fault. He wouldn't have even been in our lives if it weren't for you – and Sabrina. You do realise that, don't you?"

Tears splashed onto my cheeks. "I swear I didn't know you knew about the Blue Man too. I thought he only tormented me. I thought he was my problem."

"He wasn't your problem for twenty years though was he? You'd successfully got him out of your life. Ask yourself why – and how – he came back into your life. Think about that for a minute."

I sniffed and wiped the tears away wit the back of my hand. "Are you saying Sabrina had something to do with this?"

Stuart nodded. "She told you the story in the first place. She was there in your bedroom the first time you saw him."

I thought back to that night. The day that Louisa-Mae had sabotaged my Tech project and I had left school. The night that Sabrina had paid me a pity-visit at Aunt Tracey's house. "I'm not sure though. That's not enough to just pin the blame on Sabrina. I connected with him through the Ouija board. I found out so much about him and his life on earth – not Sabrina. Maybe he didn't want me knowing too much about him."

"Funny you bring up his life on earth." Stuart paced back and forth the room at the foot of my bed, the rhythm making me nervous. "You already know that Johnny is a descendant of Norman James McMurray, and now you say you're the reincarnation of Maureen Ann Boyd. But there's another missing part of the equation. Someone else is the third side of the triangle. Any guesses who?"

"I already know that Sabrina's brought the psychic energy that drew the Blue Man into our lives – he told me himself when I did the Ouija board a few months ago. I know she's trouble. It's because of her grandmother in Madrid. Apparently, she was a gypsy medium, or a fortune-teller. Sabrina has her psychic powers."

The Blue Man

Stuart shook his head, a judgemental grin on his face, satisfied in the knowledge that he had a piece of information I didn't know. "That's part of it, but there's more. Sabrina's Mum's side of the family are from Spain. But her Dad's side are from here, in Northern Ireland. Dungannon, to be specific."

My jaw slackened, though no words came out of my opened mouth.

"That's right. Sabrina is the great granddaughter of Martin Roberts and Maureen Ann Boyd. They raised her first born – the bastard child conceived by Norman James McMurray – and pretended that the baby was fathered by Martin since of course he was her husband. But they had three other children that he favoured instead – and all of them dark haired unlike her fair-haired first born. Sabrina's descended from the youngest. She caused all of this, wreaked all this havoc in your life."

I stared at my brother, letting his words sink in. Maybe the knowledge of the afterlife had given him a wisdom I didn't have access to. "You're right though that I'd managed to get the Blue Man out of my life for twenty years, and then I got back in touch with Sabrina and—"

"Exactly." Stuart sat forward in his chair. "Look what happened? The Blue Man tried to take your son's life and successfully stole my life away. It's Sabrina's fault. She's a harbinger of doom. She's the Blue Man's natural enemy, since she a descendant of his rival's offspring."

Fear seized me. "What can I do? I only just got him trapped in that Amber gemstone necklace I gave to Johnny."

"Don't worry." Stuart's voice was low, menacing. "All you need to do is cut her off. Stop contacting her. Tell her that you need time alone what with my funeral and everything going on. The further away you keep her, the less harm her psychic energy can bring."

Chapter thirty-nine

Sabrina – July 2021

I couldn't live like this anymore. For the past couple of weeks since I had last seen Megan, right after she had slept with Johnny, I had been avoiding him like the plague. My rational side told me that none of it was Johnny's fault; that he was simply caught in the wrong place at the wrong time and tangled up in a sinister supernatural web that Megan and I had brought on ourselves. But my paranoid side overruled any logic; if Johnny really was the physical descendant of Norman James McMurray and a host for the reincarnated evil spirit of the Blue Man himself, then I needed to keep away from him as much as was humanly possible. Over the past fortnight, I had hurried into my flat, ducked for cover into the laundry room as soon as I heard footsteps on the stairs lest they be him, or raced out of the building to take Leo on walks. It wasn't sustainable. I would end up driving myself mad if I kept it up. At the very least, living in fear of every footstep from any neighbour wasn't a healthy way to exist.

I listened carefully for the sound of Johnny's motorbike returning after one of his delivery shifts and hurried to the front door of my flat when I heard his footsteps ascending.

"Johnny. How have you been?"

Johnny stopped and turned. His face searched mine for a split second before he smiled. "Alright, Sabrina? Haven't seen you in ages. How's the wee man?"

"He's doing well, thanks. Just asleep at the moment. How are you and Claire?"

I hadn't seen Johnny's girlfriend around the building in the past few weeks; not since before I had heard him sleeping with Megan, of course.

"Claire and me aren't together anymore." He scratched his forehead, then sniffed to cover the awkward pause. "Dumped me just like my ex did."

So he must have cheated on his ex back in Stranraer too, then. "How are the girls?"

He shrugged, then smiled. "They're alright. I see them every other weekend. Getting big. I might move back over there soon to be near them. Jemma's not as mad at me as she was last year and both of the lockdowns – last year and this – were hard as I've missed so much of their lives. They're growing up so fast, don't want to miss it."

Johnny's maturity surprised me. "Kids have a way of doing that, I guess. Appreciating them, and spending time with them is the most precious thing that we can do, I suppose. Megan nearly lost her son, did she tell you that?" I said.

He opened and closed his mouth, at a loss. "I didn't know. What happened?"

"Her baby was born with a hole in his heart. There was one day when he nearly died – the same day she lost her brother. She believes the Blue Man tried to kill her baby Harry, but that she saved him and deflected the ghost onto her brother – so he took his life instead."

Johnny's serious face tremored for a moment, as though he were about to laugh, but thought better of it. "You're not serious, are you? She really believed in all that stuff about that ghost in Vicky Park from all those years ago."

I nodded. "Believed it enough that she thinks you're his descendant."

His face became animated then and he waggled his finger at me. "You know now that you say it, you reminded me of something there. When you told me all that stuff about Maureen whatever-her-name-was, I forgot to tell you what had happened. You remember that night when Megan, Louisa-Mae and Lauren broke into my Dad's flat in Holywood, back when we were at school?"

I frowned. "How could I forget?"

"Well, I forgot to tell you that she swiped a bunch of stuff – private papers, you know. Documents."

"What sort of documents?"

"Birth certificates. Stuff about my family history."

My jaw dropped. I closed my mouth, struggling to control my racing thoughts. "You mean, she could've made up stuff about the Blue Man based on your family history – just to fabricate his back story?"

Johnny shrugged. "Could have. It would explain why she knew stuff about my family names, and so on."

I paused, wondering if I should say what was on my mind – but went ahead anyway. "If that's the case, why did you still sleep with her?"

He shrugged again. "Why not. She was offering it, who was I to refuse. Her being schizo is nothing to do with sex. It's not like either of us are after a relationship."

Each to their own, I guessed; Megan and Johnny were both adults and could do what they wanted. My eyes skirted his neckline for signs of the gold chain with the Amber gemstone.

"Did you keep the gemstone Megan gave you? It seemed pretty important to her," I said.

Johnny's hand jumped to his collarbone, his fingers absently touching his bare neck, then dropped to his side again. He winced. "Oh that? I sort of broke it."

"You broke it? What happened?"

The irrational part of me reared its ugly head. Megan believed the Blue Man's restless spirit was trapped inside the Amber. If it was broken, he would be free.

"The chain snapped and it fell on the ground outside. I didn't even notice it until I saw it smashed to dust after my motorbike backed over it."

The gemstone wasn't the only thing in pieces; I felt like the last shred of my rationality had splintered too. A terrible feeling of dread and terror settling deep in the pit of my stomach.

"Are you alright there, Sabrina? You look white as a sheet," said Johnny.

The Blue Man

"I'm okay." I forced a smile and gave a dismissive wave of my hand. "I probably should get some rest while Leo's sleeping."

Johnny stood watching me, as though he was about to speak but couldn't get the words out. The dead air between us felt positively charged like it could have electrocuted either of us, if we made the wrong move.

"Johnny, I need to ask you one last thing." I gulped, composing my thoughts. "That summer, when we were eighteen. Was there ever a time – I mean, did you ever see – or sense – the Blue Man that Megan saw?"

He looked pensive for a moment as he stared at the ground. "Well, now you mention it, there was this weird thing that happened – just the once, mind you."

"Weird thing?" My voice quavered in the dead air between us.

"It was the night Megan shoved Louisa-Mae down the stairs at Sydenham Bridge. When she had me pinned down on the bed at that party in Inverary."

"What happened?"

He scratched his head. "This odd smell was coming off her, you know, like this sour smell that I can't describe. Like rotten meat."

Rotten meat. A devil, dead for a hundred years.

"I swear there was a darkness coming off her that night, like it wasn't her – not the Megan we knew. She was covered by a–" Johnny trailed off, waving his hands in circles above his head. "Shadow, or a dark energy that surrounded her."

Possession. Possessed by the Blue Man. I pulled myself out of my own dark musings and smiled, for the benefit of my old school classmate. "Thanks for sharing that with me, Johnny. It gives me some answers on certain happenings from our past."

My smile seemed to have relaxed him too, for Johnny winked. "Well, mucker. See you around."

I watched him walk on upstairs to his flat. Just as I was about to turn back inside my own flat, a creeping shadow on the stairwell behind Johnny made me spin round. My heart jumped into my throat. My chest felt as though it were getting tighter, squeezed by an invisible boa constrictor. I couldn't breathe.

I dashed inside and slammed the door then slumped against it. A horrible, guttural bellow escaped my diaphragm; a wretched, pitiful bovine sound, a wake-up call to my own ears. I needed to get help. My head was turned. It couldn't be late onset postpartum depression, could it, to think that the Blue Man was not only real, but after me? I had never fully, truly believed it over the course of the whole twenty years if I was honest; I had shared the experience with Megan though a part of me had always wondered if it were hysteria on my part. Getting caught up in the sinister madness, and dare I say, excitement that having the Blue Man in our lives had brought. But now? Now what? I was afraid. Truly, honestly in fear for my life. And Jake's. And Leo's. What kind of malevolent force had I welcomed – with open arms – into our lives? I was a wreck of a woman, pathetic. Not a woman at all. My back slid downwards against the wood and I sank to the floor in a pool of tears and despair.

Epilogue

I scrolled down through my phone, reading the last few messages Sabrina had sent me.

July 2021. *Just wanted you to know I'm thinking of you and I hope you're alright at the funeral today. I'm sorry that my boss wouldn't give me time off to come, but just wanted you to know that you're in my thoughts.*

Exactly a year ago today; maybe that's why I had thought to check back through my phone. Honestly, it had been a blessing in disguise that she couldn't get time off work, as it had saved me an awkward confrontation by asking her not to come. I looked at the next message, sent three months ago.

March 2022. *I know we haven't been in touch for a while, but just to say I'm here if you need me.*

And my response: *Thank you, that means a lot. xx*

Then another message, sent a month ago:

May 2022. *Hi Megan, just sending some e-hugs and kisses to you, Harry and Paddy. Heart emoji, kiss, kiss, kiss.*

I didn't bother responding to that one. Stuart was right. Keeping Sabrina at a distance was the best thing for my life. The less she knew about me, the harder it would be to draw the Blue Man back into my life.

I set my phone down on the coffee table and picked up the blister pack next to it. I popped the last small, white pill in my mouth and swallowed, then threw the empty blister pack in the bin. Goodbye citalopram. My doctor said I didn't need another repeat prescription of antidepressants. It was time to move on.

I looked down at my beautiful sleeping son in his cot. Noah was blonde-haired like me and unlike his dark-haired older brother and father. My cheeks prickled as I corrected that thought; Paddy wasn't his father. Noah was blonde like his biological father, Johnny Montgomery. Paddy was no longer my husband either. An image of him loading his bags into his car and driving away floated across my mind's eye. I had suspected Sabrina at first, but it turned out it had been Johnny who had filled Paddy in on the sordid details of our tryst, after I had ignored his phone call for round two. No amount of pleading or explaining that I had slept with Johnny to keep us all – me, Harry and Paddy – safe from the Blue Man could exonerate me in Paddy's eyes. A cheater was a cheater, he had said, and all trust had broken between us.

Still, I had my boys. Harry was a fragile wee thing at sixteen months, in and out of hospital for check-ups because of the hole in his heart. It had closed by the time he was six months old, and the specialists at the Royal Belfast Hospital for Sick Children had told me that such a thing was to be expected. But I knew the truth; Norman James McMurray had put a part of himself into my firstborn child on the day he had murdered Stuart, when he had reached inside my child's chest. The Blue Man controlled poor Harry's fate, forever more.

Noah, unlike his brother, was a robust baby at eight weeks old. He was alert, not missing a thing, and had a strong grip. He had the Blue Man's fighting spirit; and his genes. I stole a glance at my squat, stocky baby in his cot and his blue eyes locked with mine. For a moment, a shadow passed across his angelic features; a brooding brow, ice-cold eyes locked with an intensity borne of a century-long wait to correct a one-hundred year injustice. Black circles danced in hollow eye sockets that hadn't been there moments before, his face now sinister and skeletal, his desiccated lips pulled into a wide sneer. I shivered and blinked, dispelling the phantom gaze back into the netherworld where it now belonged; when I looked again my chubby, healthy baby watched me with smiling eyes and plump, pinks lips, full of energy, light and life. The Blue Man was gone, appeased in a physical sense through the bloodline that I now carried onwards for him through Noah, and trapped in a spiritual sense with his energy encased inside the Amber gemstone that hung on a chain around his great-grandson's neck.

My phone buzzed, the loud vibration against the coffee table alerting me to a notification. I stared at the screen; another text from Sabrina.

Speak of the Devil; funny how mere moments before, I had been delving through her texts of the past year and now a new message from her awaited me.

I was about to delete the message unread when the first few words caught my attention.

Megan, about the Amber gemstone.

Yes, she had piqued my interest in a heart-stopping, breath-catching way. I clicked on the message to open it.

I know we haven't been in touch lately and I completely understand – I'm sure I remind you of some difficult events in your life, so I'm not asking you to be in touch. But I needed to tell you this. The gemstone you gave Johnny broke. He ran over it with his motorbike last year, a couple of weeks after you gave it to him. He left it outside our apartment building in the gutter. I'm sorry, Megan. Your old friend, Sabrina.

Left it in the gutter. Throw salt over your left shoulder to blind the Devil. The Devil is behind your left shoulder.

Why did Sabrina choose to tell that to me? Why now?

My shoulders hunched closer to my neck and I cringed as I began a slow, cautious, turn to look behind over my left shoulder. For a split second a blue, shadowy figure stood in the doorway, before slipping away until it was gone from my peripheral vision. The room felt normal; no unearthly drop in temperature, as had happened before. What was different this time?

Noah gurgled, drawing my attention back to him. Norman's son. I had given him Noah; I had done as he asked. The Blue Man was free – but he wasn't coming for me. He was after Sabrina now, tormenting the living survivor of his nemesis, the man who had killed him. Martin Roberts. Sabrina McCann was the target of the Blue Man's wrath now, not me. Blue Sabrina.

***

The Blue Man

What was I thinking, stirring bad memories up for Megan, telling her about the accident with Johnny and the broken Amber gemstone? Megan had stopped replying to my texts three months ago in March – clearly she didn't want to hear from me. Maybe I was hormonal. I looked down at my growing bump, much wider and not as 'neat' with my soon-to-be second child, a daughter, than with Leo.

I had got what information I could from Johnny about Megan; after all, he was the father. He told me that Megan's husband had left her. Johnny was giving what he could in child payments for the baby's upkeep. He said the child was a boy, and that she had called him Noah. Noah, a biblical name for a person who had saved humankind. Maybe Megan's Noah had saved her.

It would seem so. Johnny had disclosed that Megan had been taking antidepressants after the death of her brother Stuart and postpartum depression.

Megan wasn't new to taking drugs – prescription or otherwise. Johnny himself had been her dealer, providing her with ecstasy, LSD, temazepam back in our teens.

Could it be that all of it – the entire presence of the Blue Man – was nothing more than a prolonged hallucination, caused by substance abuse?

Not if the creeping feeling that had been following me around for the past eight months was anything to go by.

It was in all the little things that didn't quite add up: a shadow out the corner of my left eye; a pool of darkness in the hallway when I went to the toilet at night, making me shiver. Too many little things that weren't quite explainable and the whole time, every time the heebie-jeebies needled me, Megan popped into my mind.

Megan. Maybe she blamed me for telling her the story of the Blue Man in the first place. Maybe she blamed me for kissing Johnny; for falling out with Louisa-Mae; for her Technology project getting destroyed. Maybe she blamed me for how we had become the targets of a prolonged and sustained haunting that had given both of us post traumatic stress disorder over the past twenty-two years.

I rested my chin on my palm and looked out the window of our flat.

A full moon shone high in the cloudless sky. An eerie blue light formed a halo around it and a wispy mist trailed, silvery in front. I swallowed a lump in my throat, but found myself unable to blink, as much as I wanted to close my eyes. I wanted to shut my mind from the sense of impending dread and doom sinking over me, like a blanket of unearthly fog in my mind, but I couldn't. All I could do was sit there, rooted to the window ledge, and stare at the moon.

It started as a prickle behind my left shoulder, followed by a whisper, more in my head than my ear.

Sabrina, it said. *Blue Sabrina.*

Was that me? Was that my fate? It was true, I felt blue. More blue, and down than I had ever felt.

You're mine now, Blue Sabrina.

The eerie blue light from the moon outside was in the room now, surrounding me, a living, breathing entity. Swallowing me into the deepest, darkest recesses of a phantom netherworld that I found myself sinking into, pulling me further and further away from my husband and son, from my life.

Blue Sabrina.

About the Author:

Leilanie Stewart is an author and poet from Belfast, Northern Ireland. Her writing confronts the nature of self; her novels feature main characters on a dark psychological journey who have a crisis of identity and create a new sense of being. She began writing for publication while working as an English teacher in Japan, a career pathway that has influenced themes in her writing. Her former career as an Archaeologist has also inspired her writing and she has incorporated elements of archaeology and mythology into both her fiction and poetry.

In addition to promoting her own work, Leilanie runs Bindweed Magazine, a creative writing literary journal with her writer husband, Joseph Robert. Aside from publishing pursuits, Leilanie enjoys spending time with her husband and their lively literary lad, a voracious reader of books featuring creatures of the deep.

Acknowledgements

First and foremost, thank you to my two awesome horror lovers: my hubby Joseph Robert, for all the editorial work on this novel, support and feedback and to our wee KJ who played with his kraken monsters while 'mummy was on her computer' allowing me the time to write. You both indulge me with all the scary movies and books – and love them in your own right. You guys are the best.

Thanks are also due to the following people: Heather for her fantastic proofreading work for this book; Amy Jeffrey and Ellen Collier for being fabulous beta readers; Linda McKee, Sharon Bell and David Smith for their ongoing support of my writing; Roxana Nastase, Editor in Chief of Scarlet Leaf Review, for publishing the short story version of this novel back in spring 2021, from which this novel grew; and last, but not least to you, for buying my book. Having readers keeps me motivated to write more stories, so thank you for taking the time to read and review my books. It means more than you know.

Other books by Leilanie Stewart

The Buddha's Bone

Death
Kimberly Thatcher wasn't an English teacher. She wasn't a poet. She wasn't an adventurer. Now she wasn't even a fiancée. But when one of her fellow non-Japanese colleagues tried to make her a victim, she said no.

Cremation
In Japan on a one-year teaching contract at a private English language school, and with her troubled relationship far behind her in London, Kimberly set out to make new friends. She would soon discover the darker side of travelling alone – and people's true intentions.

Rebirth
As she came to question the nature of all those around her – and herself – Kimberly was forced to embark on a soul-searching journey into emptiness. What came next after you looked into the abyss? Could Kimberly overcome the trauma – of sexual assault and pregnancy loss – blocking her path to personal enlightenment along the way, and forge a new identity in a journey of-

Death. Cremation. Rebirth.

Gods of Avalon Road

London, present day.

Kerry Teare and her university friend Gavin move to London to work for the enigmatic Oliver Doncaster. Their devious new employer lures them into an arcane occult ritual involving a Golden Horse idol.

Britannia, AD 47.

Aithne is the Barbarian Queen of the Tameses tribes. The Golden Warrior King she loves is known as Belenus. But are the mutterings of the Druids true: is he really the Celtic Sun God himself?

Worlds collide as Oliver's pagan ritual on Mayday summons gods from the Celtic Otherworld of Avalon. Kerry is forced to confront the supernatural deities and corrupt mortals trying to control her life and threatening her very existence.

Printed in Great Britain
by Amazon